HIDDEN
HOPE

Book Three of The Hidden Trilogy

Amy Patrick

Oxford South Press /September 2015
Cover design by Cover Your Dreams
Formatting by Polgarus Studio

Visit http://www.amypatrickbooks.com/ to sign up for Amy's newsletter if you would like to receive news and insider information on The Hidden Trilogy books and release dates.

CONTENTS

PROLOGUE

You'd think it would be an easy choice between Light and Dark. I mean, who would choose darkness? It's frightening, filled with the unknown, with unseen dangers ready to trip and capture and corrupt.

The light is warm. It's comforting and right. No one ever questions your sanity when you step into a bright room, go out on a sunny day, turn down a well-lit street.

But to a creature born of the dark, doesn't it also embody a certain rightness? A sense of safety? A freedom to be who you *truly* are because no one can see or pass judgment.

And there is excitement in the unknown. Like a theater when the lights go out just before the show begins. Like a secret whisper. Like a kiss in the dark.

Anything can happen.

Chapter One
Lad

The first time I saw her, I thought she was the most beautiful girl in the world. It was the last time that messed me up.

I move silently through the treetops, taking care to balance my weight with the additional burden of the two sacks strapped across my back. Finding my footing on the rough bark, I glance up at the patches of sky visible between the thick leaves, pastel colors mixing and changing as the sun slowly sinks toward its evening resting place.

My whole life is a balancing act now—my duty to my people, my relationship with my betrothed… and those rare moments I get to spend with *her*.

Ryann will be almost to the spring-fed pool by now. It's the natural choice for a meeting spot. It's always been our place—the site of our reunion this past spring—the place I finally found her again after years of longing and searching, after having all but given up on my childhood dream.

But then one afternoon there she was—a vision, a miracle—bathing there, wearing almost nothing, driving me out of my mind. She was more beautiful, more perfect than I ever could have imagined.

Thinking of that day, of all that has happened between us since, my heart gains weight until it's a stone in my chest, threatening to drag me from these branches and hurl me to the ground below.

Don't think about it. Keep your mind on your job.

My job today is delivering the saol water Ryann needs to make the sweet tea that saved her family's land and my people's home as well. Bringing her the necessary ingredient is my responsibility because the other Light Elves don't mix with humans and don't know how to communicate through spoken words.

And I *want* to be the one to do it—in spite of the pain. Continuing to see her like this, keeping our conversations limited to small talk and business, is the greatest torture. But it's also the best part of my week because it's the only time I can be close to her.

If Ryann only knew the effect seeing her has on me… well… it's best she doesn't know.

I reach the clearing and, as expected, she is there waiting. I should say something, announce my arrival.

And I will.

But first I take a moment to observe from the concealment of the thick summer foliage. My heart thumps hard from the guilty pleasure of watching her.

She sits at the edge of the pool, trailing the fingers of one delicate hand through the water. Her long chestnut hair drapes over one shoulder, exposing her neck on one side. She lifts her dripping hand to rub it, and the cooling water runs down over her collarbones and chest into the neck of her tank top.

So beautiful. I reach out and grasp the air just in front of me then draw my hand back to my side where it closes around the emptiness, forming a hard fist.

No. Not mine. Not anymore.

If all goes as planned, maybe all of this will be over soon. But will it be soon enough? Is it already too late? Every day she's with Nox is another day she steps further from my reach. Is she happy with him? *Does she love him?* Sickness builds in my gut at the thought.

During the plane ride home from Los Angeles, I started to hope that maybe she still cared for me. There was *something* still there in her eyes. A wistfulness in her voice.

Or maybe it was just *wishfulness*—on my part. Until I can tell her everything, I won't know.

CHAPTER TWO
CONFESSIONS
RYANN

One month earlier

"You need to break up with him, Ryann."

"What?" I had to make sure the words I'd just heard had actually come out of Lad's mouth and not from some exhaustion mirage or in-flight-doze-off dream. After all, I'd had perhaps the longest day of my life, starting with joining Reggie's fan pod, then being ogled, groped, and held at gunpoint, forced into a trunk, all followed by witnessing Nox being shot and then being whisked away myself to the airport for the flight home.

I glanced around. No, not dreaming. We were on the plane. The hum of the engines beneath the wings, the faraway lights below, barely visible through the night-dark windows, the sound of Emmy's soft snore from the corner where she'd burrowed into her pillow and blanket all assured me I was neither asleep nor delusional.

For the first two hours of the flight, Lad had sat alone while Emmy and I talked. It hadn't been easy to explain what was happening without giving away too much of the closely-guarded secret, to come up with a cover story for how I'd happened to be in California at the same time she'd been suddenly kicked out of her fan pod. Or for how I had access to a private plane. Or for why in the heck Lad was there with me.

Let's just say by the time she'd fallen asleep, I'd used up my yearly allotment of truth-stretching and creative license. Now Lad and I were, for all practical purposes, alone. And he was giving me dating advice.

"You need to break up with Nox," Lad repeated. "The sooner the better."

"I can't…" My words sputtered in furious indignation. "I can't believe you actually just said that to me. What makes you—"

"I care about you." He took my hand and rubbed his thumb across my knuckles in tense strokes. "And I care about him. And you're not right for each other. You need to end it—for both your sakes."

I tugged my fingers away, folding them against my stomach. "Your right to weigh in on my love life ended on the day you sent me away and told me never to contact you again. Remember that little chat?"

His green eyes pooled with pain. "That was the hardest thing I've ever had to do, believe me. I'm so sorry, Ryann. I *had* to send you away. I had no choice."

"So you're saying you didn't want to do it? I'm sorry, but I was *there*. You said it was over, and you meant it. I saw it in your eyes. I *felt* it. I've discovered one of my glamours is emotional acuity—you *meant* it when you told me not to contact you again. You said there was *no point*. And in that moment I knew in my heart you meant every word."

"You're right. I did. I thought I was doing the right thing." The admission was breathed out on a long sigh.

Lad closed his eyes. His chin dropped to his chest as his fingers clenched into fists on his spread thighs as if he were gathering strength. Finally he opened his eyes again and pinned me with a tortured stare. "I don't know what to do, what I can say. I know you hate me—I don't know how to fix that Ryann, but I want to try. Will you let me try to explain?"

My heart thumped hard, and a tremble began deep in my core, working its way outward to my hands. I'd thought there was nothing Lad could ever say that would affect me again. Now, here I was, an emotional mess after a few words from him. What was the matter with me?

I folded my arms across my chest, suddenly cold in the plane's air-conditioned interior. "So what—now you can suddenly tell me everything?"

"Well, no. Not exactly. But I can tell you some things—I *need* to tell you some things... if you'll let me."

My gaze left his face and drifted to the dark rectangle of the plane window as I replayed our devastating breakup. He'd said he wished he could glamour me into forgetting we'd ever met. He'd told me he didn't have time for my "jealousy and insecurities."

Why was he doing this to me now? Hadn't my heart been jerked around enough? Did I even want to hear what he had to say? Screw him, I wouldn't listen. A long moment passed in silence.

"All right. I'll listen," I said. "But only in the Elven way." If he talked to me mind-to-mind, at least it would be impossible for him to lie to me. At this point, it would be the only way I could believe anything he said.

Thank you. As I told you... that day.... He had the grace to look ashamed at the memory of that brutal conversation. *It was a dangerous time. The Light Council was calling for blood. Murder is our highest crime, and the murder of a king is unthinkable. Or it was. At first they refused to consider that another member of the Fae might have been responsible.*

He lifted a hand toward me. *As an outsider, a human intruder in our world, you were the most likely suspect, especially in light of the wedding. Many wanted to act first and ask questions later. There were threats on your life. When I intervened, some Council members questioned my ability to lead, in spite of the fact I was heir to the throne. They believed my objectivity was tainted because... because I loved you. For a terrible moment, I wondered myself if that were true. Because Ryann, I did love you so much I could hardly think straight.*

I turned my head away, letting my gaze bounce from Emmy, to the cockpit door, to the magazines in the seat-back pocket in front of me. Hearing him say it in the Elven way was overwhelming.

Unnerved by a powerful wave of emotion, I squeezed my eyes tightly shut to hold in the threatening tears. *I will not cry in front of him. Not after what he did to me.* I rolled my hand through the air in a silent gesture for him to continue.

Of course I knew better—I knew you had nothing to do with his death. But I had to lead my people, and I was afraid to relinquish control, even temporarily, because the head of the Council was calling the loudest to have you brought to Altum and interrogated. I had to show strength, to stand firm, to quash the fears that I was unfit to lead because of my preoccupation with a human. And I was warned that there were those who'd strongly disagreed with my father's decision to let you leave the kingdom in the first place. In order to protect you, I made a vow to them—that my involvement with you was over.

When I heard you'd gone to Los Angeles, my first impulse was to feel relief that you were out of their reach. Of course when I spoke with your grandmother and discovered the rest of it—that you'd gone in search of Emmy and immersed yourself in the Dark Elven world—my relief turned to fear.

I stared at him, reading the honesty in his eyes, remembering he had left his precious people behind to come after me in L.A. and warn me about Davis and my mother.

So maybe he *had* still cared for me when he sent me away. But why had he made it so permanent? Why had he stripped all hope and warned me not to wait for him and never to contact him? Why had he hurt me?

I gave him a hard look. *You could have told me all this then. I would have understood. You knew I would have waited for you until you'd found the murderer and settled everyone's fears. I would have waited for you—forever if necessary.*

There was a flicker of deep emotion in his green-green eyes. He swallowed, making his Adam's apple move under the smooth, tanned skin of his neck. *I couldn't ask that of you. And moving on was the best thing—for you. It was clear that my people would never accept a human, and I could not leave them. I could no longer hold onto the childish hope of avoiding my birthright. I realized I was stuck with it—forever. There is no one else to rule the Light Court.*

I searched his sincere expression, his pleading eyes. What did he think was going to happen here? That he would apologize and I would sigh and throw myself into his arms?

Not going to happen.

Good intentions or not, he had decided what was best for me without any input from me—without even telling me what was really going on. He'd hurt me too deeply. And I was building a life with Nox now.

"Why are you telling me all this? Do you expect me to say I still love you?" I huffed a bitter laugh. "I'm *never* going to say those words again. To *anyone*."

"Ryann—"

"And you can't really believe, after all that's happened, that I would throw Nox aside and get back together with you."

His shoulders sagged. "No, of course not. I'm not asking for that."

Now that I thought about it, he hadn't asked me to come back to him—just to listen to him.

"Oh. So… just what *are* you asking for?"

"Your forgiveness… for the things I said to you. For the way I handled the breakup… and Vancia."

I flinched at the mention of her name. He had been minutes away from marrying the Dark Elven princess when I'd showed up in Altum that day. Somehow, they'd gotten re-engaged since then, though he now was claiming he had been in love with *me*. And then a stinging thought flashed through my mind.

"Are you still engaged to her?" I asked quietly.

Lad visibly winced and his jaw tightened, though he held eye contact. "Yes."

Pain ricocheted through me. "I don't understand. Why do you care what I think of you if you're planning to marry her? Why bother telling me you loved me and that I should break up with Nox? Is it like, some kind of sham engagement or something?"

He stared at me with serious eyes. His voice was very quiet. "No. It's real."

A fresh wave of hurt washed over me. Why were we even talking then? The last thing I needed after this day from hell was mind games. The thing was—I could *feel* his sincerity, his desperate desire for me to understand him. We stared into each other's eyes in a standoff of bruised silence.

I was the first to crack.

"So that's it? You have nothing else to say about it? You're just going to keep sitting there looking like you want to throw yourself from the plane with no parachute. Or… maybe you'd like to elaborate a bit?"

"I can't. Ryann, I'm sorry. Can you please just think about what I've said and trust me?"

I stood up and moved into the aisle. "Um… no. You've just told me I should break up with my boyfriend… who loves me by the way… and you refuse to explain. Not exactly trust-inspiring. And you're an engaged man—we shouldn't even be talking. To borrow from our last conversation in your nest hideaway, 'I don't have time for this.'"

Marching toward the back of the small plane, I put as much distance between us as I could manage. How was I supposed to *trust* him again? Mom might miraculously have faith in love after betrayal and heartbreak, but that wasn't me. I was fresh out of trust these days.

Though I'd burrowed into the back row of seats, it wasn't far enough. I could still hear Lad's pleading words loud and clear in my mind.

Please, Ryann. There's still more to talk about. I'm worried about you.

Worry about yourself. And get out of my head.

CHAPTER THREE
GRAND OPENING

Today

I pulled into my spot in the parking lot of the Magnolia Sugar Tea Company, the nerves in my stomach boiling like the sweet tea brewing inside the sprawling white building. Today was a big day for all of us. Needing a momentary escape, I hit the music app on my phone.

The sound of Nox's unearthly voice flowed from the speaker, filling the car's interior, and like a junkie getting a fix, I relaxed. It was impossible to feel bad while hearing something so beautiful.

Out in L.A., I had fought against being subjected to Nox's singing—I had no defense against his musical glamour. But now, forced to be away from him, I had to take what I could get. I found myself turning to his songs, his videos, even interviews with him on You Tube, more and more. They were so addictive, they were almost as good as the real thing. Almost. A song couldn't hold you, kiss you—

A car pulled in and parked beside me, reminding me where I was and what I was supposed to be doing. I wrenched myself from the hypnotic memory of his kisses and opened my car door, stepping back into the real world.

It had taken nearly the whole summer to get the factory set up and running, but the abandoned Rebel Cola bottling plant across from the First Baptist Church on Main Street had been transformed and repurposed and was once again functional and employing many of the citizens of Deep River, Mississippi.

A good number of them had turned out to help celebrate the grand opening today, which wasn't surprising. In a town with three stoplights and 3600 residents, there wasn't that much else going on. Plus, we were passing out free tea samples, and people couldn't seem to get enough.

Grandma Neena greeted me as I stepped onto the factory floor, lifting one hand toward the balloons and the Grand Opening banner stretched between two giant vats. She rubbed my arm. "It's looking good, darlin'. You've done a fine job."

I grabbed her hand and squeezed it, my belly tumbling in dread of the speech I was expected to make in a half hour.

"We've done it—together. I'd never have made it if you hadn't laid the groundwork while I was scrambling around L.A. looking for Emmy."

She puffed a dismissive noise but blushed as she grinned. "It gave me something better to do than worry about *you* every minute. Everything's ready for the party. As for production, we're running low on saol water. We've got enough for this batch, but no more."

"I know. I'm meeting Lad later for a delivery."

Her face softened in sympathy. "You going to be all right with that?"

I met her questioning eyes. "Yes. We're fine. We're… friends now." My mind flashed back to our conversation on the private plane on the way home from L.A., but I snatched it back to the here and now. I couldn't go there. I'd never get through the day if I allowed myself to dwell on what he'd said that night.

Still wearing that soulful look, Grandma nodded. "Speaking of friends… Emmy and Shay still planning to come today?"

I glanced over my shoulder at the factory's front doors. "Should be here any minute. And Mom just called." I grimaced. "She's on her way."

Things were weird with Mom and me. As soon as I had gotten home I'd tried talking to her about Davis—as much as I could without revealing the secret—but she refused to listen. Of course. He was rumored to have the strongest Sway of all the Elven people, and she was totally under his glamour.

She *seemed* so happy. I wished I could just let her be. If only her new fiancé, my biological father as it turned out, wasn't the leader of the Dark Elves, maybe I could have.

The heavy steel door creaked open, flooding the interior with bright sunlight, and for an instant I was filled with irrational hope of seeing a six-foot-four, hazel-eyed god enter the manufacturing plant instead of my mother or my two best friends. Maybe Nox managed to get away from Los Angeles after all?

One decidedly short silhouette bounced into view, followed by another, slightly taller and curvier one. The door closed behind them, and I smiled and crossed the factory floor to greet Emmy and Shay.

"Wow, girl. This is amazing. You're like, for real."

Hugging Shay, I said, "Thanks. It's getting there. I need this place to be basically running itself by the time school starts, so we're not quite done."

"Is it selling yet?" Emmy asked, wandering over to inspect the nearest production line.

Retro shaped glass bottles with their magnolia-themed labels rolled by on a conveyor belt, heading for the machine that would affix caps to the top before they were placed into shipping cartons and loaded onto delivery trucks.

"Yep. The first shipment went out to stores three days ago. I hear it's doing well so far."

I had started selling my own special recipe of sweet tea this past spring out of desperation, when our family land was threatened by an IRS debt. First at Deep River's main street diner The Skillet. Then, nervous as all get out, I had taken it to the manager of our local Food Star, where Nox had *persuaded* the man to give it a try.

But it was Lad's contribution—the addition of Elven saol water to sweeten it and enhance the nutritional content—that made the tea something truly special and turned it into a beverage line stocked at more than a hundred Food Star grocery stores across the Southeast. If it kept selling well, the plan was to expand the brand nationwide.

"Is your mom coming with her hot man?" Shay's shoulder bumped mine in a teasing gesture.

"Ew, Shay. Don't be gross. He's so old," Emmy said, cutting her eyes in my direction.

Neither of my friends had any idea just *how* old Davis actually was—two hundred fifty-five years, according to Vancia. Like my friends, I'd only seen him on TV, but I had to admit he was very handsome, and of course, he looked young. He was Elven after all.

I smiled my silent thanks to Emmy. Naturally, I couldn't confide everything to her about my "real" dad— but on our plane trip back from Los Angeles, I had told her about the shocking discovery I'd made—that the father I grew up with, Michael Carroll, wasn't my biological father, and that my mom's "new" love was actually her *old* lover *and* my father.

"That doesn't change who you are. You're still the same girl I've known since preschool," she'd said, trying to make me feel better.

The problem was, it kind of *did* change who I was. When I left on my rescue mission to California, I believed I was a quarter Elven on my mom's side. As it turned out, I was only a quarter human. What's more—my Elven sperm donor was a Dark Elf—*the* Dark Elf, in fact. Or at least he had been until Nox showed up and displaced him as the ruler of the Dark Court.

I'd been in sort of a tailspin ever since. It was wonderful to be back home with my best friends again. But my mind kept drifting to my new friends, like Gigi and Kim and Bonnie, back in the fan pods in L.A. I hadn't been able to help them. I'd felt guilty about it every day since leaving them behind, but what could I really do? I'd barely escaped with my own life, and it was only because of Lad and Vancia's intervention I'd been able to bring Emmy home.

I was confident the girls in Nox's fan pod weren't being used or mistreated. I couldn't say the same for the ones unfortunate enough to be under the control of Vallon Foster and Reggie Dillon and the countless other celebrities who were, unbeknownst to their human fans, actually Dark Elves.

"So where's *your* man?" Emmy asked with a silly eyebrow waggle. She had been positively gleeful when I'd told her Nox and I had gotten together in L.A., gloating unmercifully and claiming she'd called it from the first night Nox and I had met at the ballpark.

"He can't make it. He's still in L.A." The dejection in my voice was impossible to hide. I missed him. I'd been home for a month, and we'd hardly been able to talk since then. I understood, but the sudden separation after such intense togetherness—and all we went through together— was hard to take. "He's hoping to visit soon."

"Well, he better get his tight booty back here quick, or Mr. Hot Homeschooler's gonna move back in," she teased.

Lad. She'd met him on the plane trip, of course. And of course, she was instantly fascinated. In spite of all my protests, Emmy insisted Lad still wanted me.

"The way he looked at you," she said, shaking her head. "Like he never wanted to let you out of his sight again."

"He's *engaged,* remember?" I rolled my eyes at her. "Besides, there's no *room* for him in my life, even if he did want to move back in. I'm with Nox now."

"Okay, okay. Whatever you say, but it's not over till the wedding bells ring."

"What wedding bells?" Shay returned to our group, holding three paper cups filled with tea. "Who's getting married?"

"My mom," I said at the same time Emmy blurted, "Ryann's *ex.*"

"Ooh, that's hard," she sympathized. "I can't stand it when Tisha even *looks* at Lance."

Shay and her major crush Lance were dating big-time now. She offered a cup to me.

"Oh—no thanks. I'm kinda burned out on it, you know? It's like when you work at a donut shop, and you can't stand the thought of eating donuts. Too much of a good thing."

"Well, I love donuts," Emmy said. She took the cup from my hand. "And I *love* this stuff. Give it to me. I'll drink it."

I laughed, watching her drain the cup. "I think you're my best customer."

Emmy seemed really happy since returning to Deep River. She'd immediately hooked up with Jake McKee, and she even appeared to be getting over the celebrity obsession thing lately. Of course, people here treated her like she was a celebrity herself since she'd spent time in Vallon's fan pod this summer and met lots of famous people. That suited Emmy just fine.

"I only wish I could remember more of it," she'd admitted to me on that late night plane trip.

I was glad she couldn't. I almost wished *I* could forget what I knew about the fan pods, especially when I felt helpless to do anything about it here, so far removed from the glittering, dangerous world of the Dark Elves. That's the way Nox wanted it—me here in Mississippi, far away from the center of the Dark Court's power in California.

"I'll handle it Ryann. I want you to be safe and promise me you'll stay out of it," he'd said during our last phone conversation. "Trust me, okay?"

"I do. I will," I'd promised.

The crowd inside the tea plant was beginning to thicken, and I was obliged to greet and chat with all the people who'd come to wish me well or thank me and

Grandma for creating a desperately needed new source of employment in our sleepy little town.

Mr. Marsden, the grocery store manager, was there of course. As were my old Sunday school teacher and Dena from The Skillet, Grandma's bridge club and quilting group, and so many of my friends from school and around town that we were probably violating some kind of fire department occupancy code.

"I'm so proud of you Ryann," my English teacher, Mrs. Wordle said as she sipped from her cup of tea. She added with a wink, "But don't think I'm going to let you slide in British Lit this fall just because you're running a business now."

"Oh, I know. I doubt if you would've let Jane Austen slide. Enjoy the reception, okay? I see my mom coming in."

"Congratulations honey."

I smiled at her and made my way toward the entrance where Mom had finally arrived, barely in time for my speech. She was alone, and I breathed a huge sigh of relief.

Maybe he had a change of plans.

I was in no hurry to meet my "father" in person and certainly not in front of nearly everyone I'd ever known. Besides, I'd spotted Daddy slipping in a few minutes ago, and I had no idea how he'd handle a face-to-face meeting with Mom's new husband-to-be.

"Hi Mom." I hugged her and accepted her latest round of congratulations and happy tears.

"Baby, this is amazing. My daughter is a business tycoon."

"Um, hardly. Not yet, anyway. Give me a couple weeks," I joked. "Go ahead and get some tea and cookies and stuff. Grandma's over there, and I'll be back in a few minutes after I welcome everyone."

She poked her glossy bottom lip out. "I'm so sorry Davis isn't here to see this. His plane was delayed by weather. But he wants to take us out tonight to celebrate. We're going to meet him in Oxford."

I froze in place. After an awkward pause I found my voice. "Okay. Sure. Sounds good."

It was inevitable, I guess, that I would have to see him. I'd have been a lot *less* freaked out about it if I knew how much he really knew about my Los Angeles adventures.

Lad swore to me that Vancia was on our side, that she'd never tell her adoptive father how I'd infiltrated fan pods and attempted to free Emmy, that I'd essentially worked against him.

But I didn't trust her. Sure, she'd helped save me and Nox, but she hadn't done it for my sake. She and Nox had been close childhood friends.

At least I knew she was on *his* side. She'd announced to everyone that he, not her father Davis, was the true heir to the Dark throne and had stayed with Nox in L.A. to ensure he was believed as he owned up to his real identity and claimed his rightful place of rulership. She was still there, in fact. No matter how much she seemed to despise me, I appreciated her for helping him.

"You ready, girl?" Grandma asked as I joined her near the front of the room.

I nodded and stepped toward the center of the factory floor, the machinery and huge tanks forming a backdrop for this mini-ceremony. One of the workers turned off the conveyer belts to lessen the noise.

"Hi everybody." The crowd's chatter hushed as I continued. "I'd like to thank you all for being here today. It's very exciting for me to celebrate this grand opening. I never thought something like this could happen for someone like me, and I certainly could never have done it without a lot of help."

Glancing from face to smiling face, I caught the eyes of Mom, Grandma, Emmy, and Shay. Daddy stood near the back wall, far from Mom and raised his arms above his head so I could see his dual thumbs up signs. I had to blink back tears and clear my throat before I could go on.

"The most special part of today is sharing it with all the people I love."

And here I had to stop and swallow back more tears. Not *everyone* I loved was in this room. And life was not complete without him.

CHAPTER FOUR
DELIVERY

Our heated conversation from the plane kept running through my head as I waited for Lad at the natural pool. I *really* needed to make different arrangements for the saol water deliveries. This wasn't working for me.

Sure, Lad was the only one in Altum who interacted with humans, who spoke our audible language. But I wasn't the only one who could meet with him. I would ask Grandma to do it from now on. That would work. Or maybe we could work out a drop-off sort of arrangement. Yep, that would be even better. Then I wouldn't be tempted to ask Grandma anything about what he'd said, how he'd acted.

One thing was for sure—seeing him face-to-face was too hard. And this place… it was too full of memories.

Behind me there was a rustling of leaves. I spun around in time to see Lad's feet hit the ground with a soft thud.

He straightened, giving me a shy smile. And the breath left my lungs.

Would I ever get past it? The stomach-melting, heart-in-my-throat feeling that happened every time he dropped into my life? It was ridiculous. He wasn't mine anymore. He had someone else. And so did I— someone beautiful and talented and addictively sexy.

My mind knew that, but my pulse hadn't been informed. My body's instantaneous reaction to Lad hadn't changed. I told myself it was the shock of seeing him do something so… inhuman. How *could* I feel normal around him? He wasn't normal. Normal guys didn't jump out of huge trees and land without a scratch.

"Hi," I wheezed.

"Hi." His deep, smooth voice penetrated me, never failing to mess up my nerves no matter how much I tried to prepare myself. His clear green eyes roamed over my face. "How is the factory coming along?"

I shifted nervously. "Good. Great. We had a grand opening party today, and we've already sent out our first shipment." I wanted to just grab the saol water and go, but I forced myself to be polite. "How are things in Altum?"

"All is well. The people have accepted me as their king. Things are peaceful there now."

"You must be doing a good job."

He chuckled. "Either that or the leadership glamour my father always claimed I had has finally surfaced."

I nodded. "Good. I'm glad it's going well."

The stilted conversation made me sad. It was so different from the talks we used to have, filled with humor and fun… and love.

"Did he come for the party?" Lad asked in a tight voice.

He. *Nox.* My heart squeezed hard at the thought of him, and I had to take a deep breath before responding. "No. He couldn't make it. He's busy."

Lad's response was quick, his face perking with interest. "You haven't seen him lately?"

"Not since leaving L.A. He says it's too dangerous right now. And he's running a kingdom—you know how it is."

"Yes." Lad's tone was grim. He knew how it was. His duty to his people in the wake of his father's murder had been the death of our relationship—the reason he'd sent me away and let me go to Los Angeles on a rescue mission alone, according to his claims. And then of course there'd been the beautiful Elven fiancée.

He pulled two sacks from his shoulders. The clanking metallic sound from within told me they were filled with the Elven-made flasks that held saol water. He held them out to me.

"You'll be needing this."

"Thanks." I took the bags from his hands, sensing the instant contraction of my biceps. Fae metal was surprisingly light, but even with that, the bags kept getting heavier as our tea production increased.

"Here, I'll carry them to the edge of your yard." Lad took the bags back. "You'll need more soon, I suppose?"

Here was my opportunity to put an end to this torture. I fell into step beside him, our feet scuffing quietly on the well-worn path through the woods toward Grandma Neena's house. "Yes, actually. A lot more. In fact... I think we're going to have to find another delivery method—"

"Why?" He stopped and faced me, his brows lowered over intense green eyes, his tone surprisingly harsh.

"Because... it's just not practical for you to keep bringing it to me like this. Especially with the quantities we'll need now that we're ready to produce the tea at full-capacity." I turned and resumed walking.

Lad followed. "I don't mind. And I can carry more. It isn't heavy."

"For *you*."

Lad shifted the bags to his other hand, the muscles barely flexing. "Then I'll bring it into town for you—to the factory."

"No. You have too many other responsibilities. And how would you transport it that far anyway?"

The Light Elves underground kingdom was deep in the woods on Grandma Neena's land, miles from town. No way could Lad carry larger quantities of saol water walking or moving through the trees as he usually did to get around. Not without drawing a lot of attention.

He'd had some limited contact with the human world throughout his life, going back and forth to the library. And of course, he'd ventured *way* out of his comfort zone when he'd gone to L.A. with Vancia to warn me about

Davis. But it wasn't the way of his people. Unlike the Dark Elves, the Light Elves preferred to remain completely apart from the human world.

"I'll manage," he insisted. "And I like getting away from Altum from time to time."

We emerged from the woods into the back yard of Grandma's log house. "Well, I know you have your duties there, and besides, I think I have a better solution. Follow me."

Crossing the yard to the carport, I stopped in front of a long, brown chunk of metal parked beneath it. A 1970's model Cadillac Coupe DeVille. "Ta da."

"He left it here," Lad said.

"Yes. With all the upscale cars parked outside his mansion in Malibu, Nox isn't missing this one."

Was he missing *me*? It had been hard for us to talk since I'd returned to Mississippi with Lad and Emmy. As the new Dark King, Nox's life was filled with responsibility. And danger. He was convinced now that Davis was behind his parents' deaths, but without proof, he had to pretend to appreciate Davis's "mentoring" in his new role. It was very possible many of the Dark Elves still wanted Davis as their king and were fully on-board with his plan for world domination.

While he was trying to determine who was on what side, Nox thought it was wise to keep our relationship under wraps. He was right, of course. In the Dark Elven view, humans were suitable for fan pods, but not for actual relationships.

So our phone calls were sporadic, and his promises of coming back for a visit soon were starting to seem more like a fantasy and less like reality. Compared to all the upscale *girls* out there in Hollywood, I felt a bit like this dumpy old left-behind car. I knew it was silly. On the occasions we *did* talk, Nox was sweet, his voice filled with unmistakable longing. He told me he hated to be apart from me. Told me he loved me.

"You miss him," Lad said, noticing my hand as it absentmindedly caressed the old car's hood.

"Yes. Terribly," I answered honestly. Swallowing hard, I said the polite, expected thing. "You must miss Vancia as well."

Lad's fiancée—Nox's childhood friend and Davis Hart's adoptive daughter—had stayed in L.A. with Nox, presumably to help establish his right to rule the Dark Court. They had grown up together in Hollywood, the seat of Dark Elven power. Lad and I were both outsiders in that world.

The difference was, he could be assured his partner was coming back. They were betrothed.

"Yes, of course. But she'll be back tomorrow." Lad's eyes took on that look that indicated there was much more to be said. I didn't want to hear it.

I pulled my gaze away from his and reached for the bags he'd deposited on the car's hood. "So, I should get this stuff over to the factory. From now on you can just leave the saol water here in the carport. Or you can put it in the trunk if you'd like. I don't lock the car. That way we don't even have to—"

His fingers hooked around my wrist, pulling me back to face him. "Ryann, stop. We need to talk."

I tugged my arm away, pulling toward the house, suddenly desperate to escape his presence. "No we don't. It's cool. Really—this is just about convenience—it makes more sense to have you drop it off instead of our meeting."

"Not about the saol water. Would you please stop running away and look at me?"

I stopped and forced myself to meet his eyes.

"There's something else we need to talk about… this involves you and me and Vancia."

I started toward the house again. "No. We *really* don't need to talk about that."

"*She* wants to talk to you."

The bizarre statement stopped my retreat. "What?"

"I'd like for us all to meet and talk. Since she and I… reunited and declared our intentions to marry after all, her father has removed her banishment and welcomed her back. She's discovered some things about the Dark Elves' plans… well, you need to hear it from her."

I blinked and focused on breathing slowly, trying to picture this *meeting*. What—would we grab a corner booth at The Skillet? Order some bacon and home fries and chat it up together third-wheel style? I had already proved what a failure I was against the Dark Elves' plans. Besides, I was trying to manage things so I'd see Lad *less* often, not more.

"I don't think so. I'm not sure what she thinks I could do about all this."

"Nox was right when he said you were more capable than I knew. And with your relationship to Davis—"

"We *have* no relationship. And this is an Elven thing. I'm only human. And Nox was wrong. You saw what happened in L.A. I wasn't exactly an action movie hero out there."

"I'm not asking you to be one. The gifts you do have are powerful—they could be very important—to all of us."

I shook my head. "I don't even know what I'm doing with them. And after finding out Davis is my... I've promised myself I'm not using any of my supposed 'powers' ever again." The last thing I wanted was to be like the Dark Elves who took advantage of unsuspecting humans.

Lad looked at me with sympathy. "You're not like him, Ryann. I know it was shocking news, but you need to learn to accept yourself."

"Thank you, Gandhi," I snapped.

Lad sighed. "Just come to Altum tomorrow and listen to what Vancia has to say. That's all I'm asking. I would think you'd want to know what he's up to—for your mother's sake at the very least since she's still involved with him."

He had a point. "Well, I'm going to meet him tonight. Mom and I are having dinner with him, so I'll just find out for myself, I guess."

"No." Lad's face tightened into a wince and he clenched his fists in a hard pulse. "I wish I'd known about this earlier. You must not see him in person, Ryann. Vancia says—"

"How do you know you can trust her?" I snapped. I was just about sick of his bossiness, and I was beyond sick of hearing the name Vancia every five seconds. "She's a Dark Elf. Did you ever think she might have been on her father's side the whole time? Maybe she's tricking you and using you as part of their plan."

"No." He shook his head. "You know we can't lie mind-to-mind. She's told me how she really feels about Davis. She truly wants to stop him. And she's a wonderful person."

"Well then, let *wonderful* Vancia stop him. There's nothing I can do. I'm only human. I couldn't even stop that house manager from shooting Nox. If Vancia hadn't intervened when she did, he'd be dead. You, too. She's the one with all the power." *She's the one with your heart.* "Besides, Nox wants me to stay out of it. He made me promise."

Lad's intense expression smoothed out, becoming an impassive mask. "I understand." There was a long pause as competing expressions warred across his face. Finally he spoke again. "He's not right for you, Ryann."

My insides burst into a flaming fury furnace. I was surprised a wildfire didn't start around us from the sparks shooting out of my ears. "Oh really. And who is, Lad? Who *is*?"

At first he didn't respond. Then finally, his eyes dropped to the scarred surface of the carport floor as his hands clenched tightly at his sides. "I'm sorry."

"Yeah, me too. You are a total control freak, you know that? Do you *ever* just let go and lose control?"

His response was devastatingly quiet. "Only with you."

I took a deep breath and let it out slowly, trying to control my shaking hands. "Leave the delivery here at the car next time, okay?" Then I turned and walked into the house without looking back.

CHAPTER FIVE
MEET THE MAN

The nighttime breeze lifted my hair, providing a respite from the warm, humid evening. Actually, the temperature out on the restaurant's covered balcony wasn't uncomfortable—it was the man seated across the table who made me sweat.

Davis Hart reminded me of a middle-aged soap star or one of those actors who played the heroic good-dad character in a prime-time family drama. Too good to be real. Thick, brown hair framed his handsome face. Perfect white teeth gleamed against his clear, barely lined skin.

I'd seen him on the news, but up close, his Elven-ness was undeniable. More disturbing—I could see a distinct resemblance between us. Throughout my life, people had always said I looked just like my mom, though I'd never seen it. Now I knew they said it because I didn't look at all like my dad, Michael.

"It's absolutely delightful to meet you in person, Ryann," Davis said. "Although your mother has told me so much about you, I feel like I've been present for your whole life."

"But you haven't," I said sharply, compelled to point out the obvious.

Mom's face colored at my rudeness. "Ryann," she chided in her mind-your-manners-young-lady voice.

She looked mortified. And *tired*. I hadn't really noticed it before now. All the back and forth trips to see Davis in Atlanta were taking their toll.

"No, I mean, no offense, but you can't really know someone just from hearing about them," I said.

"I couldn't agree more." Davis raised one eyebrow significantly. "That's why I'm so happy we're finally getting the chance to meet."

Ah. He was hinting that I couldn't necessarily believe everything I'd heard about *him*. Well, I suspected I should believe what *he* said even less.

I looked out across Oxford's town square, with its historic white courthouse, the quaint shops and busy restaurants forming a lively town center. Couples and families strolled the sidewalks hand-in-hand. One daddy held a small girl on his shoulders, the big yellow bow topping her hair bobbing as he walked.

We would never be a family—the three of us—Mom, Davis, and me. I was probably a traitor to Daddy for even being here, but I couldn't put it off forever. And Lad was right. For Mom's sake, I needed to have some idea what kind of guy she was engaged to. From what I already knew, I wanted him out of her life.

"Ryann, why don't you tell Davis about your college visit out in L.A.?"

"Yes, I heard you made a rather sudden decision to visit the West Coast," Davis prompted.

My heart seized. How much did he know? Was he really unaware of my interactions with the fan pods out there? Did he have any idea of my rescue mission to bring Emmy back home?

"Well, UCLA was amazing." No doubt the school *was* amazing, but I hadn't actually visited the campus. Then I added a few truths to my lie. "And I got to see a gorgeous beach, went to a couple of cool clubs."

"Meet any celebrities?" Davis asked with a wink.

My heart stopped in my chest. Why would he ask that? Strike that—I knew why—or thought I did.

What should I say? I had, in fact, met several celebrities, including Vallon Foster the movie star and NFL quarterback Reggie Dillon. But I hadn't mentioned them to Mom, so I certainly couldn't own up to it now.

"Not really. I thought I saw Ian Somerholder from a distance, but I wasn't sure." And of course I'd been at a Fae mansion party with Nox at the time, so I hadn't been able to go check him out. Probably best not to admit that part in present company.

"Think you'd like to live out there?" Davis asked with a level of interest that disturbed me. Los Angeles was the center of Dark Elven power. Did he want his newfound "daughter" to *want* to live there?

"Um, I'm not sure. I still have some time to decide about college."

My whole life felt so up in the air. If things settled down and Nox needed to live in LA. for his music career, I'd certainly be interested in going to school out there to be near him, though the thought of living so far away from my home and family *permanently* wasn't very appealing. I'd miss this place too much.

As it stood right now, I didn't have to worry about it. Nox had forbidden me to even *visit* the city.

"Well you should go ahead and apply just in case. And let me know if you need a letter of recommendation. UCLA admissions are very competitive."

"Oh honey, what a sweet offer," Mom gushed and kissed Davis's cheek. "Ryann, isn't that nice?"

"Yes. Thank you. That would be great," I muttered into my menu because what could I do? Scream, *No* at him?

A phone rang, and Davis reached into his pocket, "Excuse me, ladies. I have to take this." He smiled as he stood then walked away from the table.

Mom turned to me when he was out of earshot. Her eyebrows were drawn together. Her mouth formed a tense line. "You're not being very friendly. Davis has been so looking forward to meeting you. And he's really so incredible, if you'll just give him a chance."

I sighed. There was so much I wanted to say to Mom, but it wasn't allowed. "It's just—it's awkward. And it's not like I'm meeting just 'some guy' you're dating. It's a much bigger deal. I feel pressured, like you're both expecting something from me. I know you love him, but you can't expect me to just love him instantly because we share DNA. I already *had* a father, you know. I never bargained for another one. Don't you ever miss Daddy?"

There was a spark of response in her eyes, but it was gone so quickly I wondered if I'd only seen what I wanted to see.

She reached over and patted my hand. "I'm sorry you feel strange, baby. But I promise you, once you get to know Davis, you *will* love him. Everyone does."

No, everyone's glamoured by him. Including you. That's what I wanted to say. What I did say was, "Are you sure about him, Mom? You're not with him just because you think you should be, are you? You know, because of your past… because of me?"

She blinked several times and sat up straighter. "For heaven's sake… no. I love him."

"Why?"

Her stare went on for a few seconds. "Well… he's…" Her tone was decidedly flustered. "I don't know. It's hard to describe. I've never met anyone like him. He's handsome, charming. And he's impossible to say no to."

Check, check, and check. All the Elven qualities responsible for the proliferation of fan pods all over the world.

"I just don't understand how you can trust him again after what happened between you in the past."

She readjusted her napkin in her lap and sat up straighter, laying her hand atop mine. "I read a famous quote the other day online—it was by George Addair. It goes, 'Everything you've ever wanted is on the other side of fear.' I don't want to live in fear anymore, Ryann. I want to be happy. I want love. There were extenuating circumstances back then. I was too immature to accept them at the time. I've grown up. Davis has explained himself. He felt terrible about what happened. He stayed alone all these years, you know.

"And true love makes up for a lot, Ryann. I'm in love with him. I want to do everything for him," she gushed. "I want to spend all my time with him, take care of him, make him the happiest man on earth."

She held her hands out to the side in a what-are-you-gonna-do gesture. "Can't you understand? Haven't you ever lost your mind over someone?"

A vision of Nox onstage filled my eyes. His hypnotic, beautiful voice filled my ears. The comparison troubled me, actually.

"Just… make sure you're sure, okay? Because, you know, if you do marry him—that's forever."

She didn't know I meant that literally. But it was possible. She was half Elven. She might be immortal. I assumed once they were married and Mom was fully under his control, Davis would have to let her in on the secret.

Maybe *I* should go ahead and tell her a little early. It was against the rules, but this was a special situation. Would knowing he wasn't human make a difference? Make her back out of the wedding? Or would it drive her toward him even more? Would she even believe me?

Maybe I could drop hints, help her figure it out on her own. "Mom… when you say you've never met anyone like him…"

"Ah. I apologize again. My assistant. Sometimes I wonder who's the boss." Davis laughed at his own joke as he took his seat. "My ears are burning. Were you two talking about me?" he teased.

Mom giggled like a tween. "Maybe. Wouldn't you like to know?"

He grinned back at her. "Holding out on me, huh? Well… I'll get it out of you later." He winked at her before his eyes cut in my direction and stayed on me a beat too long.

Yikes. It was true. He *would* get it out of her later. Whatever I said to Mom, she'd be powerless to keep from him. If his glamour was as strong as Nox said it was, he could glamour her into telling him everything. Doing a quick mental rewind of our conversation, I was grateful I'd only said what any concerned daughter would say.

Mom stood. "Now it's my turn to excuse myself. I'm going to the ladies room. Ryann, would you order for me if the waiter comes while I'm gone? I'll have the shrimp po-boy sandwich and fries."

"That's too much bread and fried food. You don't want that," Davis said. "You'd prefer the grilled salmon and house salad—far fewer calories."

I gawked at him, my jaw hanging open. Was he serious?

"I'll take care of it," he assured her with a blinding smile. "Go on now. Take your time."

My entire body got hot in an instant, my blood boiling at his insinuation that Mom should watch her weight. She had a great figure, especially for a woman her age. Any man should be *thrilled* to be with her, exactly as she was.

When she was out of earshot, I said, "So you're choosing her food now?"

He blinked and gave me a look that blended surprise and amusement. "Well, you speak your mind, don't you? Your mother didn't mention the fiery temper. I quite like it. I know exactly whom you got it from."

His implication that I might be *anything* like him burned me even further. "What do you *want*?" I growled.

He laughed, his smile stretching wider. "Not much for small talk, I see. What do I want? Well… what does everyone want? Love and family. Peace and happiness." He lifted his water glass to take a drink.

"Peace, huh? Not world domination? Not Elven rule and human servitude?" It was risky, revealing my knowledge that he wasn't human. But he needed to understand that *someone* was onto him—that he didn't have total carte blanche to do whatever he wanted with my mother.

The glass paused in mid-air, then continued to his lips. He took a sip and set it down gently. "I see you've been listening to my bad press. That's all you'll get from the Light Elves like your grandmother, you know."

Obviously he assumed that was how I knew about his Elven nature, and I didn't contradict him.

His smile returned, more artificial than before. "I'm glad we can speak freely—that's the good thing about family. As I was saying, the *Lightweights* never mention the other side of the story."

"Which is?"

"My concern for our *entire* race—Dark and Light. We've become an endangered species. There is power and safety in numbers. But with our reproductive limitations we have to seek another form of power."

"Lording it over the humans, you mean."

"Royal families are always a small group, but they enjoy safety and security because they maintain control over the masses. And humans are born with a built-in desire to be ruled. They have always worshipped gods in some form or another. My plan will give them gods they can see and touch. They'll be happier for it, and our people will be protected and free. We won't be forced to hide any longer. I don't want to hurt anyone. I only want what's best for *all* of us."

"So… I'm partially human—why tell *me* all of this?"

"You're *my* child. The human part of you is miniscule, inconsequential. I want there to be honesty and trust between us. That's the only way we'll ever have a real relationship. I've already missed your childhood. I don't want to waste any more time. I want you to know me. And I want to know you."

I stared at my plate and pulled the pre-dinner bread into tiny bits. He had all the right words. But they didn't match up to what I knew of his actions. "You *really* didn't know about me all these years? Even with all your... special powers or whatever?"

"I have my talents, but I'm not omniscient, Ryann. Your mother left me. She never told me there was a baby."

My chin lifted as I skewered him with my eyes. "If you loved her so much, why didn't you go after her and get her back?"

Davis sighed and shook his head. "I was ambitious. My mind was focused on rising in the human political realm as well as in the Dark Court. A girlfriend barely out of her teens wouldn't have helped me in the former, and a half-breed lover would definitely not have helped me in the latter. Sadly, at the time I cared more about my position than about love. At your age, you can't possibly understand this, but it's a long life for us, Ryann. There is time for everything, but not always all at once. I always intended to go back to your mother. I always knew where she was—I even visited her a time or two when I traveled to Altum on business."

At my shocked expression, he continued in a placating voice. "Don't worry. She didn't even remember our interludes. I glamoured her to forget them until the time was right for us to be together for good."

"You made her cheat on my father?"

"I *am* your father. She wasn't cheating. She was mine. Just as she *is* mine and will always be. He was a companion I allowed in my absence to prevent her from being lonely."

I closed my eyes, trying to hold down the water and bread I'd had since coming here. My poor daddy. "So then you lied—about me. If you saw her at times over the years, you *must* have known I existed."

"I assumed you were his child. It's so difficult for our kind to conceive. It normally takes decades of trying, and your mother and I were... together but a few times before she left me. I only realized you were mine a few months ago when she visited Atlanta and we reconnected and spoke at length. She mentioned your birthday, and I figured it out. I knew then it was time to re-enter her life... and yours."

Ugh. This was my fault. "You came back because of *me.*"

"I told you—I always intended to reclaim her. But now the timing is right. I've reached the positions I sought in both human government and Elven leadership. That's why I allowed her to keep the memory of our encounter in Atlanta and desire me again. And yes—once I knew about you, meeting my daughter was a big motivation for me. I'm sorry, Ryann."

"Sorry for what?"

"For not being there. For not being the father I should have been—the father I wanted to be."

The look in his eyes was so sincere, the tone of his voice so serious and true. All my instincts told me to believe him. I felt myself relaxing, *wanting* to trust him.

I can't. I blinked and fought to clear my mind. This guy had plotted against Nox, against his parents and Vancia's. Probably. Shaking off the glamour-hold that was trying to pull me under, I scooted my chair back from the table.

"Mom's been gone a long time. I'm going to check on her to see if she's okay."

Davis's hand lifted in a calming gesture. "She's fine. I *told* her to take her time."

Freezing in mid-motion, I studied him with my jaw hanging open. "You glamoured her when you said that? It sounded like just a casual remark. Your Sway *is* strong."

He beamed. "Your Elven knowledge is more advanced than I expected." His gaze sharpened. "How's yours, by the way?"

"My what?"

"Your Sway."

Unwilling to let any more information about myself slip, I lied. "I don't have it."

He leaned forward over the table. "You must. You're my daughter. And the thing that attracted me so strongly to your mother, in spite of her mixed heritage, was her powerful empathy glamour. You're a blend of us. Your glamour must be remarkable. You just need to learn how to use it."

Time for another lie. I shrugged. "Well, I've never felt anything. The human part of me must be dominant."

His hand came down on the table hard, his handsome face screwed into a scowl. "No. I don't believe you." There was a pause as he studied me. "I want to hear you deny it in the Elven way."

My heart started racing. "What are you talking about?"

"You know what I mean. Communicate with me mind-to-mind."

No way was I admitting to that ability. Then he'd ask me all kinds of things I didn't want to answer truthfully. "Um, that's impossible. Does my mother know she's engaged to a crazy man?"

His eyes narrowed at me. "You are bluffing. Show me your Sway *right now*." The stern order came out loud and clear. Loudly and clearly enough that several of the nearby diners turned their heads in our direction.

Though the command was laced with glamour, I found myself able to resist it. Huh. The realization that he couldn't sway me almost made me smile.

"Better lower your voice. You're attracting a lot of attention," I warned him.

Davis glanced around. Raising a brow and laughing, he flipped a dismissive wave in the direction of our onlookers. "Them? They can't hear a thing."

Suddenly, the chatter in the restaurant grew louder.

"What? What did you say?" a well-dressed woman at the next table shouted at her date.

He shook his head. "I can't hear you."

Similar comments filled the balcony, growing louder and louder and turning more panicked by the second. Soon I could hear even the patrons seated inside as they realized they'd suddenly been struck deaf.

My heart fell into the pit of my stomach, ice cold with fear. "What did you do to them?"

Davis grinned again and gave another wave. The noise ceased in an instant. Picking up a crusty French roll and coating it in butter, he said, "No more than you're capable of doing, my daughter. I want to teach you to master your genetic gifts, to reach your full potential. We would be a formidable team, and I could really use the support of my family now—a usurper has surfaced in my kingdom. He has taken what is mine... temporarily." Leaning forward, he lowered his voice in a confidential tone. "I always reclaim what is mine."

Davis sank his perfect teeth into the roll and ripped off a chunk, never breaking eye contact with me.

I did not like him. At all. He had just threatened Nox. Who else could the "usurper" be? And I hated that he was so sure he could just take anything he wanted—and anyone.

"You know, as her daughter, I have some influence over Mom, too. And you should be aware... *I'm* looking out for her *true* happiness." I sounded way more confident than I felt. What could I possibly do against someone as powerful as Davis?

Mom returned to the table before he could respond.

"I don't remember this place ever being so loud. I could hear people talking even inside the ladies room." She took her seat. "Did someone take our orders yet? I'm starving."

Davis laughed and smiled at her adoringly. "Me too, darling. My appetite is never-ending. When I look at what's on the menu, I can't help myself... *I want it all.*"

He gave me a wink then raised his hand slightly. A waiter sped over to the table. As he and Mom placed their orders, I fought a wave of appetite-killing nausea. I was a part of this man. This insincere, power-hungry, egotistical man.

As much as I hated the idea, I wished we'd had more time to talk privately and that I *could* communicate with Davis in the Elven way because I had some questions for *him*, and I wanted some straight answers. What did he really want with Mom? What did he know about Nox, and what did he have planned for him?

Maybe Davis wasn't evil. Maybe he *had* gotten a bad rap from people who didn't really know him. But he was scary powerful. And if he could strike an entire restaurant full of people deaf, could he also have influenced a pilot to crash a plane five years ago? And killed Lad's father in cold blood?

CHAPTER SIX
STILL CONNECTED

I tried to get another few minutes alone with Mom before she left the restaurant with Davis. Over dinner she'd excitedly told me all about the quaint inn here in Oxford where he'd booked a room for them to stay the night. But he stayed close by her side and swept her away quickly after the meal.

The best I could manage was a quick whisper in her ear. "I'll talk to you soon."

Worried, I trudged downstairs to my car and slid behind the wheel. As soon as I got my seatbelt on, my phone rang. I was thrilled to see Nox's name on the screen in a FaceTime request. I grabbed it and touched the screen to answer.

"Hello?"

"Hi baby. Oh, wow—you look beautiful. How's my girl?"

Seeing his face and hearing his sweet tone choked me up. I had to blink back tears. "Oh my God, Nox, I'm so happy to hear from you."

"What's the matter? You look upset. What's going on?"

"I just miss you. And... I had dinner with Davis tonight."

His tone went dark and his expression changed, becoming an angry sneer. "I don't want you around that slick bastard."

I'd never seen Nox so intense. The hatred in his voice worried me. He was with Davis on a regular basis now. Was he able to hide his feelings from the former Dark Elf leader—or was he as transparent to him as he was to me? If Nox wasn't careful, his desire for revenge would get him into trouble.

"Calm down. I'm fine. Mom kept pressuring me to meet him, and I had to do it eventually. I think it's a good thing I did. He mentioned you."

The anger lifted, replaced by instantaneous concern. "He did? What did he say? Wait—I thought he didn't know we knew each other."

"He doesn't. He didn't mention your name. He just told me he could use the support of his 'family' because someone had stolen his throne. He had to be talking about you."

Now his eyes widened. "He asked for your help? Do you think he knows about your abilities?"

I shook my head. "I don't *think* so, unless he's a mind-reader. It's just wishful thinking. And arrogance. I think he found it hard to believe he could possibly have fathered such untalented offspring. He asked me about my Sway— and he wanted me to communicate with him the Elven way."

Nox's eyes widened. "You didn't, did you?"

"Of course not. I pretended not to know what he was talking about."

He closed his eyes and let out a breath. "Good. That's good. Vancia said as soon as he realized you were his biological child, he lost all interest in her. He's been obsessed with meeting you."

"Oh." I shivered in the hot car. "That's creepy."

"Yeah. Please try to avoid him, and whatever you do, don't let him know what you're capable of. Let him keep thinking you're just like any human."

"I wish I was."

Nox's forehead furrowed. "No you don't. Why would you say that? You're perfect just like you are."

"I *hate* that he's a part of me. I hate that whatever special abilities I have come from *him*."

"And your mom," Nox reminded.

"Yeah, but he's the powerful one. His abilities are like, super-strong. And he's bad, you know? What does that make me?" My voice choked over the last few words.

"Hey now. *You*—are good. Don't ever be ashamed of who you are. I love every part of you, no matter where it came from. Never doubt that."

"Okay," I managed to whisper.

"You don't sound very convinced. I wish I was there right now, so I could convince you." One dark eyebrow lifted as his tone turned seductive.

I laughed, blushing and suddenly feeling light-headed. "Okay, okay, I'm convinced. It's just—what am I supposed to do with it? My Sway and my glamour? I feel like I shouldn't be using it at all, considering the source."

"It *can* be used for good, you know, even if your father doesn't use his that way."

"You're sounding an awful lot like a Light Elf there, Mr. Dark King," I teased, making him smile. "Hey, enough of my whining. What's going on with you? You look exhausted."

"Yeah. There's a big party downstairs. Again. I'm sick of all this. There are literally people at my house every night now. It's like Dark Elf Central over here."

"Who are they? What do they want?"

"Well, the High Council's around a lot, trying to teach me about my 'duties' and figure out my position on all these issues—like I even have one, right? Leaders from the Dark clans around the country keep popping into town to pay their respects or whatever. And there are all these strangers who just want to *meet* me. It's so weird. I kinda wish I'd stayed anonymous."

"You had no choice. If you'd done that, you'd be dead. Thank God Vancia was there to vouch for you."

"Yeah," he said, his tone distracted as he looked away from the screen. "Hey, speak of the she-devil—she's here. Say hi to Ryann, Van."

A beautiful face leaned over Nox's shoulder, her blue eyes luminous on the screen, her platinum hair brushing his face. "Hello."

"Hi. Um… how are you?"

"Fantastic." She beamed. "I love it here. It's so good to be back home in L.A., isn't it, Nox? So many great memories here."

His face came back onscreen, though his eyes weren't directed at the camera. He was looking at her.

"Yeah, memories and practical jokes. There was a manta ray swimming in my bathtub this morning. Wonder who could have put it there?" He laughed, and the sound was joined by her musical laughter in the background as his eyes turned back to me. "We used to play jokes on each other all the time when we were kids."

I nodded, stricken by the warm tone of his voice. And the thought she'd been anywhere near his bathtub. "Sounds like fun." Suddenly fighting to speak past a painful lump in my throat, I blurted out a desperate thought. "Let me come out there. I miss you so much. I'll get on a plane tonight. Grandma can handle the factory."

Nox shook his head. "I wish, baby. But you know you can't be seen with me here. I'll have to come see you there."

"When?"

"I don't know. We've got shows all this week and next. There's not enough time in between to fly there and back. I hate this. I thought the schedule was bad when I was just a musician. It's even worse now with my new position.

Hold on a sec." He looked off screen and laughed again. "Okay, see you later."

Clearly "Van" had taken her leave.

"Sorry," he said. "Where were we?"

I swallowed and took a deep breath. "How's it been… with her?"

"What do you mean?"

"You know… being reunited, getting to know each other again. Is she like how you remembered her?"

Nox had told me not only were he and Vancia childhood friends, they'd been very close. Their parents had been best friends, and the two children had grown up together until the tragedy that had separated them and caused them each to believe the other was dead.

She had spent the past few weeks in California with him to make sure he was believed about his identity and to help him acclimate to his new role. That was, unless she was actually there as a spy for Davis. Or for another reason entirely.

"In many ways, yes, she's the same. But a lot has happened since we were twelve. She's changed a lot. I've changed. She's great, though. Reminds me of you in a way."

The remark was unexpected. And irritating. My reply came out with a sour note that surprised me. "I'm sure you'll miss her when she comes back here to be with Lad."

"Um… I guess so. Hey, everything okay?"

"Sure. Why?"

"Well, you just sounded sort of… jealous there, or something."

Time to fess up. He knew me too well. "I guess I am."

And his whole face changed, the anger and darkness returning. "I thought you had no more feelings for him."

What? "No. No—Nox—I meant I was jealous of *her* being there with *you* all this time. You thought I was jealous of Vancia and Lad?"

He didn't answer, but his expression told me he'd believed exactly that.

I sighed. "*You* are the one I spend all day every day missing. I've been listening to your songs non-stop. If I could climb through this phone right now, I'd tell you that in a way you wouldn't be able to doubt."

His face brightened a bit. He was obviously at least partially placated. But his tone still sounded a bit bruised when he responded. "He still wants *you*, though."

My heart skipped a beat as I thought back to the conversation Lad and I had shared on the plane, when he had told me point-blank to break up with Nox. There was no point in telling Nox about it. It would only upset him needlessly. "He's *engaged.*"

"It doesn't matter. I saw the way he looked at you. And he *heard* you when you called for help. There's still a connection."

"Are you still hung up on that? I told you—it's an old connection. A useless one. Maybe it only worked that one time because our lives were in danger."

"So, what about now? You live right there—so close together." He paused, the space filled with apprehension. "Have you seen him?"

"Well… yes. He brings me the saol water deliveries." I rushed to add, "But I told him just today that we need a new system for that. I won't be seeing him at all soon."

There was another long pause. Nox looked down. When his eyes came back to the screen, they were haunted. "So then… it *does* bother you to see him."

It did. But again there was no need for him to know about it—it had nothing to do with him. Or us. It was my own weird problem to get over.

"You're reading into things," I assured him. "We're increasing production now that shipments have started. We need it in larger quantities than I can transport by hand. That's all. Your car's coming in very handy, by the way."

That got a slight grin out of him. "*Your* car, you mean. And I wish you'd let me buy you a new one. That thing's so big, I bet you can barely see over the steering wheel. Wouldn't you love a nice little Mercedes coupe like mine? Maybe silver? Or red. I bet you'd love red."

"No. No fancy cars popping up mysteriously. My mom will think I've become a drug dealer… or the mistress of a rock star," I teased.

He let out a low growl. "I wish. I am *dying* to see you. I'll make it happen soon, I promise."

"Okay. I'll hold you to that."

"Look, I've got to go. And you'd better get on the road for home. Don't you have to get to the factory early tomorrow?"

"I do."

"Okay, babe. Love you."

I kissed the screen as a response.

Nox gave me a sad smile. "It's okay, baby. You'll say it when you're ready."

The sweet words punctured my heart. I hadn't told Nox I loved him yet. I couldn't. Often I felt something close to that sentiment—but when it came time to say the words, they just wouldn't come out. The only time I'd ever said them was to Lad. And exactly as Mom used to warn me, it had come back to bite me in the butt—or the heart, more accurately.

Now she'd changed *her* tune entirely, but the lesson had been burned into my soul. Loving Lad had led to excruciating pain. How could I open my heart to the opportunity for that level of pain again?

"Good night," I whispered, on the verge of tears. It was possible I'd never be ready to say *I love you*. To anyone. Maybe I wasn't even capable of that particular feeling anymore. It was so unfair to Nox.

"Night, beautiful."

As Nox's face disappeared from the screen and I tucked the phone away in my purse, I felt a whole different kind of pain. Being away from him hurt in a hollowed out, aching, needful sort of way. It might not have been love exactly—but he was a powerful addiction, and I was dying for a hit.

CHAPTER SEVEN
FOR A REASON

"Well, what did you think of Davis Hart in the flesh?"

Grandma and I sat at the old farm table in her kitchen that night, both of us up too late. We'd be sorry in the morning, but for now it was a relief to be able to talk through my thoughts honestly. When I'd returned from California, I'd filled her in on what I knew about Davis and the fan pods. As I'd suspected, he had glamoured her when they met, preventing her from realizing his Elven nature.

She'd been disappointed in herself, but I'd assured her she wasn't the first—and certainly wouldn't be the last—to fall prey to his powerful Sway.

"He's charming for sure," I said. "I don't know what I expected. A monster maybe? I think he probably *is* one, but he's got the whole beautiful disguise thing down."

She nodded. "That's what they do. Well, what did he say?"

"He asked me a lot of questions."

Her face pulled tight. "About yourself? About your Elven side?" I could tell she was just as afraid for me as she was for her daughter.

"He thinks I'm like him," I snarled. "He wanted to know what I can do."

"And did you tell him?"

"No. I don't trust him. If he knew I had any abilities at all, he'd probably campaign full-time to draw me over to the Dark Side." I said the last few words in a distinctive Darth Vader voice, making both of us laugh in spite of the serious subject matter.

She sobered up quickly. "Do you think his Sway is strong enough to do that?"

"I hope not. I did feel him trying to sway me, but I was able to resist. That's a good sign, right? I'm worried about something else, though."

"What?"

I drew circles in the condensation on my Coke can, inhaling deeply and exhaling slowly before raising my eyes to meet hers. "What if I *am* like him?"

"Ryann—why would you say that? You know who you are."

"Do I? I thought I did. But now... I don't know. I believed in a lot of things that turned out to be false." Like my parents' marriage. Like Lad's love.

She studied my face. "He hurt you very deeply."

It wasn't a question. Grandma already knew it was true—her empathy glamour doing its thing. And she'd been there for the aftermath of my breakup with Lad, seen me at my lowest.

"Yes. But I'm over it now. Older and wiser, right? Onward and upward and all that stuff."

I could tell from her expression she didn't quite buy it.

"I know you weren't happy with the way it ended between you two, but I'm a firm believer in things happening for a reason, working out exactly as they're supposed to."

I harrumphed. "So Lad was *supposed* to break my heart?"

"Not necessarily. But I believe you *were* supposed to meet him. The fates went out of their way to arrange it— twice."

That much was true. The fates seemed awfully cruel to me if all of that was for nothing. "Maybe. But I'm not sure what the point was. He's marrying Vancia. I'm with Nox."

She lifted her shoulders and let them fall. "Maybe you were supposed to meet Lad for another reason. Knowing him allowed you to learn more about yourself. And about the fan pods and the threat of the Dark Elves. You have these gifts and abilities for a reason, too. Without them, you never would have been able to save Emmy. Maybe you're meant to do even more with them."

"More? You mean the other fan pod girls, don't you?"

I'd been thinking about them a lot—constantly—but what could I possibly do to help them? It was one thing to kidnap one little Mississippian and quite another to free all of them. There had to be thousands, perhaps tens of thousands in this country's fan pods by now, not to mention what was going on abroad.

"The problem's too big. I'm not enough," I told Grandma.

"Maybe not. But Nox is certainly in a position to do something. What does he say about it?"

"He won't tell me *anything* about what's going on with the Dark Court. He doesn't want me involved. He thinks it's too dangerous."

"Well, perhaps he's right. One of my babies is already wrapped up in this mess. Maybe I need to keep my nose out of it and not encourage my other one to step into it. You can stay right here with me, darlin', where it's safe."

Sitting back into my chair, I relaxed for the first time all night. Those were the words I'd wanted to hear. If I couldn't be with Nox in L.A., this was where I wanted to be. At home where I belonged, on the land that I loved, close to all the people I loved—Grandma, Daddy, and Mom. I forced myself to stop the list right there.

This thing with the Dark Elves was way above my pay grade, anyway, and the fact that Nox didn't think I could handle it was further proof that my abilities weren't up to the task.

Looking around the kitchen, breathing in its comforting scent and feeling the smooth, warm surface of the antique farm table under my palms, it was easy to tell myself that the situation in L.A. was under control. And even if it wasn't quite, at least it couldn't touch us here.

I stopped by Channing's Funeral Home the next day on my way home from the factory. Mom had spent the night in Oxford with Davis, and I wanted to catch her here before he could spirit her away again to dinner or Paris or something.

Instead of finding her at her desk, I walked into Mom's office to see Mr. Channing going through her file cabinet. He was a nice man, if an odd one. His overly long tie and overly long hair both seemed to be getting in his way.

I stopped short, just inside the doorway. "Oh, hi. I was looking for my mom."

He flipped his hair back, put down the file he was holding, and gave me a quizzical look. "Hi Ryann. Well, this is peculiar. I would have thought she'd have told you already."

"Told me what?"

"Your mama called me this morning and resigned her position. Said she's moving. I was surprised to say the least."

"What?" I bellowed. "Moving? We're not moving." I started to charge out of the office, then spun back around to see the man's dumbfounded expression. "Thanks, Mr. Channing. I'll figure out what's going on. See you later."

Pulling into the driveway at home, the first thing I noticed was the absence of Mom's car. My nerves began bubbling on a slow simmer as I let myself into the house and walked from room to room, calling her name. Silence. Clearly she wasn't home. Had she decided to stay an extra day in Oxford with Davis?

I hit a button on my phone to call her as I pushed open her bedroom door—and nearly dropped the phone. The place looked like a double-funnel tornado had struck.

Drawers jutted crookedly from her dresser where they'd been left ajar. Her closet door was wide open, the bare hangers strewn there like plastic skeletons in a Halloween specialty store. A few items lay on the closet floor, whether dropped or left behind on purpose I didn't know. One thing that hadn't been left behind was the large red suitcase that usually occupied the top shelf.

What had happened? Why had she packed her things so suddenly?

Genuinely alarmed now, I lifted the ringing phone to my ear. The call went to her voice mail.

"Mom. Where are you? What's going on? Why are all your clothes missing? And you quit your job? Call me as soon as you get this."

Frustrated, I threw the phone onto her bedspread and searched the room further for a note or some kind of clue as to where she'd gone and why. Thinking maybe she'd left a note on the refrigerator or something, I headed for the kitchen.

My text alert tone sent me running back to her room for the phone. And yes, there was a message from her.

-I'm fine honey. Sorry I didn't have a chance to tell you first, but I'm moving in with Davis. Don't worry about me. I'm happy and where I want to be. Will call soon.

What the hell? "No," I said to the empty room. "No." This wasn't right. This just didn't happen. And it wasn't like my mom at all to take off with no warning, no discussion. She was *happy*? It had to be Sway. That was the only explanation for her bizarre desertion. I texted her back, nearly jamming my finger from typing the words so forcefully.

-Call NOW. I need to talk to you. How could you just leave?

There was no response.

I paced the house, needing to do something, but unsure of what. Grandma Neena didn't have a cell phone, but she'd be home soon. Had Mom told her about her moving plans? Probably not.

I practically charged her as soon as the squeaking screen door announced her arrival. "Mom is gone. Did you know?"

She gave me a quizzical glance over the bag of groceries she was carrying. "Gone? What do you mean?"

"I mean she left. Her stuff is gone. She told me in a *text* that she's moving in with Davis."

"What?" Now Grandma abandoned the groceries on the counter, and as if suspecting I was playing a practical joke on her, rushed to Mom's room. Her gasp was audible as she surveyed the disarray. Sitting hard on the bed, she turned to me, her eyes wide and dazed-looking.

"I can't believe this. He's taken her. He's glamoured her into leaving her own child."

"And her mother."

"Yes. But I'm stunned she'd actually leave *you* behind. Why? And why would this happen *now?*"

"Oh." I sat beside her, sinking into Mom's quilted bedspread. "At dinner last night, I did sort of warn Davis I was going to try to talk some sense into her. He must have been worried she'd listen. I shouldn't have said anything, but I wanted him to know that someone was looking out for her."

She patted my hand. "Or maybe taking her was part of his plan all along."

"Maybe. Yesterday Lad told me Vancia wanted to talk to me—about her father. He said they might need my help."

"You didn't tell me this last night. Did you speak to her?" Grandma asked.

"No. I told him I wasn't interested." My face dropped into my hands. I rubbed the heels of them against my eyes. "And she wasn't in town yet. But I should have asked Lad more about it." I lifted my head and looked at her. "I should have found out what he knew. I was in too much of a hurry to get away from him."

She gave me a sympathetic glance. "Maybe it's time you got over that—or figure out why you can't."

I slid off the bed. "I'll go to Altum tonight. Vancia should be there by now. Maybe she can give me some idea where they might have gone."

"I'll go with you. Just let me change my clothes and shoes."

"Okay, I need to call Nox first anyway."

When Grandma left the room, I pulled my phone out again and dialed him. Nox would know what to do. He'd helped me find Emmy, and he had access to all kinds of information about Davis. Besides, I needed him to talk me down from the ledge where I was teetering on the brink of full-blown panic.

The phone rang several times before going to his voice mail. I left a message. "Hi. Um… something's happened, and I really need to talk to you. Call me when you can."

I hung up and looked at the screen—6:30 p.m. That was 4:30 Pacific time. Didn't he say The Hidden had a show tonight? They were probably setting up or in rehearsals or something. No doubt the venue was crowded and loud. I probably wouldn't be hearing back from him for several hours.

Grandma came back to Mom's door. "You ready?"

"Yeah. Let's go."

It didn't really matter. Ready or not, I would meet with Lad and Vancia, and if necessary, work with them to figure out what Davis was up to—and bring my mom back home.

CHAPTER EIGHT
HE WANTS YOU

Arriving in Altum for the first time in months, I marveled anew at the underground world. The last time I'd been here—the day I interrupted Lad and Vancia's wedding—the Assemblage had been going on. Now the place was much more sedate, but no less impressive.

No one I knew would ever believe this entire kingdom could exist here underground, spread underneath who knew how many acres of my grandma's wooded land, completely hidden from human view and knowledge. I could hardly believe it myself. If I tried to describe it to Emmy or Shay, they'd think I'd gone completely against my clean reputation and gotten high.

The cavernous world was so large, the earthen walls so high, you felt more like you were in a suburban shopping mall than underground. The perimeter walls held a vast number of openings, which I'd learned led to more rooms and hallways and tunnels. The open central area, with its magnificent river, was the common area, the floor of which was filled with huts and with people—well, Elves—everywhere, going about their daily lives.

As usual, two large Elven men met us inside the entrance from the surface tunnel. I'd always thought of them as the linebackers because of their intimidating height and wide shoulders, though they'd be more properly described as guards. We followed them to the royal residence, Lad's home.

Waiting outside the huge, carved wooden doors I couldn't help but flash back to Lad's wedding day, when I'd come here with Grandma to give him the good news about our land and the tea company deal that would save it. Of course, at the time, I'd also hoped seeing him again would lead to our getting back together.

It had worked, actually. For a day.

That blissful, awful day seemed so long ago now. We were so far from the love-soaked happiness we'd shared, it seemed like that was all a dream.

As he had on that day, Lad rushed through the doors of his mansion to meet me. "Ryann—what are you doing here? I didn't expect—"

"I know. I'm sorry if it's a bad time. I know you've just been reunited with Vancia."

He shook his head and put his hand on my back, guiding me inside. "No. Not at all. I'm happy to see you. Please come in. Miss Neena, welcome back. Will you be visiting your family this evening?"

"Yes," Grandma said. "But I'm in no hurry." She gave me a questioning glance. *Want me to stay with you while you talk to Lad and Vancia?*

I answered her aloud. "No, you go ahead. I'm okay." Coward-time was over. Now it was suck-it up-and-be-a-big-girl-time. I could handle seeing him, seeing them together. I had no choice.

Lad made a noise that was somewhere between a laugh and a harsh exhale.

"What?" I asked.

He shook his head side-to-side. "I can't get used to the idea of you communicating in the Elven way with anyone but me. Your skills must have improved so much while you were in California with..." He didn't finish the thought.

But he was right. I had gotten rather good at it thanks to all the practice with Nox. I'd even discovered the ability to communicate long distance because of my connection to him. A connection I also shared with Lad.

Still couldn't read his mind, though. The way he studied me with those dazzling green eyes, his appreciative I-can't-believe-you're-here gaze made me wonder what he was thinking.

Uncomfortable, I broke the moment. "Where's Vancia?"

He blinked, as if coming out of deep thought. "This way. Thank you for coming. What changed your mind?"

"My mom is gone. She's disappeared with Davis."

His eyes widened. "How do you know she's not coming back?"

"All her things are gone. And she texted me that she's moving in with him."

"I'm sorry."

"I think he's trying to keep her away from *me*."

Lad nodded as if that made perfect sense. "He's afraid you'll undo his glamour."

The thought made me recoil in surprise. "Really? Why would he think that? He's so strong. And I told him I don't even have any."

"He must suspect, anyway. Did he try to use his on you last night?"

I nodded. "He did. He ordered me to use my Sway in front of him. It didn't work."

"Really? Wow." Lad nodded, his mouth working as he considered it. "So now he either *believes* you don't have it... or he knows you're immune to all glamour."

Before I thought about it, the words were out of my mouth. "Not *all* glamour."

He blinked rapidly, his head jerking back. "What are you talking about?"

"Never mind."

"No. Tell me. This could be important. Did you fall under someone's glamour in L.A.? Vallon Foster? Reggie Dillon?"

"Um... not Reggie... or Vallon."

Lad's eyes grew dark. "Nox. His musical glamour affects you."

"Mmm hmm. Among other things."

His chin lifted, and he studied my face through slitted eyes. "What does *that* mean?"

I looked away and shifted, my clothes suddenly feeling itchy and tight. "Well… I suspect he has multiple glamours. Like me."

I was *not* going to go into specifics, namely the other glamour Nox seemed to have—sexual glamour. Lad and I would not be discussing *that* subject.

"I see." He nodded. After a few moments of strained silence, he spoke again. "Ryann… have you ever considered—"

"I'm not here to talk about Nox. We need to focus on Davis and my mother. Let's just find Vancia. Can't you call her or something?"

He hesitated before answering. "I can't. We have to be in the same room to hear each other."

"Oh."

Interesting. Lad had heard me from across a vast city when I'd called out to him from the trunk of a moving vehicle. He and Vancia couldn't hear each other in the same house? And why did that knowledge cause a tingle of gratification in my chest?

I gave myself a mental slap. That was not something I should feel good about. I should *want* him to have a close connection to the girl he'd be spending eternity with. Still, knowing I retained a connection with him that she *didn't* produced an involuntary stirring in my heart.

Together we walked through the royal residence where Lad encountered several servants and asked them if they'd seen his fiancée.

We found her in a small room, surrounded by canvases. Her back was to us, and she was painting a scene that was clearly from Los Angeles. In fact, looking at the other canvases, in various stages of completion, they all seemed to be California landscapes and ocean scenes. Well, not all of them.

Though only one part of it was visible, one painting tucked behind the others was clearly a portrait—I couldn't see the face, but it appeared to be a guy with black hair and wide shoulders. Obviously Vancia had been *inspired* by her time out west.

"Vancia." Lad spoke to get her attention.

She spun around to face us, dropping her paintbrush.

"Excuse me for interrupting. Ryann has come with some bad news," Lad said.

"What is it?" She leaned over and swept up the brush with her fingertips, popping it into a jar in one graceful move.

I stepped forward. "My mother has disappeared… with your Pappa."

She stood from her painting stool and lifted her chin. "I no longer call him that—except in his presence. He's *not* my real father."

"I know exactly what you mean," I said, experiencing my first real moment of liking for her. Maybe working together wouldn't be so bad. After all, the enemy of my enemy was my friend. "So, I need to know where he's taken her. And why he's doing this. What does he want with her?"

"I can answer that one easily. It's not her he wants. He wants *you*."

A sick feeling curled through my belly as she went on.

"I could tell you almost to the day when he discovered you were his child. He didn't say anything to me about it, but he changed instantly. He was never especially fatherly toward me, but from that day he showed no interest in me. My value to him was solely as bait to lure Lad—and thus the Light Elves—under his control. I'm sure if he'd known who you were earlier and that *you* were already involved with Lad, I would have been discarded entirely."

The look on her face reminded me of a small girl I'd seen recently at an Oxford shopping center. She'd been separated from her mother and stood frozen in the center of a store aisle, her eyes wide and forlorn. I'd been about to offer to take the child to the mall security officer when her panicked mom appeared and swept her up in her arms, both of them bursting into tears simultaneously.

"I'm sorry," I whispered to Vancia.

I was. I knew from what Nox had told me that she'd lost her own parents five years ago. It wasn't fair for that tragedy to be followed with rejection by her adoptive parent.

She dismissed my comment with a wave and a weak smile. "Don't worry about it. It isn't that great a loss. He never actually loved me. I was always a big disappointment to him. When I told him the wedding to Lad was cancelled, he was ready to cut me off without another word for the rest of my life."

Again, my heart tugged in her direction. "That's terrible. But… Lad said you're back in contact with him now?"

"Yes. Davis told me on the day of the wedding I'd someday come crawling back to him. He never believed I could make it on my own. When I needed to get close to him again—so I could figure out what his plan was—I gave him exactly what he was expecting, what he wanted. I went and begged him to take me back. What he *wasn't* expecting—and probably the real reason he agreed to have anything to do with me again—was that I told him Lad and I had reconciled and the wedding was back on."

"I see. What about what happened in Los Angeles? With Nox? Wasn't Davis angry at you for siding with Nox? For supporting him as the Dark Elven king?"

"Oh, I'm sure he was furious. But I explained it this way—that Nox was about to be killed, and as I had discovered he was the missing heir to the Dark Throne, I *knew* Pappa would never want him to come to harm. In front of the Council and the Court, I told him I'd done what I was sure *he* would have *wanted* me to do."

"Smart," I said.

She went on. "Of course he pretended that was true. What could he say? That he wasn't happy Nox was alive? That he didn't want the rightful ruler to lead us? That wouldn't have made him look very good, would it? It would make him seem selfish and power-hungry, which is of course, the truth. But he would never let our people see that. He's the ultimate poser."

"So, he stepped down without any protest then?" I had a hard time imagining it.

Her smile was completely without joy or humor. "He's been very *talkative* since then about his *delight* over this new development and has graciously stepped back into his old position as leader of the High Council. He's made a big show of welcoming Nox and serving him in the Dark Court."

"You don't believe any of it."

The shake of her head was emphatic. "No. All I've seen in my years with him are his unending efforts to increase his own power and influence. It must be killing him inside to take a step down. I've warned Nox never to be alone with Davis. I'm afraid for him." She hesitated before adding, "That's why I stayed out there so long with him." Her cheeks flushed a deep red.

Okay... who was she concerned about getting the wrong idea? Me? Or Lad?

He seemed completely unconcerned. So either he trusted her implicitly—I *knew* he didn't trust Nox—or he didn't care that much about her motivations for spending time with his brother.

Either way, it didn't matter at the moment. What mattered now was finding Mom and getting her away from Davis.

"So, where can I find my mom? I need the address of your house."

"There are several. We have homes in Atlanta, Washington D.C., and Los Angeles. But you can't go to any of them. I'll go."

"So will I," Lad said immediately, obviously uneasy about his fiancée's safety.

"This is *my* mother we're talking about. I have to go." Seeing Lad's obstinate expression, I added, "Imagine if your mother was in danger. Could you stay here and do nothing?"

"No. Of course not. But if Vancia's right, and Davis really wants *you*… I can't let you walk into his trap."

"The first thing we have to do is locate them." Vancia stood and walked to the door. "I'm going to the surface to call 'Pappa.' I'll arrange to meet him wherever he is as soon as possible. It'll be interesting to see if he mentions to me that she's with him. I'll let you know what he says."

My eyes followed Vancia as she left the room. This was my mother's best hope? A girl I wasn't altogether sure I trusted who might just hate me. And I had to rely on her. On my own, I could do nothing to help Mom.

When I thought of her there, wherever she was with Davis, far from home, probably confused, I had to swipe away helpless tears. Embarrassed and angry they'd dared to make an appearance in front of Lad, I turned my back to him. I'd sworn never to cry in front of him again.

"Hey." His large hand came to rest on the nape of my neck. "She'll be okay. We'll find her and bring her home."

And now the tears did flow, overriding my ability to control them. "I know." The words were garbled by sobs. I swished my hands in front of my face, embarrassed. "Sorry."

"Oh Ryann. *I'm* sorry." Lad moved closer and wrapped both arms around me, pulling me close until my wet face pressed against his neck. "Don't be ashamed to cry."

He smelled amazing, as he always had. Though we were no longer a couple, the fresh, woodsy fragrance of his skin had been burned into my nervous system long ago. It would always remind me of safety. And pleasure. And first kisses. I wanted to bury my face in that heavenly scent and stay like that, letting the old feelings of childlike trust cover and comfort me.

I didn't. Pulling away, I took a step toward the door. "I should go now. I need to talk to Nox."

Lad's expression instantly morphed from tenderness to a careful blank.

I hadn't meant it as an insult. I just needed some distance from him. Too much closeness muddled my brain. Though I didn't have to explain myself, I did anyway for some reason.

"He's spent a lot of time around Davis lately. Maybe he knows something that would help. He hasn't wanted to talk to me about the Dark Elves and their plan, but I need to know whatever he knows now. He's been so worried about protecting me. I just hope he's watching his own back."

I shivered at the thought of Nox putting himself in harm's way. I hated that he was out there in the middle of the Dark Elven landscape with no one to help him.

Lad must have noticed it and guessed my fears. He stepped closer but made no move to touch me again.

"He'll be all right. Nox is a big boy. He can take care of himself. He always has."

I bristled at his tone, feeling suddenly defensive of Nox. "Because he *had* to. He was all alone in the world."

"No. He had my parents. He had *me*. What did he tell you? Because I loved him like a brother. I would have done anything for him until…"

He stopped right there, but I finished his sentence. "Until he tried to take *me* away."

His brow furrowed and he let out a tired sigh. "He didn't *take* you. I don't blame him for what happened between you and me. I have only myself to blame for that. Come on, I'll walk you home."

CHAPTER NINE
DON'T CROSS ME

We parted at the edge of Grandma's yard where the woods ended. Though I'd assured Lad I'd be fine to walk home on my own, he'd insisted on escorting me. What he didn't know was, as far as I was concerned, the most dangerous thing in this forest was him. Because he still had the power to confuse me.

It wasn't that I doubted my feelings for Nox. He deserved my loyalty, and he had it. And there was something so alluring and addictive about Nox it made my head spin. But that didn't mean the feelings I'd had for Lad had magically disappeared.

I'd thought a lot about it—why he still affected me. Maybe it was our childhood connection, or all the time we'd shared this past spring, or maybe it was that my love for him had come first, but it felt like he'd been tattooed onto my heart. No—not a tattoo—a brand. Tattoos could be removed. Brands went deeper. They couldn't be erased short of amputating a body part. Unfortunately, I couldn't survive without my heart, so I was kind of stuck with this crazy mixed-up mess inside.

Ugh. Why had I thought I could handle being around Lad again? What I needed was to spend some time with Nox.

I stepped through the back door into the kitchen, thinking of him. *Where are you? I miss you. I need you.*

The phone in my pocket rang before the thought was finished.

Heart thundering, I whipped it out of my pocket and up to my ear. "I was just thinking of you. Could you feel it?" He couldn't possibly have heard me all the way out in California, could he? If he had, that really *meant* something.

There was silence on the line followed by a voice that did *not* belong to my long-distance boyfriend.

"Hello Ryann. That was a rather interesting question. Who did you think you were speaking to? Not your mother, I think."

My heart froze. It was Davis.

I pulled the phone away from my ear and looked at the screen in horror. He was calling me from her number.

My voice shook with adrenaline when I responded. "Where is Mom? Why are you using her phone? Is she okay?"

"She's fine. I felt she'd be... happier here with me. You two are quite close. And as you are not completely in support of our wedding, I didn't want her to catch cold feet."

Anger burned in my gut. "What kind of man has to brainwash a woman into being with him?"

"What kind of daughter would talk her mother out of being with her eternal bond-mate?" Davis snickered. "I told you I always regain what's mine sooner or later. You won't cross me if you want your mother to *stay* safe and happy."

"Don't you dare threaten her."

"Do I seem like the kind of man who would hurt a woman—a *mother*?"

The sneer in his voice reminded me of what had happened to Vancia's parents. And made me fear for Nox's mother. She'd disappeared after dropping him off with her sister Mya in Altum. Nox had always assumed she was dead. Had she fallen into Davis's hands? I shuddered to think of the ways he might have tortured her before killing her, trying to get information about her missing son.

"You had better not, if you value your eternal life," I growled.

"There's that family temper again. Don't worry, little girl. I have no desire to harm the mother of my child. And there will be no need to… as long as you behave."

"What is it that you want from me?"

"Well, since you've asked, I'd like for you to join us. Then we can all be together—one happy family."

I didn't say anything, struck mute by the battle between what I wanted to say—"go to hell"—or whatever the Elven equivalent of hell was—and the thought that maybe I *should* join him. At least I'd be near my mom and could try to figure out how to get her away from him.

Before I could answer either way, Davis chuckled. "No? Well, let me know when you're ready."

And he hung up the phone.

I started shaking all over, berating myself. I should have said yes immediately. I should have asked where they were and volunteered to fly there tonight. Anger and fear had paralyzed me when I should have taken action. I hit the call-back button and listened as the call went directly to Mom's voice mail.

And then I knew. There was no decision to make. I was involved now in the battle against the Dark Elves, like it or not, capable or not. It didn't matter whether my Elven abilities were up to the task. I had to do something. Mom's life might depend on my actions right now.

Nox would just have to understand. After all, his life might depend on it, too. And the fate of the human race wasn't looking real good either at this point. I would have to work with Lad and Vancia, no matter how hard it might be. No matter how thick the awkward got.

Though darkness had fallen already, I had no time to waste. I turned off the lights in the log cabin, shut the door behind me, and headed back into the woods. Back to Altum.

CHAPTER TEN
HAVE YOU?

This time when I entered the underground kingdom, the bodyguards didn't even blink or wait for me to explain why I was there. They led me right to the doors of the royal residence and opened them. Lad met me just inside the entryway.

"Ryann—I didn't expect to see you again so soon. You didn't walk through the woods alone, did you?"

"I'm not a six year old. I don't get lost anymore," I quipped, referring to the way we'd met a decade ago.

"I still don't like you being alone out there." His expression was grim, but I saw him making an effort to control his displeasure. "Come in. Why did you return? Tell me what's happened."

"Davis called me—on my mom's phone. He wouldn't let me talk to her. I think you were right. He took her to keep her away from my influence. Or maybe as bait."

"Bait?"

"To get me to join him."

Lad's nostrils flared as he straightened to his full height. "I'm even more convinced now that you should stay here while Vancia and I—"

"No. I'm going. Don't even try to talk me out of it. I'm going to get her back and figure out what his plan is—how he intends to install Dark Elven rule over the world. If I'm the bait, then so be it."

Lad exhaled slowly. "Let's find Vancia."

His fiancée was in her own private quarters within the royal residence. Far, I noted with some perverse satisfaction, from his room. She invited us into the sitting area and sent a servant to get some food and drinks for us.

Like the studio where she'd been working earlier, this room was filled with gorgeous paintings, each one seeming to come to life on the canvas, almost glowing from within. They were like nothing I'd ever seen.

I gestured to the nearest one. "Your glamour?"

She nodded. "Yes—artistic glamour—isn't that laughable?"

"What do you mean? Your work is beautiful."

"It drove my 'Pappa' crazy—he wanted me to have a more 'useful' glamour, like music or acting—something that would attract a fan pod. All I ever wanted was to roam the world and find new subjects for my art, then sit in a room for days and let my imagination flow through a paintbrush."

"So, why does he want *me*? I don't have a useful glamour like that. And I know he doesn't actually..." I shuddered as I said it. "... love me."

"I'm not sure. But it must have something to do with his plan. He never does anything without a reason. Here's what I've been able to put together so far—I think we all realize by now the fan pods are the first step toward the goal of complete human domination by the Dark Elves. When Pappa—Davis—first informed me of my betrothal, he told me my role would be persuading my new husband..." She stopped and glanced over at Lad. "... to join the cause. Davis said the Dark Elves didn't have the numbers needed to accomplish the plan on our—their own."

So she didn't consider herself one of them anymore. Interesting. Maybe she'd already adopted the Light Elves as her people in preparation for her marriage.

Lad engaged her in direct eye contact, and I watched the two of them as they presumably communicated mind-to-mind. They leaned in close, their foreheads almost touching. Any lingering questions about theirs being a fake engagement dissipated. They'd only known each other since the Assemblage, but they obviously had formed a great rapport in a short amount of time. Maybe it happened quickly when you were two of a kind.

I worked to keep my mind focused on Mom and not my own crazy confused emotions. "How much does technology have to do with the plan?" I asked Vancia.

"What? What did you say?" She instantly broke mental communion with Lad and turned to me with wide eyes and an expression that looked almost terrified.

"Technology. TV, internet, radio waves, satellites. When I was in Reggie's fan pod, I noticed the girls were always watching recordings of his games and interviews. There were TV's everywhere, even out by the pool. And of course they were constantly reminding us to post on social media about him. Nox's house manager encouraged us to do the same thing. The girls in both houses were totally glamoured, even though I know at Nox's house, they were hardly ever with him in person." *Because he was with me as much as possible.*

Vancia's skin blanched as white as the beautiful Elven-made dress she was wearing. "That's it. That's why."

Lad touched her hand. "What is it?"

"Whenever Pappa met with the Council, their conversations were always about the latest advances in communications technology. I never could figure out why they were so obsessed with it—well except that Pappa is the Chairman of the Senate Science and Technology Committee."

"What legislation was the committee working on? Do you know?" I asked.

"I'm trying to remember. I know it was something about increasing the pace and volume of cell tower construction. Some kind of eminent domain thing, so the government could basically mandate building them anywhere it wants to and the residents of the area can't stop it."

"I remember a few years ago, someone wanted to build one near the elementary school in Deep River. There was a big petition and the people of the town were able to get them to change their plans," I said.

"Right. It happens often," she said. "Everyone wants their mobile devices, but no one wants a tower in their own back yard. This bill would essentially ensure total signal coverage, no matter where you look on the map."

I pictured one of those wireless company ads with the red dots clustered in areas of "good" coverage and spread out more sparsely in areas where it was weaker. Davis's bill could lead to a solid red map. Great for business. Bad for the world overall.

"With most of us carrying smart phones everywhere we go now, there's more opportunity for us all to watch videos and listen to music," I said.

Vancia nodded. "And more opportunity for the Dark Elven celebrities to spread their glamour."

"Do you think it might be more than that? More than increased opportunity? Maybe the electronic signals actually enhance the glamour," Lad suggested.

Vancia bounced and shifted to tuck one leg under her, waving enthusiastically. "Yes. That makes sense. That would explain why fan pods are growing so much faster now than ever before. My agent Alfred came up with the fan pod system. He started representing Dark Elven clients in the fifties, when TV first got going. He must have figured out what the signals do."

"Great. So what do we do—go around knocking down cell towers with bulldozers? That's not very practical. And what about the satellites? We can't exactly shoot them out of the sky," I said.

Lad and Vancia sighed at the same time.

"Maybe we could somehow stop the bill from passing?" Lad suggested.

Vancia shook her head. "Doubtful. I was there when Davis *persuaded* two of its biggest opponents to vote for it. By the end of the evening, they were practically ready to campaign for the thing. Besides, even if it doesn't pass, the signal coverage and device usage will continue to increase. It'll get to total coverage eventually. People don't want to go backward and give up the technology they've grown attached to. They only want more and better and faster. It'll happen sooner or later."

"You're right," I said, running my hand over my own phone in my pocket. It was my lifeline to Nox. To Mom. To all my friends. I couldn't imagine living without it. "Everyone I know is completely addicted to their phone. Me included. So... how do we stop this?"

"I'm not sure," Vancia said. "But I think we all agree the first thing we have to do is get your mother away from Davis. I spoke with him briefly and found out they're in D.C."

"Did he mention her?"

"Not by name, but he did say it wouldn't be a good time for me to join him. He said he had a companion who was under the weather and not up for company."

I sat forward in my chair. "Do you think she's really sick? She didn't look that great the other night. The longer she's with him, the more willpower of her own she seems to lose—I've watched it eroding day by day." And then a terrible thought occurred to me. "Do you think the Sway can cause permanent damage?"

Vancia looked off to the side, appearing to consider it. "That's a good question. I've always been reluctant to use mine because it weirds me out to see humans with those vacant eyes and acting so subservient. It is possible if it's changing their brain function or chemistry that someone who's subjected to it long-term could suffer brain damage."

"There was a girl from Deep River who joined a fan pod. She was gone for three years. She died, and the people at the funeral home said there were no signs of injury or foul play. Maybe that's what happened to her. Maybe she didn't like being there, and someone had to influence her repeatedly to keep her there and keep her quiet." Reflecting on my mom's tired face at dinner, I felt an increased sense of urgency. "So when do we leave?"

"I scheduled a flight for tomorrow on one of my father's planes. He's given me use of it so I can fly back and forth between my work in California and my fiancé here. We can all take off from the airport in Oxford at noon."

I turned to Lad. "You don't have to go. I know you have a lot of responsibilities here." As little as I looked forward to spending girl time with Vancia, I had to say it. I knew what his people meant to him. I had come between him and his duty to them too many times already.

He looked me directly in the eye. His gaze didn't waver. "I want to go. You're not alone in this."

When I'd asked for his help to find Emmy, he'd told me I was on my own. Now, he was insisting on helping me save my mom. What had caused such a drastic change in his attitude? Maybe he'd finally realized what a threat Davis and the Dark Elves were.

"Okay then. I guess I'll see you both tomorrow." I got up to leave, and Lad stood to join me.

After we left Vancia's quarters, I assumed Lad would offer to escort me home again, but he didn't. He stopped in the hallway, right in front of his room, and turned to face me. "Stay here tonight."

"What?"

"Your mother is gone. Your grandmother is here with her family. Stay here. I don't think it would be good for you to be alone tonight. I'd offer my room, but you'd probably be more comfortable in your family's quarters."

"Um, yeah, okay. You're right. It's so late now anyway. Well, I guess I'll see you tomorrow then." I started to walk away, assuming he'd open the door and go into his room for the night, but he fell into step beside me.

"I'll go with you. The hallways here can be a bit of a maze."

We walked together in silence. I wasn't sure if he felt awkward, but I certainly did. "So, when's the wedding?" I finally asked to fill the quiet space between us.

He blinked several times and cleared his throat before answering. "We haven't set a new date."

"Oh." He didn't explain further, and I didn't ask. Obviously he felt uncomfortable discussing the topic with me, and really, their relationship was not my business.

Arriving at the entrance of Grandma Neena's family home, I grabbed the door knob and glanced back over my shoulder to tell Lad goodnight. Before I could get the words out, he put a hand on my upper arm, turning me around to face him.

He said nothing, just stared at me, glanced away, and then caught my eyes again. His chest was rising and falling rapidly as if he'd been for a jog instead of walking slowly through Altum with me. He was even sweating a bit, his forehead glistening with a light sheen of moisture.

"Lad... what's..."

"Ryann." He took one of my hands in his. My gaze dropped to our fingers in surprise and then flew back up to meet his eyes. They looked strained.

"You haven't..." He stopped and appeared to be searching for the right words. "Have you... did you bond? With Nox? When you two were in California?"

My heartbeat instantly accelerated from cruise control to hyperspeed. I gasped and extracted my hand, which had broken out in a sweat. "*That* is none of your business."

"I know. But if you haven't... I mean... I hope you haven't. Please don't, Ryann."

My astonishment at the fact he'd dare to even talk to me about the subject, much less make such a request of me, made me stutter. "For one thing, you... *you* don't get to weigh in on that decision. For another—he's a *good* person, Lad. The things you think you know about him aren't true. I know the *real* Nox."

He nodded tightly. "I know. He is. That's not why I said it."

"So... why..."

"I..." He stopped, looked down, let out a sharp breath, then met my gaze again. "I'm just asking you to wait. Please." And that's where he stopped.

I huffed a laugh. "Well, the Abstinence Council would be very pleased with you, I'm sure, but I don't need your advice on my love life. Goodnight Lad."

I stepped inside and shut the door firmly behind me, leaving him standing in the hallway. Leaning against the interior of the heavy door, I let out a shaky breath. All of me was shaking as a matter of fact. How exactly was I supposed to face my extended Elven family after *that* conversation?

And what was Lad trying to do to me? Did he want to keep me around as his plaything while he and his fiancée planned their wedding? No thank you, sir. I had someone who wanted to put me *first*—if only we could manage to be in the same place at the same time.

CHAPTER ELEVEN
WORLD TOUR

The next morning I rose early, told Grandma good bye and to try not to worry, and headed for home. I dialed Nox as soon as I got near the clearing of our yard where there was a decent signal. I'd missed his return call last night when I'd been in Altum, far too deep for any satellite coverage to reach.

Nox's voice was edgy and strange. "Good morning. I'm glad to hear from you. I was worried last night when you didn't answer the phone—especially after your message."

"I'm sorry. My phone was…" I hesitated to tell him I'd stayed overnight in Altum. He was already needlessly concerned about my spending time with Lad. "… out of service. I didn't see I'd missed your call until just now. It's good to hear your voice."

"You too. I miss you." The bitter tone was gone, and his voice regained its usual spellbinding smoothness.

My confusion from last night evaporated. *This* was the voice that filled my heart, made my knees so weak I could barely stand, and inspired thoughts that made me blush.

"Is it an okay time for you to talk? What are you doing?" I asked.

"Um… nothing."

"Oh no. I woke you up. I'm sorry. I keep forgetting about the time difference."

Now a smile entered his voice. "No problem. I actually haven't been in bed that long—I wasn't even really asleep yet. We had a good show—tried a couple new songs. They still need work, but they went over pretty well. So what's going on? What are *you* doing?"

"Actually, I'm in the woods." I took a deep breath and told him the truth. "I just left Altum."

"What were you doing there?" The smiley tone had disappeared.

"I was meeting with Lad and Vancia. That's what I called you about." I paused before admitting the rest. "We're going to do something about Davis."

"No. No, Ryann. I've already told you I don't want you involved. It's too dangerous. You don't even know—"

"No, *you* don't know. My mom's with him, Nox. I got home from work yesterday, and she was gone. All her stuff is gone. She's moved to Washington D.C. with him. I know you don't want me involved, but I *am*. I have to be. Davis *has my mother*—and it's my fault."

"Your fault? You mean for being born? Don't be ridiculous. No one's at fault here but Davis. Listen,

Ryann. Don't do anything, okay? I'm coming home. Forget the tour, forget the Dark Throne crap. I'm coming back. I'm going to help you. We'll get your mom back."

My heart leapt at his eagerness, at the thought of seeing him again soon. There was nothing I wanted more. And just as quickly it sagged in my chest because I couldn't allow it.

"You can't. You have to stay there."

"No—"

"You *have* to, Nox. You still don't know who you can trust, who might be on Davis's side. If you go running off and leave your court, if anyone figures out *why*—that we're together—it could be even more of a danger to my mom. And to you." He started to protest until I added, "And to me."

His aggravated sigh was as clear as if we were in the same room. "You're right. Damn it. I want to be with you right now. I feel like an alcoholic desperate for a drink—I don't know how much longer I can wait."

It was amazing how accurately he'd described the exact feeling I had when I talked to him on the phone or listened to his music. It truly was like an addiction, and the withdrawal symptoms were kicking in big time.

"I know what you mean. But we *have* to wait. If Davis really is planning to overthrow you and get his position back, you leaving right now could give him the perfect opportunity. Don't worry about me—I'll be okay. We'll handle the thing with my mom."

"What are you going to do? Please tell me you don't intend to go to D.C. after her."

"I'm going to D.C. after her."

"Ryann…"

"Not alone. Vancia will be there. If anyone knows how to handle her father, it's her."

"What about Lad?"

"He's coming, too." Why hadn't I mentioned that to Nox earlier? Because I knew how he'd react, that's why.

His response was a low growl. "Why? Why is he always around?"

"He's not 'always' around. He brings me the saol water. That's it. I've hardly seen him. And of course last night we met to talk about the thing with my mom."

"And now you're going to travel with him."

"*And* with Vancia—his fiancée."

"Yeah, well…" He didn't finish the thought. Just left it hanging there.

"Well what?"

"When she was here, she never talked about him. Other than to confirm they *are* planning to get married, she didn't have much to say about him or their plans. And… well, she doesn't *act* engaged."

That got my attention. How does one act *not*-engaged?

"If you ask me," he continued. "She's not really that into him."

A thrill of alarm went through me. If Vancia wasn't that into Lad, who was she interested in? Part of me wanted to ask him to elaborate. The rest of me knew I'd sound like an insecure wreck if I did. I went for nonchalance.

"Well… that's too bad. For them. It would be a shame to spend eternity with someone you're not that into. Anyway, enough about them. Tell me about you."

Now the warmth was back. "What's to tell? I'm missing my hot girlfriend who I'm crazy in love with."

I giggled. "How's your shoulder?"

"All better. You know, accelerated healing, blah, blah, blah. Alfred was so mad at me for getting myself shot just as our first single was coming out. He was totally freaking about the tour. But my playing is back to normal, and the tour's still on schedule."

"Maybe we'll get all this resolved, and you can come see me before you leave."

"Maybe you can come *with* me—see the world, keep me company?"

"What?"

"Yeah." His voice gained excitement as the idea seemed to solidify for him. "It's the perfect solution. You can't come to L.A. because of the Council and the Dark Elves who might still be loyal to Davis. But the only ones you'd see on the road would be my bandmates. And they're not going to mess with us. All they care about is the music. And the girls. Rye—you have to come with me. We're even going to be part of the Opening Ceremonies for the Summer Olympics in Boston—don't you want to see that?"

"Of course, and I want to see you. But what about school? What about the tea company?" *What about the fact I lose my mind every time I hear you sing?* I could only imagine the mess I'd be if I traveled with the band and heard them perform night after night.

"I don't know. I'll hire you a tutor or something. And your grandma can run the company."

Grandma had already shown she could handle the factory, and what better education was there than traveling the world? I *was* desperate to be with him.

Still, something inside of me balked at the idea of leaving home, of leaving the land and my family and friends behind long-term. *And* at the thought of immersing myself in a nightly glamour-bath, listening to his music. It all left me less excited than I should have been about the idea of hitting the road with Nox. It was complicated.

"I don't know. I want to. I'll think about it. I can't really plan *anything* until I find Mom."

"Of course. Listen, I've got another call coming in. It's Alfred. I'll call again soon. Love you."

"Mmm hmm." Why couldn't I make those three little words come out of my mouth? I knew it bothered him when I didn't return his declaration. I was certainly crazy about him—almost to an obsessive degree. So what was holding me back? "Get some sleep. And be careful."

"*You* be careful. And tell Lad if he lets anything happen to you, he's a dead man."

"Nox—don't joke about things like that."

His voice was surly when he replied, "Who's joking?"

CHAPTER TWELVE
As Long As She Lives

After showering and changing, I stopped by the tea factory to check on production then headed to Daddy's apartment in Oxford. I wanted to see him before leaving for D.C.

He opened the door after the second knock, his eyes going wide at the sight of me then crinkling into the smile I'd loved all my life. "Well, there's my girl. What brings you by this morning? Everything okay?"

"I wanted to see you." I held up a bottle of Magnolia Sugar Tea. "And to bring you some fresh supplies. How are you?"

"Good. Good. Come on in." He led me into the kitchen where he pulled out a glass from the cabinet. "You want some?"

"No thanks. Being around it all day has killed my appetite for it." That wasn't the entire truth about why I'd stopped drinking my own sweet tea, but I couldn't get into it with Daddy.

"Well, I haven't had nearly enough. It's not in my local store yet. I have to wait for 'special deliveries.'"

We both laughed and took a seat at the tiny dinette set. I surveyed Daddy's appearance. He'd gotten even thinner than the last time I'd seen him. Was the poor man not eating at all?

"How are you… really?"

His smile faltered. "I'm getting by, darlin'. The job is fine." His job had never been in question. I was referring to his Mom-withdrawals, and he knew it. He sighed deeply, his shoulders rising and falling. "How is she?"

"She's…" Oh God. How did I tell him this? "She moved out."

He stood up so fast his chair fell over backwards and smacked the linoleum floor. "Moved? When? Where?"

"Yesterday. It was all kind of sudden. She's moving in with Davis. She sent me a message, but I haven't been able to reach her since then to get any more details."

He slammed his hand down on the table. Then, after a minute, righted the chair and slumped back into it, shaking his head. "I don't understand. How did all this happen—and so fast? She's not acting like herself."

"I agree. I'm going to try to talk to her. But you—you need to think about yourself." I reached across the table to lay my hand on his forearm. "About taking care of yourself, *eating* every once in a while, having some fun. And you need to find some way to move on."

"I can't." He rested his forehead against his clenched fists as he leaned his elbows on the table top. "There's something about her. I always knew she was out of my league, but there's no one else for me. As long as she lives... I'll be under her spell."

Poor Daddy. He was under her glamour, and neither he nor Mom even realized it. I was surprised it was still so strong when they hadn't really been close to each other in months. How tragic would it be if he was right—if the only thing that broke the spell for him was her life ending? As a half-Elf, she might live forever, or at least for hundreds of years. His relatively short life would come and go in misery.

And then a thought hit me. What if death *did* break the glamour? My heart rate sped up until I felt like I *had* drunk too many glasses of caffeinated tea.

Who knew how many unsuspecting humans were under Davis's powerful glamour. *If he were to die...*

We had to stop him. That much was clear. Ending his life, and therefore his glamour control, was one possible solution. And a permanent one at that. But could I *really* kill my own father? I couldn't kill *anyone*. I was a high school senior with a talent for making sweet tea—not some fierce Elven warrior.

"I don't trust that man—and it's not just his politics," Daddy said. "He's got a shifty look about him. And he's too good-looking. I mean, what kind of middle-aged man looks like that? I don't think he's changed a lick in the twenty years he's been in office. He's got to be getting plastic surgery."

"Definitely," I agreed. "And hair plugs."

He laughed out loud, but his smile fell away as he picked up his glass and rubbed his thumb over the smooth surface. "They do make the perfect couple."

"No. They don't. You two made the perfect couple."

He reached over and squeezed my hand, his fingers cold from the glass, but the gesture warmed me. "Well, I know one thing, we have the perfect daughter. I've loved you from the minute you were born. You know that, right?"

I nodded, fighting tears. This was my *real* father. "I love you, too, Daddy. You're the best dad I could ever have hoped for."

If it ever came down to it and there was a choice between his life and Davis's—there would *be* no decision. I might not be too sure about my own identity right now, but I knew who my family was.

I made it to the Oxford Municipal airport before Lad and Vancia. When they arrived, they approached my car together, walking in perfect synch. Nearly the same height, they seemed to glide toward me, their long legs matched stride for stride. Now *there* was a perfect pairing.

I watched them laughing together over some inside joke, no doubt, and my gut filled with a burning sensation—which I promptly doused with a bucketful of reality. I had no right to jealousy. Just because I'd seen him give me that same brilliant smile before, felt the shivers inspired by that deep laugh of his—none of that mattered anymore. He was *supposed* to get along with her for God's sake. She was his fiancée. And I had moved on. But something inside me kept insisting things were all wrong.

I *really* needed some time with my own boyfriend. Too bad this plane wasn't bound for L.A.

As they reached the car, and Lad saw me behind the uplifted trunk lid, he turned that sun-shaming smile in my direction. My heart did a crazy so-you-think-you-can-dance move as he left Vancia's side. Stupid disoriented heart.

He reached me and grabbed the handle of my suitcase. "Let me get that."

"Thanks. Don't you two have any bags?"

"Well, we're going to one of Vancia's houses, so she has things there already. If we end up staying more than a day, Van said she'll buy something for me. As you know, my human wardrobe selection is rather limited. I've got Scarecrow Beefcake, as you called it, and Beach Bum." He gestured to the shorts and t-shirt he now wore—the same outfit he'd worn when he and Vancia had barged in on me and Nox in Nox's bedroom in L.A.

"Follow me." Vancia strode across the tarmac toward a sleek white and gold Gulfstream, the plane we'd flown from Los Angeles here. As she neared it, the boarding steps lowered and a distinctly Elven-looking pilot greeted her.

Lad and I followed her aboard. I went to the furthest back row and settled into one of the captain's chairs, pulling out a book to pass the time on the flight. Instead of sitting with Vancia toward the front of the cabin, Lad passed her seat and came to my row.

He slid into the seat beside me and buckled his belt, angling to get a look at the cover of my paperback. "Anything I've read?"

For a moment I could only stare at him. "What are you doing?"

"What?"

"Why are you sitting here? Don't you want to sit with Vancia?"

He shrugged. "I thought we could talk on the way there—maybe figure some things out."

"What 'things?'"

"Tell me about your dinner with your mother and Davis. Did he tell you anything else that might be helpful to us?"

"Oh. Uh, well… let me think." So Lad was here on business. Okay then, what could I tell him that might help? "He warned me not to interfere with him and my mom. He told me he didn't believe me when I said I had no Sway—oh speaking of that—I talked to my dad this morning. Something he said made me think. He said he'd never be free of my mom's 'spell' as long as she lived. That was the word he used—'spell.' And I wondered… does the

Sway lift from all the influenced humans when the Elf who swayed them dies? Is that true?"

"I'm not sure. Not many Elves die. I always thought the Sway would dissipate when the one who used it on a human was no longer close to that human, but your mom and dad don't see each other anymore, and you think he's still affected by hers?"

"Absolutely. And when I was in the fan pods, I witnessed long-lasting effects even when Reggie… and Nox… weren't close by the girls."

His eyes met mine and held for a long beat. "What about you?"

"What do you mean? What about me? I told you—Davis wasn't able to sway me."

He swallowed and looked away. When he met my gaze again, his expression resembled someone about to cross a high wire between two skyscrapers on a windy day. "I'm not talking about Davis. You said Nox's glamour—or glamours, whatever—*did* work on you. What if…" Here he halted and looked away again, toward the front of the cabin.

"What if what?"

"What if… it's *still* working? I mean, what if the feelings you have for him are all…" He scrunched his face in an apologetic wince.

As his implication hit me, heat rose in my cheeks, building behind my eyeballs like steam in a teapot. "Are you suggesting the only reason I feel a connection to Nox is that he's glamoured me? That he's *still* glamouring me into believing I have feelings for him that aren't really there?"

He raised his brows. "You have to admit it's possible."

"No. It's not. I know what I feel." But did I? I *had* been questioning my feelings since coming home. I'd stressed just last night about Lad's lingering ability to affect me and about the effect Nox's music had on me.

And then I got mad. How dare he suggest my relationship with Nox wasn't real. It had certainly been more real than Lad's 'love' for me these past few months. How dare he. And besides, what if I was a little glamoured by Nox? For someone who was no longer capable of the real thing, glamour might be a pretty nice love-substitute.

I leaned forward, my voice a harsh whisper. "Nox and I spent a lot of time together in L.A., and we went through a lot. *He* was *there* for me. You know what? You should probably go sit up front with your girlfriend. I have some reading to catch up on." I grabbed my book and opened it to the bookmark before realizing it was upside down. Quickly righting it, I stared at the page and pretended to read.

Lad didn't move. From my peripheral vision I could tell he was still looking at me. I glanced over at his pleading eyes, and then quickly back to the meaningless words swirling on the paper in front of me.

Finally he sighed and rose from his seat, making his way toward the front of the cabin. He plopped into the seat beside Vancia and leaned over to say something to her. She twisted and glared at me through the opening between their seats before turning back to Lad and tipping her head in close to his.

CHAPTER THIRTEEN
THE OTHER THING SHE SAID

Upon our arrival in D.C., Lad disembarked first, leaving me and Vancia alone together in the cabin. Instead of following him off the plane, she shocked me by coming down the center aisle straight toward me.

"What is your problem?" she demanded.

I blinked several times in rapid succession. "What are you talking about?"

She stared at me, a skirmish of thoughts racing across her face. Finally she exhaled a hard breath and shook her head. "Lad and Nox both seem to think you're so smart, but I don't see it. And Davis thinks you've got some kind of glamour super powers—what a laugh. You have no idea what you're doing—with your glamour *or* with guys."

I felt my jaw drop open. What was she talking about? I *wasn't* all that experienced with relationships, but what was that to her? "Look, if you're afraid I'm trying to steal your guy, don't be. Lad and I—"

She laughed out loud. "Oh that's beautiful. Just beautiful."

Lad's head popped into the door opening. "What's the hold up, ladies? Everything okay?"

Vancia pushed past him and stomped off the plane.

He only smiled and held out a hand for my bag. "Cab's here. Come on."

"What's up with her?"

"Don't worry about it. She doesn't think you should be here—thinks it's too dangerous and that we should have handled it ourselves."

"Oh yes. She's *clearly* beside herself with worry over my safety."

He laughed. "She *is* concerned about it." Closing his eyes, he gave a quick shake of his head. "Listen, she's under a lot of stress right now, but she's actually very kind."

I rolled my eyes. "That's what I keep hearing from you and Nox—what a *great* girl she is. Still waiting for *that* girl to show up, by the way."

We didn't talk about our mission on the way to the house. Vancia was too paranoid about the driver overhearing. She'd told the pilot I was one of her new friends from Altum and seemed to think he'd buy the story. Maybe my height—typical for Elven females—helped.

When we arrived at the brick townhouse in Georgetown, the driver pulled over to the tree-lined curb in front of it. Vancia asked him to wait, and we all got out.

"Think we'll need a getaway car?" I asked as we approached the door and she pulled out her keys.

"You never know. Maybe your mother is here alone right now, and we can grab her and go. Davis doesn't know we're coming. He might have gone to work and left her here."

That would be ideal. What were the chances it would be that easy?

Vancia unlocked the front door and pushed it open. "Pappa?" she called.

We followed her into the wide foyer with its shining dark wood floors, high ceilings, and gleaming white paneled walls. Polished antique furniture decorated the rooms opening out from the foyer. There wasn't a speck of dust anywhere, and it was *cold*. It felt like I was in a museum rather than a home.

A servant rushed into the foyer and gave Vancia and then me and Lad a wide-eyed stare. "Miss Hart. Your father wasn't expecting you."

"I know, Sia. I wanted to surprise him. This is my fiancé Lad. And this is my friend… Roberta."

Roberta? Really? That's the best she could do? I cut my eyes at Lad, who stifled a laugh.

For all the housekeeper knows, you're a hundred years old, he said. *Play it cool.*

Um, I'm sorry but "Roberta" couldn't be "cool" if she tried.

"Is he home?" Vancia said.

The servant shook her head. "No Miss Hart. He's not even in the city. Your father's gone to California."

"California?"

"Yes, for a Council event. I thought you knew. I thought you'd be there, too."

"Yes of course," she responded smoothly. "I just didn't realize he'd be leaving for L.A. this early. I wanted to get some of my dresses from my closet here before I head out myself. Could you ring Francine to help me pack, please?"

The woman scurried from the room, and Vancia turned to us with a dour expression. "He told me he would be here all week. Someone must have warned him we were on our way." She tipped her head in my direction without actually looking at me. "Maybe the pilot didn't buy my cover story for her and alerted Davis. I thought he was loyal to me—he used to work for my real father. But I suppose he could have turned and be working for Davis now."

"Unless one of *us* is working for him," I said, staring directly at Vancia.

"What does that mean?" she snapped.

"We arrive and he just *happens* to have left already?" I couldn't believe we had missed her. How would we find her now? "How do we know it wasn't you who warned him?"

"Ryann," Lad cautioned with his tone.

"*I* didn't tell him. I'm trying to *help* you," Vancia said, stepping closer and looking down at me. "And if anyone's been lying around here, it's you."

"Me?"

"It's obvious you still have feelings for Lad. Where does that leave your boyfriend, Nox, huh? It's not fair to him."

I'd never struck anyone before in my life, but I was sorely tempted in that moment. That pert little nose of hers was practically begging for my fist. Instead I yelled at her. "You have no idea what you're talking about. Wait— you didn't say something like that to Nox, did you?"

"Why? Are you worried he doesn't trust you? He shouldn't."

"You mean he shouldn't trust *you*. I certainly don't. You could be working with your 'Pappa' and lying to all of us."

Lad stepped between us. "Ladies, ladies. Let's lower our voices and our adrenaline levels, okay? Ryann, for what it's worth, I *do* trust her." He turned to Vancia. "And I trust Ryann, too. Now, why don't Ryann and I go back out and wait in the car while you get whatever you need from inside the house? Then I suggest we get back to the airport as quickly as possible and see if we can get a flight to L.A."

Vancia and I gave each other one more unfriendly glance before I spun around and headed for the door with

Lad's guiding hand on my lower back. When we got out to the sidewalk I turned to him.

"What if it really was the pilot who reported us? If he knows who I am, he's not going to fly us to Los Angeles."

"If he won't, I guess we'll find out very quickly which side Vancia is really on."

"How?"

"She's the only one of the three of us who can afford to buy us all commercial airline tickets. Am I right?"

I let out a tired breath. "You're right. Or maybe Davis *wants* us to come to him in L.A. Maybe it's all part of his scheme."

"Perhaps." His brows knitted in concern. "You know, you could fly back to Mississippi."

"No. I'm going to L.A. If that's where Davis has taken my mother, that's where I have to be. I just wish I knew what he was thinking."

"I was thinking the same thing about you."

"What do you mean?"

There was a long pause as he looked at the sidewalk and off to the side, then finally at my face. "Do you want to talk about the other thing Vancia said?"

My heart flipped over. He meant her accusation that I still had feelings for him. I most definitely did *not* want to discuss that. "I don't want to talk about *anything* to do with Vancia. I'm not even sure I can stand to be on the same plane with her. If I had any choice about it, I wouldn't."

"You need her, Ryann."

"I know, I know. And so do you. And apparently so does Nox. Yay for Vancia, Savior of the World."

Unfortunately she slid into the front passenger seat of the cab just as I uttered the last sarcastic sentence. Looking back over her shoulder, she smirked.

"No, that's your job. I'm only the placeholder." To the cab driver she said, "Reagan National please."

CHAPTER FOURTEEN
PICTURE PERFECT

As soon as the car pulled away from the curb, Vancia called the pilot, who said he'd put in a flight plan to L.A.

"So we're good there?" Lad asked her.

"As far as I can tell. When we get to the airport, I'll speak to him mind-to-mind and find out what he knows, make sure he's planning to actually fly us to Los Angeles and hasn't been directed otherwise by Davis."

So we were going to L.A. There was no more putting it off—it was time to call Nox and tell him. I pulled out my phone and hit the button for his number. He didn't answer, but about fifteen minutes into our journey through the congested D.C. traffic he called me back.

"Hi. I have some news," I blurted. How would he react to hearing I was on my way to him? He'd forbidden me to come to L.A., forbidden me to work with Lad and Vancia against the Dark Elven plot, and told me to stay away from Davis. I was defying him on every point.

"Me too," he said grimly. "Davis is on his way here with your mother."

The air left my lungs with a whoosh. "Yes. That's right. How did you know?"

"I got a call from my agent Alfred. He asked to see me at his office. When I went there today, he warned me. Remember I told you I had a feeling about him—like he was trying to drop hints to me? He was a close friend of my father's. He said he'd suspected my real identity early on."

"But he's a friend of Davis's. Are you sure you can trust him?"

"He told me mind-to-mind. He's an ally, Ryann. He was loyal to my dad, and he's been pretending so he can stay close to Davis and find out what he's up to—the way Vancia is."

I darted a glance toward the front seat. "Are you sure about that part, too? Did you ask *her* mind-to-mind?"

Vancia looked back over her shoulder, obviously aware I was talking about her.

"Yes. I'm sure about her," he said. "She's loyal, and she has a good heart. So anyway, I want you to know I'll do everything I can to get to your mom when she gets here and get her away from Davis."

"Well, you're going to have some help. We're on our way."

There was a pause before he responded. "What do you mean? Who's on the way?"

"I'm in a cab with Vancia and Lad. We're headed to the airport. We'll be there tonight."

"Ryann, no. Not you. I don't want you out here."

I knew he meant because of the danger, but his vehement statement still stung. "But you want *her* there?"

He sighed. "Don't be silly. It's not like that. I'm not worried about *her* getting hurt. You could, though. The bullet could as easily have hit *you* that day. And you don't have Elven healing capacity, at least as far as we know."

He didn't have to point out to me that I wasn't like Vancia. Or him. I was all too aware of my shortcomings. "Nox—I'm coming, okay? I have to. I may be the only one who can get through to my mom and get her to leave Davis. She might not even listen to me, but I have to try." There was quiet on the other end of the line. "So... I'll see you tonight?"

Nox finally responded with a long exhale. "I shouldn't be excited to hear you say that, but I am—God I'm so selfish. What time will you arrive? I'll pick you up at the airport. And then I'm gonna kiss you until you can't breathe and squeeze that beautiful body—"

"Nox," I interrupted, breathless and blushing furiously. My voice was part giggle part gasp.

Beside me Lad shifted in his seat and let out a disgusted sort of grunt.

Composing myself, I said, "I don't know what time we'll get there. There's a possible issue with the private jet."

"Okay. Would you pass the phone to Vancia for a minute?" he asked.

I leaned forward and handed it to her. She was quiet except for a few "uh huh"s and "okay"s. Then she touched the button to end the call and handed the phone back to me with a wincing fake smile. "He said to tell you, 'goodbye.'"

Refusing to let her bait me, I turned my attention to Lad. "Nox says his agent Alfred is an ally. He told Nox Davis was on his way to Los Angeles and was bringing my mother. At least we know we're heading in the right direction this time." I smiled, feeling hopeful.

"*Geographically* speaking," Lad muttered.

"What does that mean?"

He only shrugged and gazed out the window at the thick city traffic.

When we boarded the plane, the last thing I wanted to do was converse with Vancia, but there really was no choice anymore. Either we were working together or we weren't, and I wanted to get her take on Nox's supposed ally.

I slid into the empty seat beside her. Lad had already stretched out across three adjoining seats in the rear to sleep a bit.

"So what do you think of Alfred Frey? He's your agent, too, right? For modeling?"

She looked at me, round-eyed. Maybe she was surprised I knew anything about her.

"Um, yes, I met him a few months ago when I went out to shoot a portfolio. He booked me for some jobs. I'm not really a model, you know."

She seemed embarrassed, blushing and looking away. "I mean, yes, I did some modeling jobs, but only because it's what my father—what Davis wanted. Anyway, I wasn't sure what to think of Alfred. He wasn't very nice the first time I met him, sort of dismissive. I didn't think he liked me. But a few days later I met with him privately, and he told me he'd been very tight with my mom and dad—my real one, you know? He said their deaths devastated him, and that if I ever wanted to talk about them he was there for me. I didn't know how to react. He seemed to be inviting me to be disloyal to Davis, like he was testing me or something. I didn't say anything either way. I was too afraid he'd tell Davis everything I said. But he did open that door."

"Nox says Alfred wants in on the plan to take Davis down. He trusts him."

"Well, that's good enough for me. Nox has always been really smart about people, even when we were kids."

The plane lifted off, and I sat back into my seat, swallowing a few times to pop my ears. I turned back to Vancia's profile. "You were good friends, huh?"

She actually smiled at me—a real one. "Best friends. We grew up together because our parents were best friends and worked in the music industry together. I can't remember a time when Nox wasn't in my life—except for after the accident, of course."

"I'm sorry about that," I said. And I was. I couldn't imagine anything as horrible as losing both your parents in the same day. Except maybe losing both your parents and your best friend. "You must have been blown away when you discovered Nox was alive."

The memory overtook her face, making her look exceptionally beautiful. "It was pretty much the best day of my life."

My belly sank, and it wasn't the increasing altitude. Damn her. She and Nox would make a stunning star-couple with his dark, wavy hair and dark tan next to her platinum hair and pale skin. The model and the rock star—a tale as old as time.

"Did you two ever... um... date or whatever?" I hated myself for asking, but I had to know.

Her smile turned to an expression of dreamy reminiscence. "We didn't exactly date—we were only twelve. But I had a monster crush on him. I'm not sure if he ever knew. Twelve-year-old boys aren't usually *quite* as into it as girls are."

I couldn't help but laugh. "I remember. I had this huge crush on a boy named Brian who lived two streets over from me and was in my homeroom. I'm pretty sure he didn't even know I was alive."

Thinking back to those painful days of unrequited longing, I felt a certain kinship to Vancia, at least her pre-teen entity. I grinned at her. "I can't even picture Nox at twelve."

"I have one, actually." She drew a small booklet from her purse and handed it to me.

Oh. A photo album—that's what the book was. I opened it and studied the first picture—it showed a group of people in front of a gorgeous pool. Studying closely, I picked out the tween version of Vancia.

"These are your parents?"

She nodded. "Yes. This is one of the last pictures I have of them." Pointing to the other adult couple, she said, "And those are Nox's parents."

"Right. I recognize them from TV." Nox's parents had both been famous musicians. Mom was a particular fan, so I'd seen their videos. I pointed to the tall, gangly boy with high cheekbones and shaggy dark hair. "This has to be Nox."

She grinned. "Yep—in all his dopey pre-teen glory. I thought he was beautiful, though."

"He was," I agreed. He was only a boy in the picture, but you could see the promise of his full-grown handsomeness. He was a super-masculine looking kid, and the dazzling smile was already at work, no doubt mesmerizing every little (and big) girl who crossed his path. He'd certainly put Vancia under his spell.

I flipped to the next page, and there was a picture of the two of them. He held her cradle-style in his arms over the pool, as if threatening to throw her in. Her mouth was wide open in laughter. His eyes sparkled with boyish mischief.

In the slot on the opposite page there was another picture of Nox and Vancia. In this one, his arm was around her shoulders, and hers was wrapped around his back. She was looking straight ahead, smiling for the camera, but I could tell he'd looked away just as the photo was snapped.

Instead of making eye contact with the lens, he'd turned to look at his childhood friend. The expression on his face was... absorbed. Adoring. I didn't say it to her, but it was pretty obvious she wasn't in that puppy love affair *alone*. If this photo was any indication, he'd reciprocated that childhood crush—big time.

"I always loved that shot," she said on a sigh. "He kissed me that night. Our parents went inside and we stayed out by the fire pit. I thought I would die of happiness." She paused for a long moment before continuing in a hushed tone. "About a week or so later, they were all gone."

"I'm sorry." I closed the photo album and handed it back to her.

"Wait, you have to see this one." Vancia opened the small book to the last page, which displayed a photo of a much younger Nox and Vancia. They looked about six— the age I was when I'd first met Lad, when he'd saved my life and the fascination began for both of us.

"Wasn't he adorable?" she said.

I nodded. For some reason, this shot upset me more than any of the others. I recognized something in it. I *knew* what a lifelong connection like that felt like... because I shared one with Lad. It wasn't something you got over easily. It still pulled at my soul, even after all that had happened, even though I'd forged a new connection with someone else.

Was that what it was like for Nox and Vancia? They hadn't physically bonded, but maybe they did share a bond nearly as deep, rooted in childhood friendship and first young love.

"Thanks for sharing these with me." I scooted forward in my seat, preparing to get up, but hesitated and sat back again. "Can I ask you a question?"

She gave me a wary nod.

"Does Nox's glamour work on you? I mean, can you feel it when he sings, or... any other time?"

She laughed. "Are you kidding? I knew him back when his voice was higher than mine. I heard all of his very first songs, and believe me, they were *not* good. He was there for my awkward stage, too. We couldn't glamour each other if we tried. Why?"

"No reason." I stood and glanced back at Lad, who seemed deep in sleep. "I think he has the right idea. I'm going to go grab a nap too."

"Okay. Now that I know I can trust him, I'm going to call Alfred and get him to book me on a job or two so I'll have a cover story for being in the city. Davis has been bugging me to do more modeling, so he'll be happy. Sleep well," she said.

Forcing a weak smile at her, I moved to another row of seats where I reclined but failed to fall asleep. Instead, pictures of Nox and Vancia kissing filled my mind. Not visions of two preternaturally beautiful twelve-year-olds but the current versions of those childhood sweethearts.

Worst of all, I imagined Nox looking at her the way he had in that photo, and for the first time since our trip began, I dreaded our arrival in L.A., hoping I didn't recognize that same look in his eyes when he saw her again.

CHAPTER FIFTEEN
GUEST ACCOMMODATIONS

When Nox greeted me at the airport, there was none of the kissing and squeezing he'd threatened. He gave me a brief hug and a friendly smile, which was, of course, perfectly appropriate. Vancia and Lad were right there, and *four* was definitely a crowd in this situation.

We all walked out together into the hot California sun, heading for a black limo waiting at the curb. Before we climbed in, Nox tugged me to the side for some whispered words.

"I can't believe you're actually here. You look amazing. And I just realized *how much* I've been missing you—God, I could eat you alive."

I shivered at the caress of his warm breath on my ear. I had been afraid it might be a bit awkward to see him after a month with hardly any contact. But hearing his incredible voice, looking into his eyes, and breathing in his delicious, habit-forming scent, I felt a powerful pull toward him.

A bit too powerful, actually. I was embarrassed when he drew back and I realized I had kissed him—*really* kissed him—and basically plastered myself to him right there in front of the skycaps and other passengers and anyone else who might have looked our way. I wasn't normally one for PDA, much less PDL—public displays of *libido*.

Nox let me go and stepped back with an apologetic glance. "The paparazzi are everywhere—especially here at LAX. I shouldn't be photographed with you. I'm going to hug Vancia, too, in case we've been spotted, okay?"

I nodded. Of course he was absolutely right. Showing me any special attention would make the vultures wonder who I was—then I'd find my own face plastered across the internet, and Davis would be alerted to my arrival long before I wanted him to know I was here—and knew Nox. But I couldn't help peeking as Nox pulled Vancia into his arms.

"Hey stranger." His smile was as warm as his voice.

"Hi." She sounded young and nervous as she rose on her toes to receive his embrace and quick cheek-kiss.

Emotion rolled over me from their direction like an ocean wave I couldn't avoid. Joy—wholesome and sweet.

The sensation took me back to my own childhood, to the poignant connection I'd formed with Lad—a nearly indescribable feeling you couldn't understand unless you'd been there yourself. It made me study them closer, looking for some sort of sign, for body language or *something* to explain it. What had happened during the time Nox and Vancia had spent here together?

As Nox had predicted, flashes began to pop around us. Several men with cameras crowded toward the waiting car.

"Ugh, they're like gnats or something," Nox joked as he pulled away from Vancia and ushered us all into the back seats in a hurry. "Kiss a couple people at the airport, and they come out of the woodwork."

He turned to Lad, who sat beside him. "How was the flight?"

"Fine. No issues," he answered in a tight, uncomfortable voice. I didn't have to read his mental state—he was irked, undoubtedly at the mushy scene he'd witnessed between his fiancée and his brother.

The last time Nox and Lad had seen each other was even more stressful—they'd been fighting for their lives. And earlier that same day, Lad had barged in on me and Nox making out in his bedroom.

So, yeah. We had all that going for us in the could-it-be-more-awkward department.

"Have you seen Davis yet?" Vancia asked.

"No. No word from him. I only knew he was on his way because of Alfred. Did you speak to him?"

"Yes. Alfred's arranging a photo shoot or two for me, so I'll have an excuse to go crash at my 'Pappa's' house for a few days."

"Oh, you're not staying with us at Nox's house?" I asked, suddenly cheered.

She shook her head. "No. I'm hoping to pick up some information—maybe even see your mother. I'll contact you as soon as I know something."

Nox gave me a strange look. "You won't be staying at my house either. There are too many council members coming and going. I told you—it's Dark Elf Central there now. I don't want to put you in danger, and frankly, I wouldn't be able to satisfactorily explain you."

"Oh." My spirits sank. Here I was, finally getting to see Nox again, and we wouldn't even be staying in the same place. "So, where *am* I staying?"

"Just down the beach. I bought a cottage there a couple weeks ago, planning to turn it into a guest house. Good timing, I guess. It's small and sort of outdated—haven't even had a chance to do anything to it yet. But it's clean. It's furnished. You should be safe and comfortable there." He cleared his throat. "Lad will stay there as well. It'll give us all a place to meet up and talk, whenever I can get away."

I sank back into my seat, blinking in surprise. Lad and I were going to stay together?

Nox instructed Ewan, his driver, to drop Vancia off at Davis's mansion in Brentwood. From there the ride to Malibu was quiet and a bit uncomfortable. I made small talk with Nox, but with Lad there, the easy rapport we'd worked so hard to establish during our time in L.A. was nowhere to be found.

The awkwardness increased exponentially as we began our tour of the beach house where Lad and I would spend our next few days and nights. Nox led me to a bedroom suite on the first floor. It was pink and flowery, reminding me of my great-grandmother's house in Alabama. It even had a similar smell—roses and baby powder.

"I asked the housekeeper to prepare this for you, Ryann. I hope you'll like it." Nox set my bag on the rug and closed the door then continued down the hallway, glancing back at Lad with narrowed eyes and a pointed expression. "There's another bedroom on this floor, but *you'll* be staying *up*stairs. I also had someone run out and pick up a few clothing items for each of you. I wasn't sure if you'd had a chance to pack or how long you'll be staying. They're in your closets."

Stopping in front of a narrow door in the hallway, he said, "There's a half-bathroom up there, too, but unfortunately, the only shower is in here. The two of you will have to make a schedule or something."

Next we saw the kitchen. "The refrigerator and pantry are fully stocked," Nox said. "There's a supply of saol water here. You'll be able to make your special tea." He winked at me.

"Oh. I've pretty much stopped drinking it these days. I haven't actually made it myself—outside the factory—in a while. But thanks anyway."

He grinned. "Well, even if *you* don't want any, I do. Make some for me. I don't like to drink that pansy Light Elven water, except for in your tea."

His voice curled through me, a persuasive purr I couldn't refuse. "Okay." I giggled.

Behind me, Lad huffed an impatient breath. "I guess we're all set here then."

Nox leveled an assessing glance in his direction, then brought his attention back to me. "If you need anything, let me know and I'll order it to be delivered."

"I will."

"Thanks," Lad said, his voice gruff. He opened the refrigerator door and rummaged around inside.

I turned to Nox. "Yes, thank you so much for thinking of everything. The house is great." Taking his hand, I pulled him toward the privacy of the hallway, leaving Lad in the kitchen alone. "Why did you put us in the same house?" I whispered.

"I don't like it any better than you do—believe me. But I have to keep you both out of sight. Almost nobody knows about this place since I just bought it. And I need you two close by so we can meet whenever Vancia and I can get away. Besides, you'll be safe with him."

Nox had leaned in close to answer me, and his scent washed over me like a delicious bath. My eyes closed in a slow blink. Feeling a bit dazed, I took a step closer and put my hand over his heart. "When will we have some time alone?"

Hungry eyes looked down at me. He seemed as overcome by my nearness as I was by his. "Not soon enough," he groaned.

I clung to him in a tight embrace. Now that I was near him again, all my worries about the validity of our connection were evaporating like water droplets on a hot stove top. How could I have doubted him? He was *necessary* in my life… like a drug I could never break my dependence on, a habit I didn't want to kick.

Nox was doing his best impersonation of an addict as well. His hands came to either side of my face, lifting it for his kiss.

Finally. After all these weeks apart, I was finally in Nox's arms again. I rose on my tiptoes and met his lips eagerly. When my mouth opened, he took full advantage. Within moments, his hands had left my face and wandered down my body. Mine went up to his shoulders, his neck, his hair. He felt perfect. He tasted perfect.

His mouth left my lips and went to my neck, eliciting shivers. A deep hum emanated from his throat, the melody alluring and sensual. One of his hands found my hip and urged me closer against him, and I felt euphoric, like I was falling in slow motion through open air or maybe sinking into a warm pool.

I never wanted to leave this place, never wanted to do anything other than kiss this guy. Now that we were together again, thoughts of my mom with Davis didn't even trouble me. She'd probably be fine. I didn't need to worry about her or even look for her—

Oh my God. This is glamour.

The thought jolted me out of the moment, and Lad's words on the plane rushed back at me. *What if the feelings you have for him are all glamour-induced?*

And then I remembered Lad was in the next room. I pulled away.

"What is it?" Nox blinked slowly, as if just waking up. He tried to draw my body back to his, but I shrugged away.

"We're not alone here, remember?"

Full alertness returned to his beautiful hazel eyes, and they went hard as flint. He searched my face. "Why do you care what he hears?"

I stared back at him, panic-stricken. Why *did* I care? "I... I don't. It's just... you know, embarrassing... to have witnesses."

"One witness, you mean. Screw him—I haven't seen my girlfriend in weeks. If I want to kiss her I will." He pulled me toward him again, lowering his head over mine.

"Nox," I chastised in a low voice, leaning back, though the high brought on by his kisses beckoned me powerfully. "Be reasonable. And *why* were you humming? You know I don't like it when you do that."

"You seemed to like it well enough a minute ago."

Heat bloomed in my cheeks. "Well, obviously—but I don't *want* to be glamoured. I want to know what I feel is real."

He frowned. "If you don't already know that... then maybe Vancia was right."

"Vancia?" A suspicion sneaked up on me and pounced, taking a ferocious bite out of my heart. "Is this about her? About the time you spent with her after I left? What exactly did she say?"

His hands came to his hips and he rolled his neck side-to-side as if trying to work out a kink. "This is not about her. All she did was fill me in on some missing details. And… she did warn me that you and Lad can't be seen out and about in L.A. Not only is it dangerous for you, it'll raise the alarm with Davis and his followers. This *is* the safest place for you."

"Away from you—how convenient," I muttered.

"Only for a little while. And you can call me mind-to-mind whenever you want to. I'm just a few houses down the beach." He breathed out hard. "I have to go. I've stayed away too long as it is." He grabbed my neck and pulled me close again for another quick kiss. "I'll be back as soon as I can."

Walking toward the front door and flinging it open he called out to Lad. "Later."

Lad stepped into the foyer, holding an apple. He took a noisy bite. "See ya."

And Nox was gone. The instant the door closed behind him, I felt drained, almost dizzy. I put a hand against the wall and let out a long breath.

"So…" Lad said with a teasing tone. "Want to go for a swim and cool off? Nice cold ocean right out there." He hooked a thumb toward the back door.

"I'm fine."

"Sounds like you two had a little disagreement there."

I wheeled on him and glared. "We're *fine*. Thanks for your concern. I'm going to unpack and check out my room. Maybe you should go see yours."

"Yeah. Good idea. See you later, I guess."

"Sure."

Of course we'd see each other later. There was no avoiding it. We were stuck here together.

When I'd done all the "settling in" I could possibly do and fought the ever increasing hunger pangs as long as I could, I emerged from my room and went to the kitchen in search of dinner possibilities.

Lad was already there, stirring something on the stove top.

"Hi," he said with a smile. "I found some chicken in the refrigerator. Soup sound okay?"

I pulled a large pitcher from an upper cabinet, planning to make sweet tea. Since he'd asked, I wanted to make sure there was some on hand for Nox's next visit. "Oh, you're making dinner for me, too?"

"Of course. There was also some seafood in there—shellfish and stuff—but I've never had that, and I didn't know if you liked it either."

I rummaged through the pantry, finding the tea bags, and started filling a kettle with water. "You've never had seafood?"

He shrugged. "You know I hadn't traveled far from Altum prior to that quick trip Vancia and I made out here to find you last month. I've had fish, of course, but only the lake and river varieties you can find in Mississippi. It's not like we have a seafood truck stopping by and making deliveries to Altum."

"Right. Well, you should try it while you're here. I mean, look at where we are." I gestured out the large picture window overlooking the ocean and Malibu beach. "I'll cook it tomorrow."

He grinned. "Great. A trade out."

I watched him stirring the fragrant chicken in a deep pot. The scent of garlic and some sort of herbs filled the air.

"So… I would never have suspected you could cook."

"I hope you'll like it. I don't cook that often, but I used to hang out a lot in the kitchen at home with our chef Petra. I picked up a few things. Soup, I can manage."

Noticing some chopped fresh vegetables on a cutting board near the stove, I had to smile. "I guess so. You really *are* good at everything. I kind of hate you." I set the kettle on the stovetop and turned on the flame.

Lad didn't look up from the pot, but in a more somber tone he said, "Sometimes I think you do."

"Lad—" What did I want to say? Did I hate him? No. I couldn't. He had hurt me, but I understood his reasons now. He'd been trying to protect me.

And the betrothal to Vancia was something that had been arranged for him as a child—an obligation he was determined to honor.

No, I didn't hate him. In fact, if I was being honest— part of me still loved him. My attraction to Nox didn't magically erase the love I'd felt for Lad. It was simply a love I'd never do anything about. Too much had happened. There were too many complications—and other hearts—involved now.

"I don't hate you," I finally said. "I consider you a friend. And I appreciate you coming along and trying to help my mom."

He finally looked at my face. "I'm happy to. I'm helping my people, too."

Of course. His people. Priority number one.

"This thing with the Dark Elves has gone too far now," he continued. "I could no longer ignore it and refuse to get involved." He paused a long time before continuing. "But even if that wasn't the case... I'd still be here. I *should* have been there for you before. I'm sorry Ryann. I thought I was doing what was best for you. Instead, I hurt you unforgivably."

Speechless now and blinking back tears, I walked over and gazed out the window at the sun setting over the beach. "I think I'll go for a quick walk before dinner."

"This has to simmer for about thirty minutes. Can I join you?"

"Oh, uh... okay." Didn't he realize the point of my walk was to get away from him? I couldn't exactly say that, though. Not after I'd just told him I considered us friends. Still, I searched for an exit hatch. "You think it's okay to leave the stove going like that? I'd hate to burn down Nox's new guest cottage."

He smiled as he joined me at the back door and opened it for me. "It's on low."

Left with no more excuses, I stepped out onto the deck and then the warm sand beyond it. Lad followed.

"So this is only your second time to see the ocean, right?" I asked, eager to change the topic from our earlier conversation.

"That's right." He gazed out over the color-changing water. "I still can't get over how *big* it is. I thought Altum was huge. But the world—I think my father was wrong about venturing out and mixing with humans. There's so much to see." He darted his eyes at me. "So much beauty. So much I've missed."

"Well, it's a long life. In fact, you've got forever—to travel the world or do whatever you want to do."

He leaned over and grabbed a shell from the sand, tossing it into the surf. "And yet... I can't actually *do* what I want to do."

"You mean your obligations as Light King?"

He nodded. "That, and the current crisis with the Dark Elves. I owe it to my father and my people to make... certain choices. To keep the peace, rule wisely, provide an heir someday. If there were another way...." He shook his head in dismay, knowing it was pointless to finish the sentence.

"What would you do?" I prompted.

"If all my people were safe, if the humans were safe, and the Dark Elves were content to leave them alone? I'd travel, see some of the places I've read about in books. I'd do what *I* want to do... make my own choices." He glanced quickly at my face and then back out over the horizon. "What would you do if you had total freedom?"

"Hmmm… you know what's funny? I've had about enough travel. I'd stay in Deep River, close to my friends, my family, the land, live the simple life, you know?"

"You'd probably make a better ruler for Altum than I would," he said with a sad laugh. "Who am I kidding? My life is what it is. Father always called me a 'dreamer.' I guess he was right."

"Dreams are good," I assured him. "I think we'd go crazy if we couldn't dream."

"I agree," he said quietly. The back of his hand brushed mine as we walked, almost as if he had started to take it and stopped himself. "I like talking like this with you. It reminds me of how it used to be, you know, before…"

Before Vancia came into the picture. Before Lad had rejected me and I fell for Nox. Before things got so complicated and confusing.

I liked walking and talking with him like this, too, but I didn't say so. Instead I said, "We should turn back. If we keep going this direction, supper will burn by the time we make it back to the house."

"Okay."

We did a U-turn, walking through the shallow waves lapping the shore, and headed for our new home-away-from-home. The sun had almost reached the horizon line. Its orange glow bathing Lad's face and golden hair made him look like some otherworldly creature. Which, of course, was what he was. He'd never looked more beautiful and less human to me.

Catching me looking at him, he gave me a sad grin. "Do you ever think about living forever?"

"No," I answered honestly. "Because I'm not sure I will. Until recently, I never even knew it was a possibility. Chances are I *will* have an extended lifespan compared to most humans but not immortality. Who even knows? Why?"

He shrugged. "I don't know. I think about it sometimes. Everyone talks about it like it's a gift, but it doesn't really seem like one, you know? I mean, it's almost depressing. Eternity just seems so... *long*."

I hated the look on his face. Haunted. Trapped.

"You know... you *can* choose. Your birth doesn't have to determine your whole life."

"It does, though," he said.

"It has so far. But if you really want to, you can change things, have the life you want. I think eternity wouldn't seem so long, it *would* seem like the amazing opportunity it is, if you were happy with your life. Everyone should look forward to the future. Including you. Maybe your mom could rule in your place."

"Has to be a male." He winced, anticipating my reaction. "Elven law."

"*So* sexist. All right, there must be some eager council member in the Light Court who'd be happy to take your place. Like Davis did in the Dark Court when both Nox's and Vancia's parents died and they all believed he was dead, too."

"And look how well that turned out," he said with a grim smile.

"Okay, maybe that's not the best example. But what I'm saying is, there's always somebody who wants to rule. Let them do it. Abdicate your throne, if that's what you want."

"You make it sound so simple."

"Maybe it is."

We'd reached the back door of the beach cottage. Before going in, Lad slid an arm around me and pulled me close for a quick hug. "Thank you. You always know the right thing to say—even if it *is* just a dream."

I grinned up at him. "Happy to help."

Vancia came around the side of the house. "I've been knocking. Where were you?" She didn't sound jealous, exactly. Annoyed would be more accurate.

Bristling at her accusatory tone, I opened the door and went inside, letting Lad answer.

"Getting some fresh air. Dinner's ready. You hungry?" he asked her as they followed me in.

Sniffing the air subtly, she visibly relaxed. "A little bit, now that I smell food." Walking over to peek inside the pot, she said under her breath to Lad, "You need to be careful."

"I know," he said, sounding like a henpecked husband already.

Clearly the conversation wasn't intended to include me, but I couldn't help but overhear and wonder. Was she *that* afraid of him being seen out on the beach? Would he be instantly recognizable to the malevolent Dark Elves who might want to harm him? Or was her warning about something else?

CHAPTER SIXTEEN
WRESTLING MATCH

"All right—everybody grab a bowl." Lad ladled the fragrant soup into a heavy ceramic bowl and set it on the countertop.

Reappearing from the bathroom, Vancia lifted the dish and carried it to the nearby dining set before coming back for the other bowls. So... maybe she wasn't a *total* princess. She didn't expect to be served.

Inspired by Nox's suggestion, I had made my special recipe sweet tea. I filled glasses with ice and the sugary concoction and carried them all to the table, choosing a chair across from Vancia for myself. It was odd to sit down family-style with her and Lad.

She watched as I took a long drink from my glass, eying her own.

"So you've been drinking saol water for a while?" she asked.

"Well, I had it a few times after meeting Lad. And then he suggested I use it in my sweet tea, but I actually haven't been drinking it lately. I haven't wanted to waste it."

"Waste it?"

"Well, yes. I make sure all the saol water he delivers goes into my sweet tea for the business. And, I don't consume the merchandise. We need to sell all of it we can. It's a precious commodity, you know?"

She nodded, taking a sip from her own glass. "Wow. This is good. I'm surprised you can resist it."

I didn't want to get into the real reason I had stayed away from drinking it. It reminded me too much of Lad. In my mind, saol water would always be inextricably linked with him, with our first encounter as children when he'd used it to save my life.

Though I'd brought a vial of saol water with me on my first trip out to L.A., I had ended up keeping it in my purse and taking peeks at the copper flask from time to time. I hadn't had the heart to drink it and experience that euphoric, warm sensation I'd only ever felt in Lad's presence. My heart didn't need that vivid reminder.

I hadn't actually had any—or even tasted my own sweet tea—since before I'd gone on that rescue mission to bring Emmy home. Taking another swallow now, though, I had to admit there was nothing like it. No wonder the Magnolia Sugar Tea Company was enjoying such robust early success.

"So, how did it go with Davis?"

"Did you see my mom?"

Lad and I asked our questions at the same time, just as Vancia spooned in a mouthful of soup.

She looked from one to the other of us and swallowed. "It went well, I think. He seemed to buy my explanation that I was here to work. He was disappointed *you* weren't with me." She nodded to Lad. "But I assured him I'd just seen you and would see you again shortly, and that I was doing my *job*."

"Did he ask you about the engagement?" Lad said.

She stared into his eyes. "Of course. I told him the truth—that it's on, that we haven't set a date because your mother's still in mourning."

"What about Mom? Is she with him? Did you see her?"

"She's there. I didn't speak to her. She was in the room with him, but she didn't say anything or even look up. I think she was pretty deep under."

Worry pooled in my belly. "I knew it. There's no way she'd go this long without calling me or Grandma unless she was glamoured. How did she look?"

"I didn't get a good look at her. The room was sort of dark. She's alive, though, and she'll stay that way as long as he needs her for his plan."

"Which is... what?" Lad asked.

Vancia shook her head. "I'm still not sure. He did mention the Boston Olympics, though. Seemed pretty fired up about it."

"Oh—Nox said he and the Hidden are going to perform there, at the Opening Ceremonies. Maybe he's found out something about it. Have you spoken to him today?"

Vancia paused and her gaze fell to her bowl. "Not face-to-face."

What did that mean? Had they been communicating mind-to-mind? She said she'd been at Davis's house when she wasn't working. How far was that from Nox's house? Were they able to communicate long distance the way we had that one time?

It occurred to me I hadn't heard Nox's voice in my mind since coming back to the city. But then, I hadn't been here that long, and in spite of his invitation earlier, I hadn't yet reached out and tried to send him a message. I would have to try it later this evening, as soon as I got some time to myself.

As it turned out, it wasn't necessary. Toward the end of dinner there was a knock at the door. We all looked at each other. We couldn't answer it. No one was supposed to know we were here.

A minute later my phone buzzed with a text from Nox.

It's me. Let me in.

I flew to the door and opened it. "I'm so glad you could come back tonight. I wasn't sure if you could get away."

"I wasn't either. And I don't have long." He stepped in and gave me a quick peck on the lips. "I need to put my car inside." He crossed the hall to the kitchen and then the garage door. "Be right back."

We heard the sound of the garage door opening, his car pulling in, the garage closing again. And then Nox came back into the kitchen.

"What did you find out, Van?"

She recapped her reconnaissance for Nox while Lad and I listened.

"Good work," Nox said, squeezing her arm with a warm smile.

Vancia's face glowed at his praise. She never looked like that around Lad. Did Lad notice it? Did Nox?

I would have loved to attribute it to their childhood friendship, but my glamour for emotional empathy didn't allow me such blissful ignorance. Unable to resist, I extended my glamour senses in her direction.

Yep. I was picking up attraction. Big time. Of course any female within a mile of Nox exuded the signs of attraction—that was what he did to women.

But this was... different. It was *more*. Nox didn't seem to notice. He was engaged in deep conversation with Lad.

"What do you know about the Olympics in Boston?" Lad asked him.

"Alfred says it's the next step in taking the plan worldwide. There are already fan pods across the globe. There's going to be a performance during the live broadcast of the Opening Ceremonies featuring all of Alfred's top clients—kind of like a modern version of "We Are the World." Not just singers, but actors, athletes, models—recognizable names and faces joining together for this big one-time-only performance. Only this song isn't about feeding hungry children. It's going to be a message influencing the humans to accept Elven rule."

"Oh, I get it. The electronic signals enhance the glamour," I said. "And if it's all of Alfred's biggest clients, that's going to be a whole lot of glamour up on the same stage at the same time."

"And it'll be broadcast across the world. Okay, I guess I get why Davis was talking about it like it was such a big deal," Vancia said. "Something like that will push the Elven takeover ahead by years, maybe decades."

Nox grimaced. "Well, he's already got me and the band on the roster to be there, so at least I'll be able to monitor it from the inside and see what's going on. I'll let you all know as soon as I get a look at the song lyrics."

"Too bad *you* don't get to write them." Vancia gave Nox a shoulder nudge. "You could throw in something 'international' about sombreros and mezcal. *If* you can even remember them."

He barked a loud laugh but calmed quickly, going red in the face and darting a guilty glance in my direction. "We took a quick trip over the border a couple weeks ago," he explained. "I may have been a tad *overserved*." He pointed at Vancia in a mock-threatening way. "Which is totally your fault for suggesting I needed a break from the Dark Court. I owe you one hangover."

It was clear he *did* recall at least some of the trip—the happy memory was all over his face. Funny, he hadn't mentioned a spontaneous getaway to Mexico with his childhood sweetheart in any of our phone conversations.

"All right mister. It. Is. On." Vancia pushed the remaining dinner dishes aside and placed her elbow on the table, presenting her cupped hand to Nox in an obvious invitation to arm wrestle.

He grinned widely. "Really? Really? Do you really think you can take me on now? I've filled out a bit since seventh grade, you know."

She raised one arched brow and looked him over. "Obviously. But I wonder if you're still *afraid* of losing?"

Straddling a chair, he planted his elbow opposite hers on the tabletop. "All right. You asked for it. No mercy rule."

She met his grin straight on. "No mercy."

The two of them clasped palms and began grappling with each other. I was surprised at how well Vancia was holding him. Either that or Nox's threat had been an empty one and he was taking it easy on her.

As their wrists and forearms intertwined, the two of them stared into each other's eyes, alternately grimacing and laughing. Yet another thing they shared from childhood apparently—a fondness for arm wrestling.

I tried to enjoy the show as much as they were enjoying putting it on but failed. Leaning against the edge of the sofa, I waited for Vancia's territory marking exhibition to end.

Perhaps noticing my expression or how quiet I'd gotten, Lad sat on the sofa back next to me. He leaned close to my ear. "You okay?"

You know what's pathetic? When your old boyfriend feels sorry for you because of how your new boyfriend is interacting with another girl. With *his* girl, no less.

Lad's sympathetic reaction made me study the arm-wrestlers more closely. Their hands were clasped tightly around each other's, their faces close together and bright with amusement. If I used my emotional glamour on Nox right now, what would I feel?

I shouldn't. I was almost afraid to. And it wasn't right to invade his privacy. Besides, I trusted him.

But still.

I couldn't help myself. I had to know. Extending my senses toward the two of them, I let myself feel what they were feeling, and the sensations nearly knocked me backward onto the couch cushions.

I literally winced as my mind was assaulted with a combination of enjoyment, excitement, and pleasure. And it wasn't all coming from Vancia. Nox liked touching her, too, liked competing with her, having her sole focus and devoted attention.

Unable to stand being in the room any longer, I jumped up and speed-walked into the kitchen, opening the freezer and looking for nothing in particular, letting the rush of frigid air hit my hot face.

"Ryann?" The quiet voice behind me was filled with concern.

"Want a cold drink?" I asked Lad in a loud, overly bright tone. "I'm getting some ice."

He opened a cabinet and pulled out a glass, silently handing it to me. When our eyes met, his were filled with pity.

I snatched the glass from his hand and whirled back around, filling it with sweet tea and downing nearly the whole thing, wishing fervently he'd just go away. I didn't need his pity. And really, he should have been worrying about his own business.

He should be at least as upset as I was. Why wasn't he furious with his fiancée for flirting so outrageously with Nox? Maybe he couldn't sense their hot-blooded reaction to each other as well as I could.

A crashing sound followed by raucous laughter drifted in from the living room.

"All right, all right. Enough," I heard Nox say. "I give. We're going to break something."

"Yeah, run away now that I've kicked your ass." Vancia laughed.

"You didn't kick my ass. I got tired and let you win. Besides, I didn't want to hurt you. Hey, where's Ryann?"

Ugh. He'd just *now* noticed I'd left the room?

Nox's big frame filled the doorway to the kitchen. He glanced between me and Lad. "Hey guys. What's up?"

Vancia was right behind him, hanging onto his shoulder, still laughing. "I think you did hurt my arm."

His eyes danced with amusement as she once again succeeded in drawing his attention away from me. He looked down at her. "Are you kidding? The only thing hurting around here is my ego. I nearly got beat by a girl."

"Again," she teased and laughed out loud as he made a face at her. Glancing at us, she explained. "We used to compete with each other over everything. I was taller than him pretty much our entire childhoods. And faster."

He gave her a droll look. "Thanks for revealing my secret shame to my girlfriend, Van."

Her smile faltered a bit at his last few words, but she rallied like a champ. "Oh you better watch out—I know *all kinds* of juicy secrets about you." She grabbed his hand with both of hers and attempted to pull him back into the living room. "Want to go for best two out of three? If you win, I'll keep my mouth shut about the time we skinny-dipped in your parents' hot tub."

Slicing a glance back at me, Nox's face went serious. He yanked his hand from her grasp, causing Vancia to stumble backward and nearly fall.

He moved toward me with a wary expression. "You disappeared. Everything all right?"

I nodded. "Sure. I came in to get a tea refill. Want some? You must be thirsty after all your..." My gaze went to the empty doorway, through which Vancia had disappeared. "...exertions."

His eyes narrowed as he studied my face. *There's nothing going on, Ryann*, he told me silently.

I turned away and filled a new glass with ice. *Okay. Whatever.*

He stood beside me, watching me, but I didn't look back at him. I couldn't. I didn't want him to see the tears beginning to form in my eyes. Not when it was probably stupid to feel this way.

He'd just told me in the Elven way that nothing was going on between them. I knew it was true—on *his* end at least. But I couldn't deny what I'd seen—what I'd felt passing between them. It wasn't just a childhood friendship. There was a connection between them. Here and now.

Vancia was clearly aware of it. I wasn't sure if Nox was. Maybe he was in denial. Maybe he'd felt that way about her so long he didn't even recognize it for what it was. Maybe I was losing my mind.

He sighed. "Unfortunately, I have to go. Walk me out?"

I nodded and followed him to the door and into the garage where he'd parked. He leaned against the car and drew my body in between his spread thighs. When he dropped his head to kiss me, I shocked myself by drawing back. I didn't want his lips on mine—not right now.

"What's wrong?"

I squirmed back away from his close embrace. "You like her."

"Of course I like her. We've been friends all my life."

"Not like that. You *really* like her."

He let out an exasperated noise and tipped his head back so I was looking at his Adam's apple. Dropping his chin so we were eye-to-eye, he said, "Ryann—no. Don't be ridiculous. I love *you*. You know that. I've told you a hundred times."

I nodded. "Yes. You have… but you're acting different."

"So are you."

"I'm not. I'm still the same."

"You didn't want me to kiss you earlier with Lad nearby."

"That was… that was nothing. I just felt uncomfortable."

He blew out a long breath and pulled me close again, pressing my cheek to his chest, stroking my hair. The gesture was meant to be comforting, but his inhumanly rapid heartbeat under my ear served as a reminder of our vast differences.

"I miss you, Nox. I miss *us*. I feel like you don't talk to me anymore, like everything's changing. I have no idea what your life is really like now."

"It's lonely. It's strange. I don't tell you a lot about it because I don't want you to worry."

"I'm already worried, so you might as well tell me."

"Well… I'm surrounded by people I'm not sure I can trust. Some have told me how relieved they are I've returned and stepped up to lead instead of Davis. They didn't approve of his lust for Elven domination. Others smile and nod, but I don't know *what* they're really thinking. There are bound to be some who are still loyal to him and who actually wanted to follow his plan. But I don't know how many and how strong they are. Until then I can't say anything against him and change directions. Hopefully Vancia can help me with that kind of information. That is, *if* she can manage to stay around Davis long enough without him figuring out what she's up to. If she can manage to stay safe."

His brooding expression hinted he'd been spending a lot of time worrying about her.

"Are *you* safe?" I asked. "Aren't you worried there might be some sort of coup by the ones who *are* loyal to Davis?"

"Of course I think about that. Am I safe? I guess the answer is I don't know. I try to stay in public most of the time. When I'm not, I keep the ones I know are loyal to me—like Ewan—close by. I avoid being alone with Davis so he can't play his mind tricks on me. And I try not to draw suspicion to myself. Which reminds me, as much as I hate to leave, I really do need to get home. You think I can get that goodbye kiss now?"

I nodded against his chest, and he gripped my shoulders, moving me back a few inches to give himself access to my face. I didn't reject him when he kissed me this time.

It was a good kiss, a pleasant kiss, but something was different. The usual thrill wasn't there—at least for me. I guessed too much had happened tonight for the magic to be there. I wasn't sure how he felt about it, but he ended the kiss after a short time without pushing things further, which was a first for him in my experience. "More" had always been Nox's middle name.

"Okay," he said, dropping another soft kiss on the tip of my nose. "I'll be back as soon as I can. Make sure we talk before you try pulling off some big rescue operation for your mom, okay? I want to help."

"Okay. Good night. Be careful."

Nox climbed into his car, opened the garage door, and backed out. I stood watching his retreating headlights until he swung the car around onto the Pacific Coast highway and disappeared from sight, back to his world.

CHAPTER SEVENTEEN
I KNOW IT WHEN I SEE IT

Vancia was right inside the doorway when I opened it to enter the kitchen.

"What are you doing? Were you *listening* to us?"

"No," she said, but her high nervous tone betrayed her. "I was about to take out the trash. Lad said the garbage can is in the garage."

"Where is he?"

"He went for a walk on the beach."

"Alone?"

"Yeah." She rolled her eyes. "I guess he needed some space."

The look on her face was accusatory—there was no other way to put it. But why was she trying to make me feel guilty? I had every right to spend some alone-time with Nox. *She* was the one who'd been inappropriate.

"I'm not surprised after the way you threw yourself at Nox tonight," I said.

Her jaw dropped open, but she didn't deny it.

"You're in love with him," I said matter-of-factly. I knew it. She might as well know I knew it. When Vancia didn't respond, I went on. "You accused *me* of being unfair. Talk about unfair—how do you think that makes Lad feel?"

Her laugh was a harsh sound. "Oh, *now* you're worried about Lad's feelings. So what if I *was* in love with Nox? He was mine long before he was yours."

"Really? How can you even ask that? You're *engaged* to Lad—that's what. If you have feelings for someone else, you should tell Lad."

"Why? So you can move in and comfort him? Offer him a shoulder to cry on? You'd like that wouldn't you?"

"No, I—"

"He'd like that, too," she went on. "I don't know what you did to make both of them so crazy over you, but *that's* what's *unfair*."

Her words pierced my heart like a blade. "You're wrong. Lad is very committed to marrying you. He told me himself just today."

"Yeah." She snorted a bitter laugh. "He can't *wait* for the 'happy day' when we're bonded forever." She dropped the trash bag to the tile floor. "You know what? I don't know why I'm wasting my time talking to you. If you're too blind to see what's going on here, I can't help you."

Pushing past me, she hurried to where her own car was parked in the driveway.

"Vancia. Vancia—" I followed her out of the garage. The cool night air offered little relief from the blazing heat rising from my neck to my forehead. When she turned back to me, one hand on the car's door handle, I said, "What do you think is going on here that I can't see?"

She let out an exasperated breath. "Nox and I are meant to be together. It's obvious. I feel it. He feels it, too. It's what our parents always intended, and if they hadn't been killed, it's what would have happened."

I lifted my shoulders. "Things change. You're betrothed to Lad. Nox loves me now."

"He thinks he does. He doesn't know *how* he really feels because your Sway is blocking his vision."

A huge invisible hand closed around my throat. Lad had suggested the same thing a few days ago, only he'd been talking about Nox's glamour affecting me, not the other way around. I shook my head slowly, fighting for breath. "That's not true."

"I lived with Davis, Mr. Sway King himself, for five years. *Believe me*, I recognize it when I see it. Let him go, Ryann. You'll both be happier." She climbed into her car and slammed the door closed.

Staggering back into the house, I collapsed onto the sofa in front of the dark, lifeless fireplace, staring into its empty black interior. *She's wrong.*

Wasn't she? My mind went back to the conversation I'd had with Daddy before I'd left Mississippi for D.C.

About how he'd be "under her spell" as long as she lived. It was obvious Mom had swayed him, even though she was unaware of her own Elven-ness.

Could I be unknowingly swaying Nox? I knew his singing and his sexual glamour affected *me* powerfully. But was it really so different than the normal pull people felt toward each other when they fell in love?

And then my mind shifted to the love Lad and I had shared. It had happened slowly, naturally. His Sway didn't work on me. And after he'd pushed me away the way he did to protect me, I was pretty sure mine didn't work on him, either. Otherwise, he'd never have been able to let me go.

If Vancia was correct, and Lad *was* still in love with me, it was the real thing. And if I had any lingering feelings for him…

The back door opened, and Lad came in from the beach, surrounded by an ocean breeze and the fresh scent of the California night.

"Hi." He gave me a shy smile. "Everything okay now? You and Nox made up?"

"Everything's great." I stood from the couch as Lad dropped onto it. "I'm heading to bed now. See you tomorrow."

Concern knitted his eyebrows. "Okay then. Sleep well."

I did not sleep well. It was weird to be spending the night in the same house with Lad. I couldn't stop myself from picturing him one floor above me, stretched out in his own bed. Was *he* sleeping? Or was his mind going in a million different directions like mine?

I rose late the next morning to find the house quiet and still. Lad was obviously still in bed. Padding to the kitchen in search of coffee, I opened the cabinet and smiled. Nox hadn't failed me. There was a bag of Vanilla roast and a package of mini half-in-half containers. *He does love me.*

While the coffee brewed, I went to take a shower. The soapy water ran down my body, and I tried to let it wash away my worry. Being stuck here, forbidden to leave and without the ability to contact Mom, was beyond frustrating. I hated not knowing what was happening to her. And waiting around for Vancia to do something seemed foolish. I wasn't exactly her favorite person. Why would she go out of her way to help my mother?

By the time I turned off the spray and reached for a towel, I had half a mind to sneak out and go to Davis's house on my own. After wringing out my hair, I wrapped myself in a towel. Yep. That was what I would do. I would call a cab and go over there. Trying *something* was better than nothing. And it would be better than spending the day cooped up here with my ex-boyfriend.

I opened the bathroom door, planning to dress quickly in my room, then slip out of the house before Lad woke up. If he were awake, he might try to stop—

"Good morning."

My heart seized and then bounced around my insides like a super ball. Lad stood in the hallway just outside the bathroom, holding a steaming mug of coffee.

"Uh, hi." I tugged the edge of my towel further down over my thighs, then realized that left more of my chest uncovered. I shrugged it back up again, wrapping both arms around myself in a fight for modesty. "I thought you were still in bed."

He looked like a born-and-bred California beach boy in turquoise board shorts and bare feet. His upper body was bare as well, and drops of water still glistened on his skin. I swung my gaze away to keep from gawking at the expanse of tanned skin, wide chest, and broad shoulders in front of me. Not to mention those cologne-ad abs.

His eyes swept over me, from my wet hair and clean-scrubbed face down to my pink-painted toenails and back up again. He gave me a slow grin. "No. I got up early—went for a swim—you should try it. The ocean feels great, even better than the spring-fed pool."

I struggled to get enough air to answer him. "Sounds nice." Did he not realize I was standing in front of him basically naked?

He lifted the mug toward me. "Your coffee. I was going to put it in your room for when you got out of the shower."

The aroma of vanilla combined with ocean air and Lad's own enticing scent made my stomach growl and my insides shaky. "Okay, thanks." I let go of the towel with one hand and awkwardly reached for the mug, desperate to get rid of him and escape to the safety of my bedroom.

His gaze followed my fingers, then traveled up my arm, across my shoulders and downward, lingering at the top edge of my towel where a hint of cleavage was visible. His voice was decidedly distracted when he answered.

"No problem. I'll… uh… see you in a minute when you're… yeah. See you in a few minutes."

Speeding down the hallway, I darted into my room and shut the door behind me, my heart still zooming around my chest cavity like a jet ski on the ocean.

I'd wondered when Nox had told me on the phone that Vancia was acting *not-engaged* what that had looked like. I was pretty sure I'd just seen it in action. There had been desire in Lad's eyes that was completely inappropriate for a man who was spoken-for.

I strongly considered hiding out in my bedroom all day, but my growling belly and the need for a second cup of coffee finally won out.

Dressed and starving, I emerged from my room, determined to act like nothing unusual had happened. Lad was sitting on a high-backed stool at the kitchen counter. He smiled widely when he saw me.

"I'm looking forward to the seafood feast you promised to cook for me today."

"Oh, it's a feast now? I recall saying I'd cook some shellfish."

"Might as well cook all the seafood in there—it won't keep for long according to the cooking website I found this morning."

I grinned at him. "Getting domestic, are we? You're right, though. We should eat it all today. Maybe for lunch and supper."

"Can't wait. Listen, I really just came in for a drink myself. I'm about to head back out. There's a guy out there giving surfing lessons. Want to come along and try it?"

"I don't know." I picked up my phone from the counter and checked it. There was a message from Nox.

Spending the day with Vancia. Hopefully we'll make some progress.

I tried not to grimace. Hopefully, they wouldn't make anything *other* than progress. If Vancia had anything to say about it, they'd probably be making whoopie by the end of the day and be bonded for life.

Great. That was a lovely mental picture to dwell on. And what was I supposed to do all day other than obsess about what *they* were up to? Lad would shut me down on going to Davis's house or even into the city where we might be seen and recognized. I'd already finished the book I'd brought with me, last night when I couldn't sleep. Sitting around here all day doing nothing was going to drive me crazy.

"Okay, sure," I told Lad. "Surfing lessons sound fun. I'll head out after I eat. Hopefully there's something in there I can wear in the water."

"Okay, great. See you out there." Lad gave me a big smile and slid off the barstool, headed for the door.

After quickly cooking an egg and eating, I went to my room to change. Thankfully Nox had supplied a swimsuit, which I found in a dresser drawer. It was a *full-coverage* suit to say the least, one of those retro styles that might have been risqué in the fifties but today looked like something my mom would be comfortable wearing.

After that insane Versace number I'd been forced to wear for Reggie, he'd probably given the servant sent to shop for me specific instructions to avoid anything sexy. Whatever. I wanted to enjoy the water and pass some time, not turn anyone on.

It turned out Lad was as good at surfing as he was at everything else requiring strength and coordination. Me— not so much. I did get the hang of it after a few hours. Sort of. At least Lad didn't laugh at me, though I could tell he fought the urge hard when I wiped out. Repeatedly.

By afternoon, we were both starving. We toweled off on the deck and went inside. When I emerged from my room once again showered, and in a sundress, he'd already taken the shrimp and sea bass out of the refrigerator.

"I cut up some fruit," he said, clearly proud of himself.

"Great. I might eat everything raw if I don't have something to snack on."

He laughed. "I know what you mean." Pinching the tail of a shrimp, he dangled it over the counter. "Although these don't look too appetizing. They sort of look like bugs."

I eyed the grey transparent creature with its black bulging eyes and multitude of legs. "You're right. I've never noticed before. Once you taste them, you won't care what they look like," I assured him. Opening the refrigerator door, I pulled out a stick of butter and a jar of minced garlic. "Especially after I cook them in *this.*"

"Well, I'm going to shower while you work your magic. Unless you need some help?"

"No. I got it. Go ahead and… shower."

I had to swallow hard as I watched Lad's retreating form go down the hallway. His bare back, sloping down to a narrow waist. The strong legs and big tanned feet. The sight sent me back to the time we'd gone to the waterfalls and natural waterslide together, when he'd issued the edict that we'd be no more than friends, and it had nearly killed me not to reach out and touch that delicious-looking body.

I'd tried everything I could think of back then to make him admit he saw me as more than a friend. Now it was me who was in denial.

I cared deeply for Nox, and I would never cheat, but I had to admit the way I saw Lad was not *friendly.* Maybe you could never feel that lower level of emotion for someone after you'd spent so much time kissing them— and fighting the powerful urge to go beyond kissing.

No, we weren't boyfriend and girlfriend anymore, but we weren't just friends, either. Hearing the shower turn on, it was my turn to battle the mental image of him in a towel. *Out* of a towel. I grabbed my phone and checked it again, hoping for a message from Nox. Nothing. *Super.* What were we going to do for the rest of the day, stuck here together?

CHAPTER EIGHTEEN
DANGEROUS GAME

Lad was a big fan of the seafood feast, though really, I couldn't be sure if the credit should go to my cooking or the teenaged-boy appetite.

"So, want to go out to the beach again?" he asked, rubbing his flat belly. He'd gotten fully dressed after his shower, and for many reasons, it was best he stayed that way.

"Um… I think I've had enough sun for today. You go ahead, though."

"No, that's okay. I'll stay here."

I wandered around the living room, dejectedly surveying the empty bookshelves. Nox said he'd bought the cottage fully furnished. Obviously the previous owners weren't readers.

Opening the lower cabinet flanking the fireplace, I discovered a possibility. They weren't readers—they were gamers.

"Do you like board games?" I looked up over my shoulder at Lad.

"Sure." He squatted beside me to inspect the contents of the cabinet. "We had games in Altum. Not these, of course. Do you know these games?"

"I do. Daddy loved playing games at night. Let's see… I don't think Monopoly is right for you—since you've never used money. Hmmm… we've got Parcheesi, Pictionary…"

"What's Twister? That sounds fun."

"No. Definitely no Twister." That was the last thing I needed—the two of us reaching across each other's bodies, limbs twisting together, collapsing in a heap on the floor. No way.

"Here we go. Let's play Scrabble." I grabbed the box and pulled it from the shelf. "You like to read. You like words."

He nodded, considering. "Scrabble. Doesn't sound as exciting as Twister, but okay."

The game was fun for a while, until I could no longer tolerate the humiliation of being trounced by someone for whom English was a second language.

"I like this game," Lad announced.

"I *bet* you do. Did you read *all* the books in the Deep River library?"

"Almost, but not all of them."

We went back to the cabinet where I opened a box that looked something like a card file. "Hey, want to watch a movie? They have some DVDs here."

Based on the outdated titles, I was starting to suspect the cottage's previous owners might not have visited the property for a number of years. Either that, or they were major 80's aficionados.

"Oh, I've never seen a movie," Lad said.

"Really? Oh, right." I shook my head. "Okay, well, look at these and see what looks interesting. I don't know what you'd like."

Lad thumbed through the small collection, reading the titles and inspecting the cover photos. "What about this one?" He held up a DVD with a sinister-looking, scissor-wielding doll on the cover. The title read *Child's Play 2*.

I wrinkled my nose and shook my head. "No scary movies."

He laughed and picked up another. "How about this one? *The Blue Lagoon*. Looks tropical."

It also looked like a romance starring a couple of mostly naked teenagers. "Um...no."

He flipped through a few more and held up another case. "Basic Instinct?"

"I never saw that one, but I remember my parents saying it's really good. I think it's a murder mystery."

"Okay, that sounds interesting."

We popped it into the DVD player and, after a few minutes of fumbling, figured out the remote. The movie started off great—very intense and mysterious, interesting characters.

And then there were the scenes my parents *forgot* to mention. The sexy ones. And by that I mean two people with no clothes on totally going at it.

I squirmed on my side of the couch, my face in flames. Lad was on the far end, sitting very still. I darted my eyes over at him. He never took his from the screen.

What was he thinking? I knew he was a virgin, like me. And he was a movie-virgin as well. What a selection to start with. I didn't know if I should say, "I'm sorry," or "You're welcome."

When I glanced back at the screen and saw the man sliding down the woman's body, kissing a path along her bare skin as he went, I popped up from the sofa like a Whac-A-Mole.

"I need a drink. You?"

Without waiting for Lad's answer, I practically ran into the kitchen. My phone was on the counter, its blue light blinking. I picked it up and checked the screen. I'd missed a text from Nox about an hour ago. *Shoot.*

Nox: What are you up to?

Oh nothing. Just watching soft porn with my ex.

Ryann: Watching a movie. *(true)* **Missing you.** *(sooo true)* **What are you doing?**

Nox: I'm at a party. One of those see and be seen things Alfred arranged. Wish you were here.

I sent him back a smiley face emoji followed by a heart. But his next text made me wish I could take it back. Or replace it with one of those little red-faced guys with horns.

Nox: Vancia says hi. She and some of her model friends are here.

I swallowed a surge of bile before texting back.

Ryann: How nice. Have fun.

Yeah, it was insincere, but what girl would love to hear that her boyfriend was at a hot Hollywood party with his hot childhood sweetheart and her hot model girlfriends?

Nox: Don't be mad. Alfred wants us all to be seen together—image stuff. Blah blah blah

Ryann: I know. It's fine.

Nox: I'll probably be out really late, so I'll go ahead and say goodnight now.

Ryann: Night.

Now I was steamed for another reason entirely. Was it *really* all the agent's idea? Or was Vancia behind it?

She was the one who'd cautioned him to keep Lad and me out of sight until she could get the lay of the land with her Pappa. And she'd found a reason to spend all day with Nox. Now she was going to be "out late" with him and his bandmates and the other models.

Could I really blame her though? She'd basically announced her true intentions to me. And if I was aware of her feelings toward him, could Nox really be oblivious to them? He wasn't dumb. He certainly seemed happy enough to go along with anything she suggested.

I re-read our conversation, resisting the urge to throw my phone across the room.

What about Lad? Did I have a responsibility to share my suspicions with him? I sat on the bar stool, staring down at my screensaver while I considered it. He wasn't stupid, either. He'd seen them together, and he was entirely capable of asking Vancia himself—in a way she couldn't lie her way out of. He didn't seem concerned. *No—it's their business.*

I went back into the living room where thankfully the on-screen lovers were finished with *their* business and dressed once again. At least *they* were satisfied with their evening.

Lad glanced back over his shoulder. "Hi. No drinks?"

"Oh! I forgot. I'm sorry. I'll be right back."

Hurrying back to the kitchen, I filled two glasses with saol water. When I returned to the living room, Lad had stopped the movie.

"What's going on? You didn't like it?"

He wore a sheepish grin. "No. I *did*. But I don't want you to be uncomfortable. I can finish it later when you go to bed or something."

"Okay. That's probably a good idea," I said in the most casual tone I could manage.

"Yeah," he agreed. Eying the phone in my hand, he asked, "Talk to Nox?"

"No. He texted. He's out. With Vancia." My voice sounded so dejected I was embarrassed. I rushed to cover it. "And his band and her friends, too."

"I see." He paused for a minute, astutely reading my expression, maybe waiting for me to say more. When I didn't, he rose from the couch. "So… I'm hungry again. Did you see anything in there for dessert?"

"I wasn't really looking."

He smiled. "I have an idea. Stay here."

"Okaaaay." I dragged the word out, wondering what he was up to. I heard rummaging around in the refrigerator and the pantry. Was he making something?

Lad left the kitchen and went down the hallway. "Stay there," he cautioned.

I sat on the sofa, drinking my water and waiting for… whatever he was doing. When he returned, he was holding a long, white sock. Remembering how one of the movie characters had tied the other's hands to the bed with a scarf, I had a moment of panic.

"Close your eyes please," Lad said and stepped behind me.

"What? Why?"

"I'm going to blindfold you."

The panic increased. "Um…"

"Don't worry. This is going to be fun. I promise. It's a game."

"I don't know…"

You can trust me Ryann. I'd never harm you.

I knew he'd never hurt me… physically. But there was more than one way of hurting someone. Lad had already done that, and though I hated to admit it, he could easily do it again. Still, I found myself allowing him to tie the clean sock around my eyes and then pull me from the couch by two hands. My belly simmered with excitement, with the thrill of the unknown.

"Come with me." He led me a few steps and then guided me to sit.

A cool counter top was under my hands when I rested them. So we were in the kitchen.

"What kind of game is this?" I asked.

"A guessing game."

"What am I guessing?"

"You'll see." I heard a drawer opening and shutting, a scraping noise. And then Lad's voice. "Ready?"

"I guess so." I giggled, even though nothing was funny. My nerves were going crazy.

"Open your mouth."

"Oh—wait a minute—"

There was laughter in his voice. "I'm going to feed you. Don't worry—there are no raw onions in the house. Come on—open up."

I wasn't at all sure I wanted to play this game. Reaching for my blindfold, I started to protest. "I don't think—"

His warm fingers wrapped around my wrist, stopping me. "Come on, Ryann. Let's make the best out of our situation. There has to be something good about being stuck in a tiny house full of food while our significant others are out enjoying the L.A. nightlife together."

He had a point. A good one. But this situation was ripe with risk. I was frozen in indecision, my hands still hovering in the air, prepared to remove the blindfold and end this dangerous game. Finally, I let them drop slowly to the counter top again and opened my mouth.

I could literally feel Lad's smile, his satisfaction filling the space between us. He placed something on my tongue. It was sweet, squishy, kind of melty.

"Do you know what it is?"

"Yes. A marshmallow."

Lad laughed. "Good. I didn't know what those were, but they looked dessert-y. I tasted one before I gave it to you to make sure."

I chewed and swallowed.

"Next," Lad said, and I opened my mouth again.

This food was small, curved, firm. I bit into it, and tart juice filled my mouth. I thought I knew what it was, but it was strange—without seeing it I wasn't quite sure. "A cherry?"

"No. It's a slice of plum."

"Oh, weird. Okay, I'll get the next one. Hey, what do I get if I win?"

"You don't have to eat raw onions."

I laughed. "I thought you said we didn't have any."

"You never know," he said and put another piece of food in my mouth.

This one made me smile as I chewed. After I'd swallowed, I said, "Chocolate. Hershey's original."

"You know your chocolate." He sounded impressed.

"Oh yes sir. Better give me a harder one or you're going to lose this game and be the one eating raw onions."

"Okay then." He placed another item on my tongue.

It was dry and furry. I instinctively spit it out into my hand. "Blech. What *was* that?"

"Just kiwi." He laughed so hard his words came out mangled. "You said to give you a hard one."

"I said difficult, not disgusting."

"Okay. I'm sorry. One more. I promise this one won't be gross. Come on, you trust me, don't you?"

I sighed but answered him. *I do.*

And it was true. Lad had looked out for my best interests nearly my whole life. He'd defended me, protected me—even to the point of giving me up when he believed it was the best thing for me.

Cautiously, I opened my mouth again. I heard the scrape of a spoon and then my mouth was filled with sweetness. Cool Whip. The spoonful must have been overflowing because it spilled out of my mouth and dribbled down my chin. I laughed and swiped it with my tongue, trying to capture the escaped whipped topping.

Something hit my empathy glamour like a sledgehammer. A powerful emotion, a desperate sensation of grappling for self-control. Without seeing his face, I knew Lad was staring at my mouth, that he was fighting the urge to kiss me. That he wanted me.

Jerking back, I scrambled to pull off the blindfold, nearly falling off the stool in my rush to put some distance between us. Our eyes met, and the message was there, too—even more powerful.

I backed away from him, shaking all over. "I should… I need to—"

Lad stepped forward and steadied me with a strong hand. His face was inches from mine, his eyes filled with heat and unmistakable longing. His breathing was fast and audible.

My head shook back and forth. "We can't. It's wrong. I'm not with you anymore. I'm with Nox."

Lad's expression was not apologetic. He edged even closer. "Are you? It seems like Vancia is with him."

"For tonight. And what are *you* even thinking? You're engaged to her."

Lad's face tensed. A battle of emotions played out across it. "I can't keep going on like this. I can't keep the truth from you anymore."

My heart exploded in a riot of activity. "What truth? What are you talking about?"

He waited a full minute before answering, never breaking the intense eye contact we shared. "I don't want to marry her. You must know that already. All it would have taken was one minute of your emotional glamour, and you'd have known how I really feel about her. About *you*."

The internal riot turned into anarchy. "I haven't used it on you."

"Why not?"

"I… I don't know."

"Have you used it on Vancia? On Nox? If you have, you already know what I'm about to tell you. Hell, even if you didn't have glamour—you saw them last night together."

I shook my head. "But you *are* marrying her. You told me mind-to-mind."

He heaved a heavy sigh. "We've told everyone we intend to marry... because it was the only way she could get close to Davis again. And we have to be convincing. We have to *mean* it—in case he uses his glamour on her to make her tell the truth. Or on anyone close to us." He gave me a significant look.

"Like me?"

He nodded. "Like you. She can't resist him. You seem to think you can. I *hope* you can—because I'm not supposed to be admitting all this. It could get all of us killed." He grimaced, clearly angry with himself. "I shouldn't have told you. I can't seem to control myself around you anymore. I've barely been hanging on."

My fingers groped for the edge of the counter, and I grabbed it as if it were a ledge on a cliff I was climbing. "So the engagement... it *was* fake? The whole time?"

He nodded. "Right from the beginning. Even when you were out here in California, falling for Nox. I never wanted her. I never loved her. Only you. It's always been you, Ryann. Deep down, you *know* that. And for her... it's always been Nox."

I shut my eyes and sucked in air desperately. I felt like I was about to pass out. How could Lad be saying these things to me, after all this time? How could he *do* this to me?

Shaking my head, I chanted my response like a mantra. "It doesn't matter. It doesn't matter. I'm with Nox. Even if I wasn't, I could never be with you again. It hurts too much."

Instead of looking wounded or even disappointed, Lad's expression smoothed out. He looked almost satisfied.

"It wouldn't hurt if you didn't still care. And I would never, ever hurt you again. I will never leave you again. I know now I *can't* live without you, even if it is the 'right' thing. I want you, Ryann. I need you. I have to have you in my life, and I'll wait for you as long as it takes."

"No," I whispered, backing away from him again, the tears overflowing my eyelids as I squeezed them tight against the terrible, wonderful words. My back met the wall behind me. There was nowhere left to run. And I *had* been running—from Lad, from my own feelings.

He stepped forward, stalking me in a slow, steady pursuit. His voice was quiet but so intense I could feel every word sinking into my skin. "I don't even care about anything else anymore—about the humans, about stopping Davis and the Dark Elves."

His confession poured out like water flowing from Altum's underground river. "I'm only here for *you*. You're all I've ever wanted, Ryann. You're all I'll ever want. If you would let me, I'd make that very clear to you right now. I'd pick you up and carry you up to my room, and we'd be bonded forever. Then no one could say or do anything to stop us from being together."

He surged toward me, taking my face in his hands, pinning me between the wall and his powerful body. And then his mouth was on mine. My heart shattered as our tongues met. Over and over again, his lips moved against mine in greedy, possessive caresses that paralyzed my limbs and burned through every thought and protest in my mind.

It wasn't like kissing Nox—I wasn't mesmerized or helpless-feeling, there was no sense of strung-out euphoria. But I still couldn't stop what was happening. Maybe I was overcome by all the sensations—the taste of Lad's mouth, so sweet and familiar—the feel of his hot hands cupping my face—the way his body lined up perfectly against mine—the echo of the innocent girl inside me experiencing the irresistible pull of first love.

Maybe I was stunned by the blatant announcement of his desire to sleep with me here and now and seal the deal.

Whatever it was, my brain and body weren't making a solid connection at the moment. Emotion was in full control. All the pent-up feelings I'd ever had for Lad were gushing out of me like water from an open spillway. If Lad possessed empathy glamour, he'd be positively drowning right now.

I had been telling myself I didn't have the capacity to feel this level of passion anymore. I was wrong. It was all still there. And I could no longer control it… or deny it. I loved this guy. I needed him. I wanted him as much as he wanted me.

The phone rang in my purse across the room, and my senses returned in a rush of shock and guilt.

Oh no. Lad—stop.

He didn't break contact with my lips. *Ryann. Please. Let me.*

His starved craving for me, finally unleashed after all this time, flowed all around and through me, driving my empathy glamour insane.

I forced my hands between us, pushing at his chest. Finally, he broke the connection. Physically, at least. It was possible the other connection between us had never been broken.

Lad's eyes were burning with green fire and filled with triumph. "It's still there between us. I can *feel* it, Ryann. I know you feel it, too. Admit it."

I stared at him for a moment, my head and heart still flip-flopping in a crazy hormone-infused dance. "No. Yes. Maybe. It doesn't matter—if there *are* any feelings there, they're not enough. And they're about two months and one heartbreak too late. I've moved on. Nox loves me, and he trusts me. That shouldn't have happened. It won't happen again."

His expression hardened. "If he *really* loved you, he'd be here tonight. He'd be willing to give up his throne for you—the way I was. Or he'd march you right into the middle of the Dark Court, announce to everyone his intention to bond with you, and tell them all to stick it. That's what I'd do."

"Lad." My breaths were fast and shallow and making me light-headed. I leaned harder against the kitchen wall for support. When I finally felt steady again, I pinned him with a don't-mess-with-me look. "Do you really think she's in love with him?"

"I know she is. She told me. And *she's* the one who called off the wedding that night in Altum. She told my father she couldn't marry someone she didn't love because there was someone else out there she *did* love."

All the air left my lungs now, leaving me gasping again. All this time I'd believed Lad's father had changed his mind that night and released him from the obligation. "But... she *is* planning to go through with the wedding."

"Yes. She has a strong sense of duty." He laughed bitterly. "Looks like no matter what I do, I'm destined to end up with a girl who prefers my brother."

I opened my mouth to argue that I didn't prefer Nox to him—I'd ended up with Nox almost by default. But then I shut it again.

I did care deeply for Nox. Whether I loved him or not, he deserved my loyalty. And Grandma Neena said everything happened for a reason. Maybe things with Lad had happened the way they did so I would end up with Nox. Maybe *he* was my destiny.

But if Vancia had loved Nox all these years, had searched for him and saved his life, maybe *she* was *his* destiny. My mind was churning like the ocean outside our back door.

I met Lad's eyes again. "How do you think he feels about her? He doesn't seem comfortable talking about the time they spent together here recently. Did she tell you anything?"

My phone rang again, but I ignored it. Emmy, Grandma, Daddy—whoever it was could wait. I had to hear the answer to this question *right now.*

"She said they reconnected. There was instant closeness and chemistry. She thinks there's definitely something there. It *does* seem that way, based on what I've seen."

I nodded. I'd thought the same thing watching them interact. I had to admit I wasn't in love with Nox. Could I be if I still loved Lad? But the idea of Nox with someone else gave me a weird feeling, a shaky sense of panic. What would I do without him? I thought back on the past few weeks apart from Nox, on the strange, insistent need for him, the sense of longing that was almost painful.

Picturing Nox and Vancia *together* at the party tonight increased the bizarre shakiness—as if she had stolen the prescription pills I needed to stay alive. What were they doing right now? Dancing with each other? Leaning close so they could hear each other over the party noise? Or maybe they'd gone off and found a quiet corner somewhere so they could talk more intimately. Or do other intimate things.

I took a deep drink of the saol water in front of me, trying to calm myself. A hard knock on the front door made me jump up and nearly tip the glass over. The knock was followed by repeated raps loud enough to rattle the picture frames on the walls.

We shot each other a wide-eyed look. Lad stepped in front of me, and we moved to the front hall in tandem. He looked through the peep hole and let out a tense breath that was nearly a hiss.

"It's Nox."

CHAPTER NINETEEN
UNDER THE INFLUENCE

When Lad did nothing, I urged him on. "Well, open the door."

He opened it, and Nox burst in, hands clenched into fists, his expression determined and battle-ready. His eyes went first to Lad then behind him to land on me.

He rushed to me, grabbing my shoulders. "Ryann. Why didn't you answer your phone? I thought something was wrong."

"I'm fine," I said weakly. "I heard it ring, but I didn't pick up... we were talking."

He let out a heavy breath. "You scared me. I tried calling you mind-to-mind but you didn't respond."

Holding my chin with one hand, Nox tilted my face up toward the light. I saw the moment he realized what my smudged makeup and lack of lip gloss meant. His eyes went very dark, and his mouth set in a grim line.

Without another word, he took my hand and pulled me to the door, glaring at Lad as we passed him. Lad's expression was no more pleased. His whole body was rigid as if he was about to spring for an attack, but he didn't move and stayed silent.

Nox's yellow Mercedes was parked at the curb. He yanked the passenger door open for me then marched around to the driver's side without waiting to see if I'd get in. Of course I did. I was dreading the conversation we were about to have, but I was still glad to see him—delirious almost—that he was here with me and not at the party with Vancia.

He started the engine and pulled the car onto the Pacific Coast Highway, driving way too fast right out of the chute.

"Where are we going?"

"I don't know. Nowhere. We're just driving." He glanced over at me, then back at the road ahead. "So…"

"What?" My voice was very small.

His was scary calm. "You know what. What was going on there before I *interrupted?* What were you two doing?"

I slunk lower in my seat and crossed my arms. "Nothing. Having dessert."

Nox snorted, his face scowling. "I'll bet." He stepped on the gas, causing the engine of the sports coupe to roar.

"What are *you* doing here? I thought you were staying out late at the party. With *Vancia.*"

"Why are you saying it like that? You know I have to do that stuff. I wanted to be with you. Alone. I snuck away from all of them and called because I wanted to hear your voice. When you didn't pick up I came to check on you."

"Because you're suspicious of me and Lad?"

"Because I was worried something had happened to you. *Should* I be suspicious of you and Lad?"

"No."

"What happened between you two?"

"I told you already."

"Yeah, you told me you were talking and having dessert." Nox jerked the wheel, sending the car careening into the parking lot of a beachside café. It stopped so abruptly, my seatbelt tightened against my chest. He put the car in park and twisted in his seat to face me, skewering me with his gaze.

"Ryann—I've seen you a time or two after you've been kissed, remember?"

My face burned, and my eyes watered. "Yes," I whispered. "He did kiss me. But it was nothing. I stopped him."

"Did you want to?"

"Stop him or kiss him?"

Nox gave me a loaded glance. "You know what I'm asking. Do you want him?"

"No," I said, but the hesitation beforehand was long enough to make Nox let out an angry curse and slam his hand against the steering wheel.

"I *knew* better than to leave you in that house with him."

"Do *you* want Vancia?" I challenged. "Because you have to know she wants *you*. And you're spending all your time with her. You were here together for a month while I was back in Mississippi. That was a lot of getting-reacquainted time."

"She was helping me. We're old friends."

"She told Lad she's in love with you."

His eyebrows nearly hit his hairline. "She did?"

"Yes."

He sat back in his seat and raked a hand through his hair, staring up at the ceiling. "What do you want me to say, Ryann? I told you I'd always be here for you, and I keep my word. I've made it clear how I feel about you."

"Or how you *felt* about me. Admit it. Things are different now. She's back in your life. I want to talk about how you feel about *her*. You were childhood sweethearts. You skinny-dipped in your parents' hot tub, for God's sake."

He cut his eyes over at me. "She shouldn't have mentioned that."

"Did you like her back then—you know, *like* her like her?"

He shrugged, working his mouth in an uncomfortable twist. "I kissed her. It was puppy love."

A thought occurred to me. "Has *she* tried to kiss *you*? You know—since then?"

When his eyes swung around to meet mine, they were filled with confirmation of my fears. Well, not fears exactly, now that I thought about it. They confirmed some deep inner knowledge I'd only just become conscious of.

"Once," he admitted. "We'd both had a lot to drink. That night in Tijuana. I stopped it."

"After how long?"

"What? Are we going to get out our stopwatches and compare the length of our forbidden kisses? What are we doing here, Ryann?"

I sighed as my face dropped into my open palms. "I don't know."

Silence filled the car. Finally, Nox said, "I don't either. You're right. Something's different. But you and I and Lad and Vancia—we've got to put all this... *whatever* aside and work together right now. People's lives are hanging in the balance. Another reason I came to see you was to tell you... a girl from Reggie's fan pod washed up on the beach tonight."

I lifted my head and stared at him. "Oh God. Who? Do you know her name?"

"I'm not sure. It was something like Karen, or Kirsten... oh, Kerri. Yeah, that's it."

My hands flew up to cover my mouth. "One of Emmy's suitemates was named Kerri. Oh my God. What happened to her?"

"The official story is she went out swimming alone and drowned. But you and I both know, those girls don't go anywhere alone. I think it was a Sway O.D."

My throat felt swollen and sore. "We have to help them. My mom's not the only one in danger. The whole world's in trouble if things keep going like they are." I grabbed his arm. "Can't you end it right now? You're the Dark King. Can't you just disband the fan pods?"

"I *could* do that. I might wind up murdered in my sleep if I do."

"Oh God, Nox. Don't say things like that." My hand went to his shoulder, which was knotted with tension. I began rubbing it, and he let his head fall back on the headrest, closing his eyes and sighing in pleasure. Maybe it was exhaustion.

"I'm kidding—sort of. But I've already figured out there *are* people close to me who are still loyal to Davis. And Alfred has warned me not to make any sudden policy changes. It's not a dictatorship. The Dark Council still has a lot of power, and I need to work with them, no matter what I decide to do. I think our first order of business has got to be finding a way to control Davis. He's been pushing for a faster and faster takeover… encouraging Alfred to set up new fan pods as quickly as possible. Alfred says he's dragging his feet as much as he can. And Vancia told me about the new cell phone tower construction. That's not good. The Sway will blanket the earth before long."

"I wish there was a way to tell the humans to just turn it off or something."

"Well, you probably could—with *your* Sway they'd listen. Of course, it'd take you your whole life to go around to each fan pod and sway each member. Not to mention the fact that as soon as they were onto you, the

Council would send someone to take you out. Obviously, I'm not going to let you make yourself a target for assassination."

"Remember that thing I said to Lad in your suite the day he found us… um…"

"Making out half-naked?" Nox lifted his head and gave me a wicked grin. "Yeah—I remember the day. Don't remember what you said, though."

"I said no one was *letting* me or *not* letting me do *anything*. You were the one who said I was more capable than anyone knew. If I'm so 'capable,' then I can handle it."

Nox reached out and stroked my cheek with a fingertip. "I wish we could go back to that day. I'd have locked the damn door, and none of this would have happened."

I shivered at his touch, experiencing an unusual new sensation inside… almost like… aversion? "We can't hide from the world. We would have eventually *had* to come out of your suite—if only to avoid starvation."

"Yeah. But you would've been *mine*, and no one would have been able to take you away."

"Or take *you* away." I thought of the look on Vancia's face when she'd burst into the room and seen him for the first time in five years. And the way he'd looked at her, too.

Nox stared into my eyes as he leaned in toward my mouth. The sexual glamour was coming off of him in waves I could feel, smell, taste, and almost see.

I leaned in, too, hooked once again, not caring *why* I wanted to kiss him, only that I needed to, needed it like I needed oxygen and water and Hersey's chocolate. The fact that I'd been kissing Lad fifteen minutes earlier seemed inconsequential. It seemed like a hundred years ago.

But when our lips connected, something was off. My pulse wasn't racing, my mind wasn't swimming in a sea of lust-soaked bliss. That subtle sense of aversion was back. I pulled away, clear-headed, and studied his face, trying to figure out what had changed.

He gave me a quizzical look in return, blinking as if coming out from under hypnosis.

His ring tone blared through the car, making both of us jump. Grabbing the phone from the console, he checked the screen.

"Damn it. I've got to get back. Audun is there. He's on the Council—the next in command after Davis. He's looking for me. I didn't tell anyone I was leaving. They all think I'm taking a leak or making out in a corner with a pod girl or something."

"Okay."

Nox gave me another long look. "I wish I didn't have to take you back. It seems like something's always coming between us." He slid his hand into my hair and nuzzled my neck, apparently intending to launch into a new make out session.

A minute ago he'd said he needed to get back to the party as soon as possible. Had he forgotten already? As sharp and *un*-glamoured as I felt, Nox still seemed to be under the influence of something.

"Nox, you have to go. The call from Audun?" I prodded.

"Oh, shit. You're right." He straightened in his seat and started the engine.

As he drove me back to the cottage, I sat in troubled silence. There was a strange sort of tickling in my mind, a disturbance that danced around the edges of my thoughts, as if I were struggling to remember something I'd forgotten, like song lyrics or a name. But in this case, I couldn't even identify what it was I was striving to figure out.

It was so strange—I'd longed for closeness with Nox during the time we were forced to be apart. And when I saw him at the airport and that first day at the cottage, his touch and kisses had drowned me in a deep pool of glamour ecstasy.

But for some reason, his hold on me seemed to be slipping. As I'd told Lad, I had no intention of breaking up with Nox. So what had changed?

I watched his strong, beautiful profile, illuminated in the dashboard lights. Sensing my gaze, he gave me a sexy, sideways glance. He still seemed as smitten as ever. What was wrong with me?

CHAPTER TWENTY
REFILL

When we pulled up to the cottage, Nox dropped me off at the curb with an apology. "I'm sorry I have to leave in such a hurry." He kissed me. "Okay—jump out and let me make sure you get in the door safely before I go."

I did as he said, hurrying to the front door and turning for a quick wave before opening it and going in. The house was dark. Lad had gone to bed already. I guessed he'd finished the movie alone, or maybe he was too angry and just went to his room.

I shut the door quietly and locked it, then slipped my shoes off before walking to the kitchen for some sweet tea. Now that I'd started drinking it again, I couldn't get enough, and I was parched.

Filling a glass, I carried it with me back through the house toward my room.

"Did you kiss him?"

I jumped and slapped my palm over my hammering heart, sloshing tea all over my other hand and onto the floor, nearly dropping the glass to the tile.

The growling voice had come from the dark living room. I changed course and walked into the room, searching for Lad. Only his silhouette was visible, slouched in a chair, facing the lifeless TV set.

"What are you doing in here? Why are you sitting in the dark?"

"Did. You. Kiss. Him?"

The question was more emphatic this time. Angrier. And that got my temper going as well. I flipped on the light, causing Lad to squint in the sudden brightness.

"If I did, it's none of your business."

"It *is* my business because your welfare is my business, and he's glamouring you."

His astute assessment of the situation unnerved me. And the fact that Nox's glamour *hadn't* seemed to work on me tonight made it worse.

"He didn't sing," I said as if that was any sort of defense.

Lad rolled his eyes. "You said he had more than one glamour, and I have a pretty good idea what the other one is. I saw how the girls reacted to him in Altum. Yes—even though we're less affected by it, glamour can still work on other Elves."

I wasn't about to confirm that speculation for him. The last thing I wanted to do was discuss Nox's sexual glamour with Lad. "Well, he has a right to kiss me. He's my boyfriend."

Lad rose from the chair and stepped toward me, his hands out as if he meant to grab me and shake me. Instead he grabbed the air in tight fists. "Only because I pushed you away. You would *never* be with him if that hadn't happened. And it shouldn't have."

I took a step back. "Well... it did."

Lad's hands came to rest low on his hips and his head dropped, hanging down as he stared at the floor, silent, for long moments. Then he looked up, glanced around, and grabbed the DVD case with Sharon Stone on the cover and threw it against the wall where it struck with a loud crack and clattered to the floor in two pieces.

I fell back a step, shocked. I'd never seen him lose his temper like this.

He held up one hand in a calming gesture. "Sorry. I'm not mad at you. I'm mad at myself." He let out a growl of frustration. "I don't know—maybe I *should* let you go. Maybe he's better for you. Maybe you belong here, with him, in the Dark Elven world. I can't compete with the fame and the fancy cars and mansions on the beach. And I sure as hell can't compete with sexual glamour." He collapsed back into the chair, once again sullen and staring at the floor.

What he didn't know, what I *wouldn't* say, was that when we'd been together, I'd found him every bit as enticing as I found Nox—without any glamour at all. My fascination with Nox hadn't begun until after I'd arrived in L.A., after I'd—

"Oh my God."

Lad's head lifted. "What?"

That thing that'd been poking gently at my brain? It had just reared back and sucker punched me.

"I didn't feel... you know... something for Nox until we got out to L.A. together. That's when I stopped drinking this."

Now his eyes were bright with interest. "Tea?"

"Tea... made with *saol water*. I've been drinking it again since I got here, and I've noticed... well... when I was with him tonight—I felt different. Last night, too, after dinner. Something had changed." I lifted the half-empty glass. "I think maybe it lessens the effects of glamour. I've seen the same thing with my friend Emmy, too. Once she started drinking my tea on a regular basis, she was a lot less interested in celebrities. And she's always been *really* into them. At first I thought it was some sort of residual effect of having been in the fan pods, but maybe it was the saol water in the tea."

Now Lad's expression was fully alert and engaged. "Maybe that's why Elves are less susceptible to glamour than humans. I assumed it was genetics, but maybe it's the saol water."

"We should test it. If it's true... then all we have to do is convince the whole world to drink Magnolia Sugar Tea, and they'll be released from the power of the Dark Elves," I said facetiously. Easy-peasy. Nothing to it.

"That's not a bad idea," Lad said with a totally serious expression and tone.

"Um… I was joking. How would we get everyone to drink it? It's only carried in 110 stores right now. And it's brand new. Hardly anyone's ever heard of it."

"I don't know yet. But there's something to that idea. Let's discuss it with Vancia the next time we meet."

"Yeah. Can't wait for *that*."

"So… you really feel a difference from drinking it?" Lad asked.

I nodded. He nearly jumped out of the chair and charged past me to the kitchen.

I followed him. "What are you doing?"

"Getting you a refill."

CHAPTER TWENTY-ONE
RESCUE

The next morning I had a text from Nox saying Vancia had called a meeting at our cottage. I assumed we'd be talking strategy for rescuing Mom. She was supposed to be on the lookout for opportunities, any times that Davis might leave Mom alone. It would also be a good chance to discuss my saol water theory with both of them.

When Vancia opened the door, I could tell immediately something was wrong. Nox arrived moments later, and his expression confirmed something was up— she must have already told him about whatever had happened.

"Davis figured it out," she said when we were all gathered in the living room.

Lad was sprawled in the same chair where he'd been sulking in the dark last night. I was in another, facing the small sofa where Vancia and Nox sat side-by-side.

"His spies were at the party last night—they saw us together." She gestured between herself and Nox.

Of course, my first thought was to wonder what they had been doing together last night that had raised such alarm with Davis.

"And…" Lad prompted.

"When I got home he cornered me and asked me directly mind-to-mind about… my feelings." She blushed. "He used his Sway on me. I couldn't lie. I'm sorry."

"So what does this mean?" I demanded.

"It means I'm kind of useless to the cause now. He knows I was working against him. And… he knows the engagement—oh." She stopped herself there, looking toward me with a panicked expression.

Lad spoke up. "It's okay. She knows."

Her eyebrows pulled together in an angry V. "Since when? I thought we couldn't *tell* her."

"Tell her what?" Nox said, throwing his hands out to the side.

"The engagement was a ruse—so Davis would let me come back home."

Nox stared at her, clearly taken aback by her confession. But then, he shifted and nodded, his face looking like a guy on the verge of solving a Rubik's cube for the first time.

She glanced around at all of us. "He also kicked me out of the house. I blew it. I'm sorry."

Taking in her downcast expression, Nox set a comforting hand on her back. "It's all right. You couldn't help it. His Sway is too strong."

When Vancia let out a sob, his back-patting turned into a slow, comforting rub. He leaned his forehead against hers and lowered his voice. "Don't worry about it. You tried your best."

"Where am I going to go?" She sniffed. "He banished me from all of his homes."

"You'll stay with me, of course. There are plenty of rooms at my house."

Under another set of circumstances, I might have been more concerned over Vancia's sudden homelessness and Nox's proposed cohabitation. Things were changing so fast I could hardly keep up. But all I could really care about in that moment was Mom.

"Does this mean we're not going to try to rescue my mother?" I asked, sounding as desperate as I felt.

Vancia shook her head. "It doesn't have to. I think tonight might be the best chance you'll get. They're going to see the Philharmonic at the Hollywood Bowl. I know where his box seats are. Of course I can't be seen there, or he'll immediately know something's up. But you three could go."

"That's what we'll do then," Lad said, coming to his feet. "Because I think it's even more critical to get Ryann's mom away from him as soon as possible. Now he knows for sure there's a faction working against him. Because of last night, he has to strongly suspect you're in on it with her." He nodded to Nox. "It may speed up the timetable for whatever he has planned. And if Vancia's right, and Ryann's mom is critical to what he's doing…"

"Right," Nox said. "Okay, so let's talk about how we're going to do it."

The three of us arrived at the iconic clamshell-shaped music venue in one of Nox's cars. I was in a disguise, of sorts, heavily made up and wearing a designer dress, sunglasses on, my hair poufed in a glamorous style I'd never normally wear. I did my best to hide my face as paparazzi appeared from seemingly nowhere, calling Nox's name and shouting questions as they snapped pictures of us getting out of the car.

"Who's the lucky girl tonight, Nox?"

"Give us a peek at your face, sweetheart."

Nox tucked me against him, rushing us past the photographers toward the main gate. Lad was still in the car, staying in the back seat as the driver drove it to the parking lot. According to our plan, he would meet up with me later at a designated point near the West gate where, if everything went well, I'd be waiting with Mom.

Nox and I found our seats. He'd purposely purchased tickets several rows behind Mom and Davis, so we could keep an eye on them throughout the show. The plan was to ensure that Mom would separate herself from him at some point.

Nox had paid a server to inform Davis and Mom that the management was thrilled by their attendance and sent complimentary champagne with instructions to keep it flowing all evening. Knowing Mom as I did, she'd be delighted by the gift. She loved champagne. I also knew her teensy bladder would guarantee at least one trip to the bathroom during the concert—probably more than one.

When she reached our row, I would avert my face until she'd gone by, then slip out and follow her. The idea was to get her alone, far from Davis's reach. Then I'd use my own glamour to convince her to come with me to the West gate where Lad and the driver would pick us up.

The orchestra was barely into the second movement when I saw her whisper to Davis and slide out of their box toward the steps. Picking up my program, I covered my face until Nox told me she'd passed us. Then, with a quick glance at him and a squeeze of his hand, I slipped out of our row and followed her to the bathroom.

Waiting by the sinks, I waved on the other women who motioned for me to take the next available open stall. Yes, I looked like some creepy restroom stalker, but I couldn't take the chance that Mom might somehow make it out of there without me seeing her.

She emerged from a stall and went directly to the sink on the opposite end from me, not even glancing at my face. She washed her hands and studied her makeup in the mirror, looking for touch-up opportunities, no doubt. She might be a glamour-bot, but she was still my mother.

"Mom?"

Her eyes flew to my face. She blinked several times. "Ryann? Is that you? Wow, honey, you look beautiful." Her head tilted, and her eyebrows quirked. "What are you doing here?"

"I came for you."

She rushed forward and embraced me, then pulled back with a beaming smile as my words registered. "Did Davis bring you here as a surprise? I've been telling him how much I miss you."

I pulled her toward the restroom exit and through the door as she was talking—there was no time to waste on explanations. We'd have to walk and talk.

"No, Mom. He didn't bring me. I came on my own, because he—"

"Ryann, what a lovely surprise."

Davis's voice behind me nearly made me jump out of my skin. Had he followed her to the restroom as well?

I whirled to face him. "Davis. I… just ran into Mom in the ladies room. You can imagine my shock." I laughed uncomfortably, already aware my lie wasn't going to convince him. "When she said she was moving in with you, I assumed she meant Atlanta or D.C. I had no idea y'all would be in L.A."

Stepping closer and wearing a predatory grin, Davis pinned me with his eyes. "And I had no idea you were such a fan of symphony music. Or that you were planning a return trip to California so soon." He lowered his voice into what I now recognized as his Sway tone. "What are you doing here?"

Okay. So he was trying to glamour me into telling him the truth. Obviously he was suspicious, and he should have been—me being at the same location as him and Mom so far from home was incredibly damning. I'd have to make my next lie very convincing.

"I was… following your daughter."

His eyebrows flew up over eyes wide with shock. "Vancia? I wasn't aware you knew her."

"I don't, really. I know her fiancé. We… he and I… we used to be together. We were in a relationship before…"

"Before he and Vancia were to marry," he said, finishing the thought for me. He gave a little *huh* laugh. "Remarkable."

"She took him from me. And I followed the two of them out here to L.A. to try to convince him to uh…" Here I allowed my voice to fill with mortification that wasn't hard to fake. "… to take me back and break up with her. But I lost them in traffic after the airport. This was the only place I knew they'd be going. I was hoping to catch him alone for a few minutes."

I sniffled a bit for dramatic effect, sweeping my hand across the fancy dress I wore. "I even got all dressed up, hoping to dazzle him. But I haven't seen them here tonight. And then I ran into Mom in the bathroom."

He studied me with a sharp, assessing gaze. "Yes… well… I'm afraid it's a wasted trip for you. Vancia was… unable to attend tonight after all." His eyes went to the side, and his tone took on a calculating note as if evil hamsters were busy turning wheels inside his brain. "She didn't *mention* her betrothed was in town. How *interesting*."

Oh no. I'd accidentally implicated Lad as an accomplice in Vancia's plot against her Pappa. Hurriedly, I concocted yet another lie. Hopefully, he'd buy it because as far as he knew, he'd glamoured me into total honesty.

"Well, Lad said they were off and on, that she had a lot of secrets and they argued a lot. Maybe they had a fight. Maybe he's flown home already." I attempted to fill my voice with the kind of unashamed hopefulness a lovestruck girl would feel at the prospect her ex-boyfriend might soon be her once-again boyfriend.

It seemed to work for Davis. He nodded, his eyes going soft with something akin to sympathy. "Perhaps. And I have some news about their 'relationship' that might please you—she has betrayed him with another boy. Your Lad may be very open to the idea of reconciling with you."

"Do you really think so?"

He lay a fatherly hand on my shoulder. "Yes I do. And I'll do whatever I can to help you in this matter. I'll find out whether your young man has returned to Mississippi or remains yet in the city."

Fabulous. Now he'd be actively looking for Lad. What had I done? And what could I do but keep playing along? I would warn Lad as soon as I saw him.

"Oh, could you? That would be amazing," I gushed.

Davis smiled. "Certainly. First thing tomorrow. Tonight we have a show to enjoy, don't we my dear?" His question was directed at Mom, who nodded robotically and looked right through me with hollow eyes.

"Where are you staying, Ryann?" Davis's voice still held the force of his Sway. I guessed he was making one last credibility check before deciding whether he believed my cockamamie tale.

"I stayed at a motel near the airport last night. But it was kind of scary. I was hoping I'd find Lad today and not have to stay there another night."

Seemingly satisfied, Davis gave me a soothing smile. "Don't you worry about that. You'll join us for the remainder of the concert and stay at my house tonight. I'll send someone to pick up your bag." Staring down into my eyes and no doubt turning his Sway up full-force, he said, "You will spend the next few days here with your mother and me. And then we'll go to the Olympics together in Boston Friday. How does that sound?"

I tried my best to make my tone and expression empty as I nodded in agreement. "Good. It sounds good."

"Excellent. Let's return to our seats."

Dang it.

I had no choice but to go with him. I followed him and Mom down to the pricey seat section where someone miraculously left their box seat chair and made room for me, swayed of course.

As I sat and watched the orchestra, I focused my mind and sent a message to Lad, who was probably frantic with worry that I hadn't met him at our rendezvous point by now.

Plan's a bust. Davis caught me with Mom.

His reply was immediate. *Are you okay?*

I'm fine. But I'm going home with them tonight. At least I'll be with Mom and get another chance at swaying her.

I don't like it. Just get away from him.

I don't have a choice—he thinks I'm under his influence. I can't let him know I'm immune.

There was a long pause before I heard his voice again. *Be careful.*

I will. You be careful, too. He'll be looking for you. I let it slip that you're in town. Sorry.

Don't worry about me. You take care of yourself.

I messaged Nox next, telling him basically the same information. There was no answer. Had he left the Bowl? Was he out of range? Or had something happened to him?

My pulse beat in a fluttery rhythm until I spotted him returning to his seat toward the center of the amphitheater. I tried again.

Didn't you hear me?

When?

A few minutes ago. I was talking to you. You didn't answer.

I'm sorry. I didn't hear anything. What's going on? Why are you sitting down there?

I ran into Davis when I was trying to rescue Mom. I have to go home with them—he thinks I'm swayed. And I lied to him about where I've been staying. Can you get my bag to a seedy motel near the airport? I told him it was at the American Inn. Davis is going to send someone to pick it up.

I'll leave right now and take care of it. But we need to talk about how to get you out of there. Should I summon him to my house?

I don't know. Maybe. Give me a chance to talk to my mom first. At the very least I'll see you Friday at the Olympics Opening Ceremony.

Oh no…

Yep. Davis just gave me a golden ticket.

CHAPTER TWENTY-TWO
SWAY DANGER

We all rode home together in the back of Davis's limo. Mom, having fully enjoyed the complimentary champagne, fell asleep on the ride. She lay slumped against his shoulder.

He asked me a few questions in a hushed voice, all of them having to do with Lad—how we'd met, how long we'd dated, how serious things had gotten between us.

Keeping in mind it's always easier to remember and repeat the truth than lies, I was as honest as possible. "I loved him. I believe he loved me, too. We'd still be together if Vancia hadn't come along."

Davis nodded. The more he heard, the more pleased his expression grew. "I wish you'd told me sooner," he said. "I'd have done more to facilitate your relationship. And kept Vancia out of the way."

"Why would you do that?" I asked, honestly perplexed. His whole scheme to draw the Light Elves into the battle had revolved around using Vancia to influence Lad.

"Because you're my daughter," he said. "I want you to be happy. I want you to have what you want. And... it would have been good for *all* of us to have such a fine young man in the family."

Ah. So he didn't care *which* of his daughters was with Lad, influencing him to join the Dark Elven plot. He'd just realized he backed the wrong horse in this race. Now that he'd heard my story, he was happy to switch up his bets, like any gambler who'd gotten a hot tip.

"I'm glad you're here, Ryann." Davis stroked my mom's hair as she slept. "It will be good for us to spend time together as a family. Your mother has missed you terribly. And you'll enjoy attending the Olympic Games with us."

"I'm sure I will. I've never been."

"Of course you haven't. You've been buried in those woods your whole life, poor child. But your life has changed. You're about to discover a whole new world of wondrous opportunities—now that you're with *me*."

His tone was so certain, so smug. He really believed he was doing me a favor by taking me into his "family." The glow of his white teeth in the dark limo was eerie as he smiled at me. I forced myself to return the smile. It was what he expected. And now that I *was* with him, I could *not* let him know his glamour didn't affect me.

Not until I was ready to reveal I had some of my own.

Davis's house was immense. So large in fact, I didn't see Mom until nearly noon the following day. I finally found her outside by the pool.

"Sweetheart!" She bounced up from her lounger to hug me. "I'm so thrilled you decided to fly out and join Davis and me. What a terrific surprise. He said you were really tired and to let you sleep in today. Did you get a good rest?"

"Um, yeah… I did," I lied.

Mom didn't seem to have any memory of seeing me last night at the Hollywood Bowl. Maybe Davis didn't trust me quite as much as I thought he did and had wiped her mind in case I'd gotten in a few words last night and managed to plant some seeds of doubt before he'd apprehended us.

"How's your California vacation been so far?" I asked.

"Oh it's beautiful here. I almost hate to leave for Boston next week. But the Opening Ceremonies are supposed to be fantastic. I'm so happy you're coming with us. Things are perfect now. I've been complaining non-stop to Davis about how much I miss you."

"Didn't you think about that before you decided to move out?" I hadn't meant to ask it, but I couldn't help myself.

She looked at me, blinking rapidly. "Move out? What do you mean? We're just doing some traveling. I'd never move out and leave you, baby."

Oh. So *she* hadn't been the one to pack all her belongings and take them from the house. Or the one who'd texted me that day to inform me. Or if she had, she'd been swayed into forgetting it all.

Speaking of that, it was time to get busy. Chances were, we wouldn't have much uninterrupted time together.

"Mom." I took her hand and waited until she was looking directly into my eyes. "I need for you to listen to me. Davis is not who he says he is. He's been manipulating you."

She shook her head, her brows lowering over confused eyes. "What? Why are you saying this, Ryann?"

I opened my mouth to explain, but a stream of blood ran from one of her nostrils over her lips and dripped onto the lounger cushion.

"Oh my God. Your nose is bleeding." Grabbing the fluffy white towel folded over her chair back, I held it out to her.

"Thank you." Her voice was muffled as she brought the towel to her face. Her eyes squeezed tightly closed, and she raised her other hand to massage her temple.

"What's the matter? Are you okay?"

Her head bobbed in answer. "I'm getting another migraine, I think. I've started getting them lately—nosebleeds, too."

"Maybe you should see a doctor."

"It's not that bad. Davis says it's probably a pre-menopause thing or something." She rose from the chair, the towel still pressed to her nose. "I do think I'll go lie down for a while, though, and get out of the sun. I'm sorry, sweetheart—I wanted us to have lunch together. I hate for you to be alone on your first day here."

"Don't worry about it." I walked slowly beside her as she made her way into the house and down the hall to the master suite. Her gait was unsteady, and with my hand wrapped around her arm, I noticed how thin she was. She'd lost weight, and didn't need to. What was happening to her?

At the doorway to the bedroom, she turned to me with an apologetic smile, looking embarrassed. "I'll lie down for a while, and then I'll feel better. We have an event tonight I don't want to miss. We'll have fun then, okay? Ring for a servant when you're hungry. They'll fix you anything you want—they're so helpful."

"Sure, okay. Just feel better soon."

She nodded and stepped into the dark room, closing the door behind her. I stood outside it for a long time, surveying the expensive artwork lining the hallway, making note of the high ceilings and pristine stone floor. The hallmarks of luxury were everywhere I looked, but all I wanted was to be back in Grandma Neena's rustic log cabin in the woods, back with my family safe and sound.

Safe. We certainly weren't safe here. In spite of the posh surroundings and the bright California sun streaming through the place, there was a dark sense of foreboding hanging over me. Something was really wrong with

Mom—something more sinister than a migraine, which she had no history of, by the way.

She'd seemed so happy and healthy when I'd first walked outside and seen her by the poolside. How could things have changed so quickly? What had happened?

And then it hit me. I had used my glamour on her. That's what had happened. *I'd* caused her sudden illness. That had to be it. Hadn't she said she was getting migraines and nosebleeds frequently? It had to be because Davis was using his Sway on her constantly. That was how he was keeping her with him all these months, how he was keeping her away from her daughter, her mother... from Daddy.

It must have been causing damage to her brain. And when I'd added my own opposing Sway to the mix, she'd gotten a blinding headache and nosebleed instantly. Her mind must be very fragile at this point.

Oh my God—how was I supposed to rescue her, to get her out of here now? I'd been counting on using my Sway. I couldn't risk doing any more damage. I would have to look for a chance to whisk her away the old fashioned way—kidnapping. But how? And when?

Tonight wouldn't be soon enough. Wait—she'd mentioned some sort of event tonight. Hopefully it was somewhere outside of this house and would present an opportunity for us to escape together at a moment when Davis was otherwise occupied.

CHAPTER TWENTY-THREE
THE DARK COURT

Lifting the hem of my full-length gown, I climbed into the back of the limo waiting in the courtyard outside Davis's mansion.

The gown was a navy Herve Ledger bandage dress that clung to me everywhere and plunged at the neckline. Obviously, it hadn't come from my own suitcase.

True to his word, Davis had sent a courier to pick up my bag from the East L.A. hotel I'd claimed to stay in. Thankfully, Nox had packed my things from the beach cottage and gotten the bag to the hotel in time. But of course, nothing in it would have been appropriate for the evening's event, which would be quite formal according to Davis.

Instead, the slinky gown had been hanging in my guest room closet when I'd returned from the pool. It was creepy how things seemed to get automatically done around this place. It was even creepier how well the dress fit, as if it had been made specifically for me.

Coordinating jewelry and a pair of sky-high heels—also designer by the looks of them—waited on my bed. These Dark Elves weren't afraid to show off their figures, their money… or apparently their daughters. Subtle, my outfit was not.

Settling into the limo, I strapped on my seatbelt and watched as Mom allowed Davis to fasten hers as if she were a child being secured into a car seat by a parent.

I had to grit my teeth to keep from growling. "So, where is this thing we're going to?"

"At a mansion in Malibu," Davis answered. "A young friend of mine owns it. He's throwing an impromptu gathering tonight." Leaning across to me from the opposite-facing seat, he whispered, "It's a meeting of the Dark Court. I've been summoned. Don't worry—I think you'll enjoy it."

He leaned back with a smile. "Your mother is very excited. There will be many celebrities present. And my friend… he's royalty."

She beamed and nodded. "I've never met a king before."

Oh God. I closed my eyes and clenched my hand to my rolling belly. We were on our way to Nox's house.

The transformation of his beachfront mansion astounded me. When I'd first been here a couple months earlier, it had been large and beautiful, but since then someone had gotten hold of it and made it elegant, fit for a king. It certainly didn't have the feel of Nox anymore, but it did seem perfect for the crowd here tonight.

It was like watching the pre-Oscar night telecast Emmy had forced me to sit through every year since we were eleven years old. Everywhere I looked, there was a famous face, each one more beautiful than the last.

In one corner, a big band ensemble played jazz standards, and at the piano sat a famous singer-songwriter I recognized as a judge from a popular television singing competition. What the heck was I even doing here? I fit into this world—Nox's world—like a shoe fits a salmon.

Though it was still early in the evening, some of the party goers were already dancing. Most were chatting with each other, laughing, their glittering gowns and jewels throwing prisms of light around like a disco ball. Black-clad and white-gloved servers moved deftly through the crowd, offering small but delicious-looking hors d'oeuvres.

Somehow when I'd pictured a gathering of the Dark Court, I'd expected something… darker. I'd never seen so much sparkle in my life, not even at the rooftop party I'd attended at Vallon Foster's mansion with Nox and his fan pod.

Davis seemed to be in high spirits, greeting nearly everyone he saw and introducing my mother as his wife and me as his daughter. Of course I wanted to correct him. But one of those statements *was* true, and the other was soon to be if I didn't keep my cool and do something to stop it.

When a particularly handsome and intimidating-looking man approached us, Davis grasped his hand and introduced him as Audun, a member of the Dark Council. He could have been Davis's brother they looked so much alike with their similarly defined cheekbones and slightly menacing smiles. The more Audun spoke, the more I realized *how* alike the men were.

"Ryann, it's delightful to meet you, and what a gift for your father to find a child just as he has lost one." He was referring to Vancia, but I wasn't sure I was supposed to know about that, so I didn't respond, just stood there smiling like an idiot.

Turning to Davis, Audun asked, "I see the family resemblance. Does she also share your abilities?"

Davis shook his head. "Apparently not."

Audun pursed his lips in a genteel pout. "Too bad. She's lovely... for a mix. Could have been useful to us."

I met some other members of the Council, including an elegant red-haired woman called Thora and her voluptuous ginger daughter Ava, who I learned was a successful model. When I'd seen the Light Elves, I'd found them fantastically beautiful, even without makeup or any sort of artifice. They were perfect in their natural state. But these Elves were different. They had a darkly alluring quality, almost to the point of being irresistible.

What did it say about me that I found them more beautiful? Once again, I worried about the dark side of my nature, about my genetic birthright. In his anger, Lad had suggested maybe I belonged in the Dark Court, with my biological father and all these people. Could he have been right?

My thoughts were interrupted as Davis suddenly bent forward at the waist in a bow so deep it seemed done in sarcasm rather than deference. I looked around to see what had caused such bizarre body language and realized other party-goers were doing the same thing.

And then I saw him, moving through the crowd like a ship parting the sea. Nox was magnificent in a scheme of black and white. His tux was undoubtedly designer-made, the elegant lines somehow making him look even taller and more beautifully proportioned than ever. His skin was tan against the crisp white collar, and his hair was slightly gelled and styled back from his face in a perfect complement to his already flawless bone structure. If the girls back in Deep River could get a look at him like this, their eyeballs would pop right out of their heads.

Oh no. My own head snapped to the side to take in Mom's expression. I'd come to a terrible realization—she *knew* Nox. What would she do when she saw him here? Should I attempt to sway her into not recognizing him? I dismissed that idea immediately. Any further mind control and she could suffer permanent damage.

Turning back to Nox, I took note of his formal attire, his slicked back hair. He did look different than he had in

Deep River. Maybe she *wouldn't* recognize him in this setting, so far from home, in a completely different context from our old life.

But then really, how many guys of her acquaintance were six-four and stunning? We were screwed. Those unique hazel eyes alone would give it away.

He came to a stop in front of us. Davis straightened. He held up my hand and my mother's.

"Your Highness, may I present my wife Maria and our daughter Ryann."

Nox gave us a devilish smile, no trace of recognition in his eyes for me or my mother. Nodding graciously, he said, "Welcome to my court, ladies. I do hope you enjoy yourselves this evening."

"Thank you." I somehow managed to breathe without wheezing.

"Thank you," Mom mumbled, showing no signs of recognizing Nox. Or any excitement, though in the car on the way here she'd been so jazzed to meet a king.

It was disturbing, but it was also extremely convenient. For the first time, I was actually happy she was under deep Sway. I could only imagine the scene that would ensue if she told Davis that Nox and I knew each other.

"You are full of surprises, my friend," Nox said to Davis. "I thought you had only one lovely daughter. You've been holding out on me." He winked at me, causing me to blush hotly.

What the heck are you doing? You can't flirt with me right now.

Nox's grin widened, and Davis noticed. He glanced between us with a disquieting gleam in his eye.

See? I accused. *Now he knows something's up.*

You're the one using mind-to-mind communication right in front of him.

He can't hear us.

"My apologies," Davis said in an overly solicitous tone. "I would never willingly keep information from you. I certainly would have told you about Ryann. Unfortunately, I didn't know about her myself until recently. We should arrange for the two of you to get better acquainted, shouldn't we, my dear?"

He looked down at my mother's face as she nodded woodenly and murmured, "Yes."

"Oh my. You'll have to excuse us." Davis pulled a handkerchief from his pocket and tucked it into Mom's hand. "Your nose is bleeding again, my darling. Here, let me show you where the powder room is."

Before leading her away, he whispered into my ear. "If you don't have glamour, I'll eat my hat. That boy is totally under your spell."

His next words were for both me and Nox. "You two chat a bit—we'll be back in no time."

My mind reeled from the double-blow of Mom's sudden nosebleed and Davis's parting words. He thought Nox was under my Sway. He'd read the attraction between the two of us, and that was the *first* thing that had come to his mind.

Vancia had said it.

Lad had said it.

And now I had confirmation. Nox didn't actually love me. I had swayed him without knowing it. Without meaning to.

As soon as Davis and Mom were out of earshot, Nox said, "How are you? Is everything okay? You have a strange look on your face."

Fighting to pull myself from a swirling abyss of dismay, I asked, "Did you throw this party to get me here tonight?"

He nodded. "Of course. And it worked. How are you? He hasn't hurt you, has he? Vancia says he can be very cruel."

"No. I'm fine. He trusts me. But he is hurting my mom—his glamour is damaging her brain. She's getting constant migraines and nosebleeds. We've got to end this thing soon."

"Agreed. What can we do? Maybe Alfred and I can make a list of those we know are loyal to me and take him down by force."

"That sounds too dangerous. And it won't solve the larger problem—the plot that's already started among the Dark Elves. I have a suspicion if you take Davis out, Audun will be more than happy to step into his role as Dictator-In-Chief."

"No kidding. That dude is mercenary, and you should meet his *kid*."

I glanced over my shoulder, surveying the room, feeling the need to speak quickly in case Davis returned. "I have another idea."

"Let's hear it."

My nerves bubbled as I realized the implications of what I was about to tell him. "Lad and I figured out that saol water seems to dampen the effectiveness of glamour. That may be why it doesn't seem to work as well on other Elves as it does on humans."

"Okay, so what—douse the planet in saol water?"

"Well, obviously that's impossible. But… we could get more people drinking it. You know Davis is taking me to the Olympic Opening Ceremonies in Boston next week. There's going to be worldwide media coverage. If I could somehow get on TV and encourage people to drink Magnolia Sugar Tea, they'll be less susceptible to Dark Elven Sway. If enough people drink enough of it, the takeover could fail. People would fight back instead of following orders like sheep."

Nox nodded enthusiastically. "That could work. And I'm the band leader for the song. If Davis doesn't bring you onstage, I can. I had an idea myself, something along the same lines. We may need both of them—there's no guarantee we can keep people drinking your tea or get it to everyone in the world who's been swayed. You may not even be able to produce enough in time."

"So what's your idea?"

"An *alternate* song for the Opening Ceremonies."

"You're writing one?"

"Yes, what Vancia said the other night got me thinking, and I've been working on it ever since. And the message is a *little* different than the one Davis wants to get across. Of course as the band leader *and* their king, that pack of celebrities is going to sing whatever I tell them to."

"Instead of swaying the world to accept Elven rule, your song will do the opposite. That's *great*, Nox." In my excitement, I embraced him, then quickly realized what I was doing—I was supposed to have just met him. And even more troublesome, Davis's comments were still banging around in my head.

I tried to pull away, but Nox held me tighter, whispering into my hair. "God you feel good. And you smell good. I miss you, Ryann. I need you with me."

I slid my hands between our bodies, pushing slightly against his chest to make him release me.

"Nox. There's something else we need to talk about. I think you should start drinking more saol water, too."

"What? Why?"

I swallowed hard. "Have you ever thought that it might be glamour that drew us together…that keeps us hooked on each other?"

"Well, you're definitely addictive, but no. I know how I feel about you, Ryann. Whenever you're around, I'm half out of my mind."

"That's *exactly* what I'm talking about."

He looked out over the ballroom for a second, his eyes coming back to meet mine in a searching gaze. "I don't see the problem. You're saying we're *too* attracted to each other? Isn't that how people who are in love always feel?"

"It's how drug addicts feel. It's how my mother feels about Davis." At his scowl, I tried to explain. "Think about it logically for a minute— *if* our connection is completely fueled by glamour, then it's no more real than Mom's 'love' for Davis."

He harrumphed. "And I suppose what you feel for Lad is real."

"Felt."

After giving a wave and a fake smile to someone across the room, he returned his gaze to me, his lips pulling into a grim line. "Right—what I walked in on last night looked like real *ancient* history. If you'd rather be with him, just tell me."

I closed my eyes and exhaled slowly, very aware of the boiling jealousy in Nox's glamour-drunk heart. I was warring with myself, too. Maybe it was still the glamour at work, but part of me wanted to be wrong, still wanted to hang onto him in spite of my feelings for Lad. Nox felt like home base to me now—he had been my center, my safety this summer.

"This has nothing to do with Lad. I'm talking about you and me. After he introduced us tonight, Davis said that—"

"Oh, Ryann, there you are honey."

Mom and Davis had found us. Well, we weren't exactly hiding, but still, it was horrendous timing—I hadn't been able to tell Nox what Davis had said about my

Sway. Nox didn't want to hear it, I didn't really want to say it, but if he *was* being swayed by me, he needed to be aware of it—he deserved to know.

"Looks like you two are enjoying each other's company," Davis said with a satisfied smile.

Nox's cool, calm demeanor made a miraculous comeback. "Yes, it's lovely to meet your daughter. She's not only beautiful but charming as well."

Davis and Mom laughed, beaming like proud parents, and then Mom abruptly stopped laughing.

"Oh my goodness—I've just realized how I know you. You're from Deep River. You're the boy Ryann was dating there—the musician." She glanced over at me for confirmation. "Ryann? What's going on? This is Nox, right? Why is he here? How can he be a royal if he's…"

Her expression was the portrait of confusion. But hers wasn't the one I was concerned with. It was Davis's face that scared me.

"If you'll excuse me," he glowered at Nox. "I'd like to have a word with my daughter."

Nox shot me a worried glance. "Of course. I should go and mingle."

Call if you need me.

I nodded, and he walked away, leaving me alone with my baffled mother and Davis, whose glower had become a murderous glare.

"You told me you were involved with *Lad* in Deep River." I could tell from his penetrating scrutiny his suspicion of me had returned full-force.

"I did. I was in love with him."

"Your mother said—"

Again, I kept my response as honest as possible. "Yes, I spent some time with Nox. We went out a few times, mostly as friends. He went to my school. I didn't know who he really was—he was pretending to be a human student. It never went very far. I could only see Lad," I told him truthfully. "He had my heart completely."

Directing his gaze across the ballroom to Nox, who was chatting with a group of beautiful women, Davis seemed to consider my words.

"I see. But I suspect Nox would have *liked* to have had it. Still…" His assessing gaze came back to me. "I find it odd you didn't mention you already knew Nox when I introduced you two. Neither did he." He paused for a moment before continuing. "I've thought better of our living arrangements. It turns out there's not enough room in my house for all of us. And concerning our Boston travel plans, I think it's best if your mother and I go together—just the two of us."

"What? But—"

"And don't try to follow us. If you happen to 'show up' there as you did here, there will be consequences. Come along Maria."

He spun around and stormed away, dragging my bewildered Sway-brained mother with him.

Oh God, this night had gone horribly wrong. Davis was onto me, and Nox was angry with me. I had to find him. Scanning the ballroom floor where he'd been moments earlier, I searched the crowd, but he was nowhere in sight. I crossed the room in the direction I'd last seen him and turned a circle in the center of the dance floor.

Spotting the top of a dark head of hair in the distance, I made my way through the party room toward the front of the house. It was him. He was standing at the foot of the grand staircase, looking up. I almost called out his name, but then I caught a glimpse of what he was staring at.

Vancia stood at the top of the stairs, looking out over the ballroom, searching the crowd without noticing the solitary figure gazing up at her. She wore a pale pink, beaded, floor-length gown that could only be described as a princess dress. She looked more gorgeous than I'd ever seen her, which was saying a lot.

Nox didn't move. I tiptoed to the side and slipped behind one of the large columns that anchored the room. From this angle, I could see his face.

He was enrapt, mesmerized. Though I wasn't completely sure I wanted to know the answer, I extended my emotional glamour toward him and read his feelings.

Just as I'd thought, he was overcome by her beauty. Maybe seeing his childhood playmate looking so much like a woman—the kind of woman men dreamed about— was overwhelming for him. There was wonder. There was also desire.

Unable to take it anymore, I turned away. And I *knew*. If I weren't in the picture, Nox and Vancia *would* be together. And he'd be happy with her. She'd already admitted to me she wanted nothing in the world more than to be with him.

The worst part was their attraction was completely genuine—no glamour involved. What he and I shared couldn't compete.

I stumbled back into the ballroom and grabbed a crystal flute of something bubbly from a passing waiter's tray. Draining it in a few swallows, I chased him down and took another glass. It was going to be a long night.

CHAPTER TWENTY-FOUR
CONTEST

Clearly my glamour gift was *not* alcohol tolerance.

I woke up in the back seat of a moving vehicle, dizzy, disoriented, and once I spotted Nox's bemused expression, mortified. We were in a limo. I had no memory of how I'd gotten there.

"Oh God. Tell me I didn't fall asleep at your party."

"You fell asleep at my party." He laughed, the usually melodic sound ringing in my ears. "I would have hoped you'd find the Dark Court a bit more interesting."

"I am *so* sorry. Did I do anything embarrassing?"

"Not unless you consider stripping and dancing on the DJ booth embarrassing."

My eyes bulging in horror, I sucked in a painfully large breath.

"Just kidding. Apparently you wandered off to a dark corner by yourself and passed out on a sofa. I went looking for you—nearly searched the whole house before I found you curled up there. You looked like a little girl playing dress up with your fancy gown and makeup, sleeping during a rave."

At my humiliated groan, he pulled me to his side and kissed the top of my head. "Don't worry about it. There were so many people I had to talk to, it would have been hard for me to spend time with you anyway. It's really no big deal. You may not feel so hot in the morning, though."

He leaned forward and took a bottle of soda from the bar, then reached into a tiny cabinet and extracted a small white packet. Tearing it open, he emptied two white capsules into my hand. "Take these."

I followed his instructions, my head spinning from the motion of tilting it back to swallow.

Nox studied my face. "You look green. How much champagne did you drink?"

"All of it?"

"Come here." He pulled my head to his chest. "Close your eyes again and sleep. That's the only thing that'll help at this point."

I didn't think I could fall asleep again. My brain was buzzing with questions. Where was Vancia? What had happened between them after I'd passed out? Why wasn't she riding with us?

But I didn't ask any of it. Instead, I closed my eyes and breathed deeply of Nox's amazing citrusy clean scent. I focused on the solid feel of his chest against my face, the sound of his rapid heartbeat, and the comforting rhythm of the air moving in and out of his lungs. It kept my mind off the nausea. It was also likely the last time I'd ever be so close to him.

If he did take my advice and start loading up on the saol water, our time together would likely end. My glamour would no longer affect him. Then we'd really know whether Vancia and Nox were soul mates as I suspected.

Obviously I would let him go. I'd step back and let them each be with the eternal partner they were born to love and bond with. I supposed there was still a chance he'd feel the same way about me *without* the glamour. Only time—and a healthy dose of saol water—would tell.

I must have dozed off after all because the next time I stirred, I was alone, lying on something soft. Well, not completely alone—there were voices nearby— male voices. I struggled to lift my eyelids, but they were made of triple-reinforced steel. I gave up and instead strained to hear the conversation.

The voices were low, but the tone of the exchange was tense. It was Nox and Lad, and they seemed to be arguing.

"... you allowed her to drink that much. Why didn't you watch out for her?"

"I tried, but I was busy. I have to keep up the act around the Court—they're not supposed to know that I know her well. Besides, she's a big girl. She doesn't need a protector."

"There's your problem right there. You should *want* to protect her, whether she needs it or not. You shouldn't let anything stand in the way of taking care of her—not even her."

"And there's *your* problem. Maybe she wants to make her own choices, not have someone make them for her the way you did when you sent her away."

"You should be thanking the gods every day that I *did*. It's the *only* reason you ever had a chance with her."

There was some sort of low curse, and then quiet. The argument must have gone internal. I struggled again to open my eyes and managed only a crack. I was on the couch in the cottage. Nox and Lad must have been just on the other side of it near the kitchen.

Using all my strength, I fought to push myself to my elbows, but managed only an inch or two before the guys were arguing aloud again and my brain was spinning.

"It doesn't matter how I got her," Nox was saying. "She's mine now. And you need to get that through your thick head. You're used to getting everything you want because you're the *heir*, the prince. But this time, I win."

"It's not over yet," Lad muttered. "She still cares for me. She could still come back to me—unless that is, you keep her trapped with your glamour."

There was an extended pause. When he spoke again, Nox's voice was steely, but there was something fragile at the edges of his words, as if he wasn't completely convinced of their rightness. "I would never do that. Her feelings for me have nothing to do with glamour. They're real."

"Keep telling yourself that. Or better yet—drink the saol water and let's find out who she *really* loves."

This was getting out of hand. They were talking about me as if I were a bone and they were two stray dogs, snarling and pulling it between them. I had to stop it before the fangs came out.

I gripped the sofa back and hoisted my three-hundred-pound head, pulling myself to a sitting position. "Guys," I said, my voice having all the strength and stability of a sheet of wax paper. No response.

Digging deeper, I managed slightly more volume. "Hey—what's going on?"

Both their heads snapped in my direction. Both rushed over to the couch.

"Ryann? You're awake," Lad said, sounding worried.

"Are you all right sweetheart? Want a drink?" Nox asked. "I'm sorry we woke you. Want me to carry you to your bed?"

Lad glared. "I'll take care of her—you've done *enough*. I'm sure you need to get back to your guests, anyway. Thank you for bringing her home."

"It's not *your* home," Nox muttered.

He scooped me in his arms. Carrying me down the hall to my room, he pressed a kiss into my temple as we passed Lad. My eyes drifted open in time to catch Lad watching his fiercest rival carry me away. His eyes—those incredible green eyes I'd loved my whole life it seemed—followed me down the hall.

Nauseated by the sight and the rocking motion of Nox's gait, I closed my eyes again and rested my head against his shoulder. The softness of the bedding materialized under me and Nox's warm arms and body were gone. But not far away. His weight depressed the edge of the mattress, and I felt the gentle stroke of his fingers on my cheek.

Forcing my heavy eyelids to part, I looked up at him. He was smiling.

"Hi beautiful."

"No. I bet I look a mess right now."

"You're stunning. You were the prettiest girl there."

Remembering the way he had stared at Vancia, I shook my head, which was a mistake. Waves of motion sickness swamped my stomach and brain. "I don't fit in your world. Those people—all that money and fame. Vancia fits there. She fits you."

His finger lay across my lips, stopping my slurred words. "Hush. You're talking nonsense. She and I are just good friends."

"No. The water. You have to…"

I felt the warm press of his lips on my forehead. "Go to sleep sweet girl. We'll talk in the morning."

"Nox… drink it. You'll see."

His voice was a warm hum of amusement. "Okay, babe. If it'll make you happy. Do you need a drink?"

My eyelids drifted shut again, unable to stay open any longer. "I am *never* drinking again."

His breath was warm on my face as he leaned in close. "You're wrong, you know," he whispered. "I'll always want you." He left a soft kiss on my cheek and was gone.

CHAPTER TWENTY-FIVE
Night Terrors

You might have thought it would be a sour stomach and a frantic midnight run to the bathroom that would awaken me, but actually it was the sound of breaking glass.

I sat up straight in bed, mouth parched, head throbbing, certain I was having a nightmare. A rush of cool ocean air against my skin and the outline of two large figures moving toward me in the dark told me otherwise.

There were people in my room.

I scrambled from the covers and toward the bedroom door, a terrified scream shredding my throat. Throwing the door open, I ran into the hallway and nearly crashed into Lad as he landed with a thud at the bottom of the staircase. He'd jumped from the balcony above.

"What is it?" he shouted, grabbing my upper arms.

I looked back over my shoulder to see the dark figures emerge from my room. Lad stiffened and rose to his full height, pulling me behind his body.

"Run, Ryann," he ordered and crouched to challenge the two men.

I guessed from their size they were Elven. What were they doing here? What did they want?

"We don't want trouble," one of them said. "Just give us the girl."

Lad literally growled, his hands fisting, arms trembling in rage. "Over my dead body."

"No problem," the other man said and moved toward Lad.

I ran into the kitchen, searching frantically for my purse. Where had I left it last night? Had I even brought it home from Nox's mansion party? I needed my phone to call for help.

My eyes landed on the wall phone near the pantry. Of course—it was an old house—they'd have had a landline. I grabbed the receiver and held it to my ear, dialing 9-1-1. Then I realized there were no beeps, no dial tone.

The phone wasn't connected.

Running back to the living area, I encountered a full-out brawl. The sounds were awful—nothing like the silly action movies I'd seen. Fists striking flesh, grunts of pain and effort, crashes as the men struggled and slammed through the room in the dark, taking out furniture and knick-knacks.

Lad was outnumbered. I had to help him. I dashed back to the kitchen for a knife.

Scrambling through the drawers, I finally wrapped my fingers around the hilt of a butcher knife—the one we'd used to slice watermelon two nights ago—and charged back into the living room, prepared to use it on one or both of the intruders—if I could get *to* them and manage not to stab Lad in the process.

Gripping the hilt, I chased the brawling group past the sofa and coffee table, but before I reached them, the three men smashed through the large glass window at the back of the house, landing on the deck in a writhing pile of glass and swinging, grappling limbs.

For a moment I stood there, stunned and struggling for breath. Was Lad okay? One of the intruders got to his feet and jumped off the deck, running toward the water. Lad broke away from the other enough to grab the back of his shirt and throw him from the deck onto the sand below. He jumped down after him.

The night was dark, the moon covered by hazy clouds so there was only the barest illumination on the beach and the ocean beyond it. I came out onto the deck, still clutching my knife.

"Lad," I yelled into the darkness. "Are you okay?"

One of the shadows looked back at me, then resumed pulling another struggling figure toward the ocean. With all of them being so large and of similar build, I couldn't tell who was dragging whom. *Oh God, please let Lad be okay.*

The fight must have made it to the water because now I could hear splashing in addition to the sounds of the struggle. I fervently hoped it was a one-on-one battle now. My eyes strained in the dark for any glimpse of Lad.

And then all was quiet. The night was a black curtain obscuring my view of the fight—or any survivors.

After long, frantic moments of searching the darkness, I did see something, a faint silhouette making its way in my direction across the beach.

It's Lad. My heart leapt in the kind of elation I hadn't felt since the last time his life had been in jeopardy and then saved.

And then the shadow was joined by another, both of them trudging slowly through the sand, side by side.

Horror filled my mind, coming out as a scream as I ran back into the house toward the front door. Where was Lad? I ran for all I was worth, sobbing and bursting from the front of the cottage. I stopped short at the sight of a limo parked at the curb. Had Nox come back?

Oh God. No. It was a different limo. *Davis.*

Unable to go back or forward, I darted toward the side of the house, hoping to scale the ivy-covered fence and land in the neighbor's yard.

A pair of brutally strong hands grabbed my hips and hauled me backward. Craning my neck around, I saw one of the men who'd broken into the cottage.

Screaming, I kicked and struggled, but his grasp was too strong for me. The limo's back door opened, and the thug dragged me over to it and forced me inside, pushing my head down so it didn't strike the door frame as I fell into the seat.

He slammed the door.

There was a click.

A small circle of light illuminated the face of the man inside.

Davis smiled at me as if we were sitting down to afternoon tea instead of meeting after midnight in the back of a car, me in my sleep tee and scared out of my wits.

"Hello my dear. Looks like you've had quite a night." He reached forward as if to pat down my disheveled hair.

I reared back, away from his touch. "What are you doing here? What have they done with Lad?"

"Yes—I see that you 'found' your long lost love. Your boyfriend *would* have been fine, if only he'd continued sleeping. Or if he'd stepped aside and allowed you to come along with my men. I had no problem with him. As it stands now, I'm afraid…" Davis let his sentence drift off with a shrug and a raised brow.

Oh God. *Lad.* A sob escaped my chest. He had risked everything to protect me. He'd given his life. I had a horrific flash of his lifeless body sinking in the dark waves.

Weeping, I shrieked at Davis. "You're a monster. You're a murderer. Why are you doing this? What do you *want?*"

Wholly unaffected by my display of grief, his voice remained serene. "Well, I realized tonight that even though you don't have any glamour gifts, you *can* still be useful to me."

"I would *never* do anything for you. I hate you!"

Another click. A second light came on, revealing my mother sitting in the seat across from us. She looked terrible. Her cheeks were sunken, her eyes hollow, underlined by dark shadows.

"Yes, well… you've already seen an example tonight of how far I'm willing to go to get my way," Davis said calmly, almost pleasantly as he gestured toward the dark windows and the men standing guard outside. "If I would sacrifice an Elven prince for the cause, what are a few more lives to me? I have orchestrated the removal of beings far more important than *him*." Here he glanced over at Mom. "…or this weak woman… for the greater good of my people."

"Nox's father. Vancia's parents. You killed them."

He lifted his brows and shrugged in a *what are ya gonna do?* gesture.

"And Lad's father Ivar? And Sophie Jerrick?"

"I've told you… I will do whatever is necessary to restore this world to its rightful order."

"Are you… are you saying you'll kill my mother?"

He shrugged again. "I fear she doesn't have much time left anyway. She is so frightfully frail. But it would be so easy for me to take your grandmother. Your 'Daddy.'" He let the word fall off his tongue as if it were a particularly sour grape. "I don't have to kill them right away. There are things that are more fun—for *me*. I have a particularly loyal—and strong—subject right here in L.A. who would love to 'take care' of them for me. Perhaps you've met him? Plays football? Has a penchant for soundproof underground rooms?"

I struggled for enough breath to respond. "Reggie."

"Ah—so you *did* have a little fun on your college exploratory visit last month. I thought so. My own flesh and blood... working against me." He made a facetious tut-tut sound with his tongue.

"I hate you."

He chuckled. "Be that as it may, you *are* going to help me." Reaching across the space between them, he lifted mom's limp hand and kissed it. Then he squeezed it until I could hear her knuckles pop. She didn't even flinch.

I reached toward her. "Stop. What do you want me to do?"

The limo had started moving sometime during our conversation. I hadn't noticed, only realizing it now because the motion stopped. Davis tapped the glass of one window, causing me to look outside and see where we were.

Nox's mansion. He'd brought me back here. But why?

"As I said... you don't seem to have inherited any truly useful *Elven* traits, but you *do* seem to hold a certain... appeal, shall we say, for young Elven men."

I looked out at the house again. Its windows, which had glowed with golden light during the party, were dark now.

"You will gain entry," Davis instructed. "You will go to his private suite, accessing it by any means necessary."

He stopped talking. I stared at him, waiting for him to finish. His eyes were black in the limo's low interior light.

"And you will kill him." He grabbed my hand, pressing a tiny vial into my palm. "Make sure he drinks this."

The wind left me. "No," I wheezed, shaking my head vehemently.

"Oh, I know you consider him a friend. But look at it this way—you've already caused the death of your true love—it's all downhill from here." He laughed as the locks popped and the door beside me swung open.

I sat in stunned stillness for a moment, then slowly, numb with shock and grief, started to climb out.

Davis grabbed my wrist and issued a final threat. "Don't think you can fool me, girl. Don't try to run. And *don't* try to warn him. The young ruler's house is full of my spies. I'll know if you've done your job." Lifting Mom's hand again, he pressed a lingering kiss to her skin. "Or not."

Shuddering, I scrambled from the car, obeying him. What I wanted to do was kill him. My poor mom. I got one last glimpse of her before the door swung shut and the limo pulled away. Her expression hadn't changed at all, but a single tear streaked down her face.

CHAPTER TWENTY-SIX
MISSION

I stood outside Nox's front door, shivering in my t-shirt, though the night was warm. What was I going to say to him? What were we going to do?

My mind slipped back again and again, replaying the last moments I'd seen Lad—his body crashing through the window, the fierce way he struggled with my attacker on the beach, protecting me with his own body. He was so alive, so vibrant in my mind. In my heart. How could he be dead?

A servant answered the bell. It was Ewan, the one person in Nox's household I knew for sure was loyal to him.

"I need to see him."

Ewan nodded and stepped back, allowing me to enter. Within seconds, Nox was rushing into the foyer, his face covered with concern. He was dressed for bed, shirtless and wearing dark sleep shorts.

"Ryann… what are you doing here so late? What's happened?"

I burst into tears.

"Tell no one," Nox said to Ewan as he lifted me and carried me on quick feet down the hallway to the master suite, passing the guards flanking the door. Once inside, he set me down and took my face between his hands, staring into my eyes.

What happened? What's wrong?

You have to ask me out loud. I darted my eyes at the two guards who stood at their posts just inside of the double doors. *There are spies here. Davis sent me—he said I'd be watched. He can't find out I can communicate with you this way.*

They're trustworthy.

I shook my head insistently.

Nox nodded his understanding. "What happened? Are you all right?"

"Lad…" I got choked up and had to start again, barely getting the unbelievable words out. "Lad is dead. Some men broke into the cottage, and there was a fight."

Nox's eyes went wide in horror. *Is this true?*

Yes. I nodded. "He's gone." The tragic news came out on a sob.

"Oh God. My brother." Nox's strangled words ended in a hoarse cry as he let me go and staggered back. He fought to compose himself. "Who would do this?"

"I don't know," I cried. *It was Davis's men. They were sent to kidnap me from my bed. Lad was trying to protect me.*

And I lost all ability to speak or communicate rationally. The entire horror of the night's events rolled over me, sapping the strength from my legs. I started to collapse to the floor.

He's gone.

Nox swept me up in his arms again and carried me around the corner to his bed, laying me gently on the surface and crawling in beside me, holding me close as I wept, our tears mingling.

Some time later when we had both calmed a bit, he spoke again, continuing our silent communication. *The guards can't see us here, but they can hear us. I'm going to kiss you. Make it sound like we're over here... uh... you know. That way they won't wonder why we're not talking out loud. Besides, that's what I'm supposed to be doing in here with girls.*

Okay. I nodded, remembering my brief time in his fan pod. That's what the girls were there for—the entertainment of the Dark Elves—and of course to parlay their *love* into increased popularity for the celebrities.

Nox's mouth came to mine, moving gently, though he probably should have been rougher about it if we were supposed to put on a show for the benefit of possible spies. As always he was a great kisser. And smelled amazing.

And I felt... nothing.

Maybe it was the trauma of Lad's death. Maybe it was the saol water depressing the effects of his sexual glamour on me. Whatever it was, his magnetic hold on me had been broken.

Did he feel the same? Had he taken my advice and started drinking more saol water? Vancia was somewhere in this house. Was he thinking of her when he kissed me?

I was definitely thinking of Lad. Tears streamed down my cheeks as I kissed another pair of lips, clung to another guy's arms while my heart screamed for him. How was I supposed to go on? Imagining living the rest of my life without him, I wanted to die myself. The pain of loss was unbearable.

And that's when I realized... Nox had always been the safe choice for me.

As sexy and self-assured as he was, as much as other girls wanted him and worshipped him, he'd pursued *me* from the start, made his devotion clear—he was a sure thing. It had probably been all due to glamour, of course. The point was, he'd never been a real threat to my heart. Maybe that had been part of the attraction for me all along.

Now Lad—he had been dangerous. Because he had the ability to hurt me. When someone owns your heart, they have power over you. That had terrified me.

It had kept me running scared, even after he came back into my life and declared his love again, told me he'd never stopped loving me. Now he was gone forever. I'd never have the chance to admit to him that I still loved him, too. That I'd never stopped loving him. I stifled a new round of sobs.

That was why I'd never been able to say those words to Nox. It wasn't that I was no longer capable of love—it was that I'd already given my heart away to Lad—no take-backs. There wasn't anything left to give to someone else, even someone as precious as Nox.

Somehow keeping his mind off of Lad's death and on the current crisis, Nox continued to question me as we stage-kissed.

Why would Davis have you kidnapped? I thought he didn't want you around anymore.

He thought of a new use for me.

What?

Killing you.

Nox pulled his face away, staring into my eyes. *What? He actually sent you to kill me?*

I nodded. *He threatened to kill my mother if I don't. And Grandma Neena and Daddy, too. He gave me poison. I'm supposed to get you to drink it.*

I opened my hand to show him the vial. He lifted his head to get a look at it, then closed his hand over mine and took my mouth again, kissing me harder and adding a passionate groan for the sake of our listening audience.

Alfred told me Davis wasn't thrilled by my return from the dead. But he never said he was this determined to get rid of me.

Maybe Alfred doesn't know. Maybe Davis figured out Alfred is no longer loyal to him and doesn't confide in him anymore. There are definitely spies in your house. I don't think you should trust anyone at this point.

Except for you. Unless you really are here to kill me. He smiled against my mouth.

I pulled away, and our eyes made contact. *I could never—no matter what he holds over my head…* "You know I love you."

He stared at me, frozen. Finally, he blinked. *Is this part of the act?*

Oh. Had he misunderstood my meaning? I opened my mouth to clarify when motion at the edge of the bed made us both jump.

Nox leapt to his feet in a battle stance, prepared to fight off whomever had surprised us right there in his bedchamber. Was it one of the guards checking to make sure we were really fooling around? Had Davis sent someone else as insurance in case I failed or refused my mission?

"Who are you?" Nox demanded. "How did you get in here?"

I scooted across to the bedside table and flicked on the lamp. There, standing at the end of the bed, shivering and dripping wet, was Lad.

CHAPTER TWENTY-SEVEN
TELL HIM

I stared in disbelief. Nox seemed paralyzed as well. And then I launched myself at Lad, touching his cold skin to prove to my astonished mind he really was there and not an apparition brought on by grief and stress.

"Lad—how did you—where did you—" My heart pulsed in an ecstasy of furious beats. He was there. He was real. He was *alive.*

He shrugged away from my touch, stepping back. "I climbed up to the balcony." His expression was hard, but otherwise he seemed in pretty good shape for a guy who'd been in a battle-to-the-death an hour ago.

"But… those men… and then you didn't come back. I thought you were dead."

"Apparently." He shot a significant glance over at Nox, who still stared at him in shock.

Nox finally snapped out of it and took a step toward Lad. "I'm so glad to see you. I never thought I'd—"

"Yeah, you seemed *real* broken up over my 'death,' brother. Sorry to interrupt you two. I thought you might need some help—when I went back into the house and saw Ryann was missing, I thought they might come after you next. Or that maybe you'd help me rescue her. I guess I shouldn't have bothered. You're both obviously just *fine*."

He turned and strode toward the open doors to the balcony extending from Nox's suite.

I chased after him. "Wait—Lad. What happened? How did you get away from them?"

He spun to face me, wearing a guarded expression. "I pretended to drown. I've swum in lakes all my life—I can hold my breath a long time."

Now his eyes narrowed as he studied me, my tousled hair, my kiss-swollen lips. "How did *you* get away? I thought *Davis* sent those men, but I guess…". His eyes drifted to Nox.

"Wait—you think *I* sent them?" Nox said. "Why? To beat you up and scare Ryann to death? How could you even think something like that?"

Lad's gaze went to the rumpled bed where he'd found us and back to our faces.

"Oh God, Lad, no." Silently, I added. *It was Davis who sent them. And he has spies in this house. Maybe even in this room. He sent me here to kill Nox. We weren't actually… we were bluffing for them.*

About all of it? he asked.

Nox broke in. "I had nothing to do with your attack—but we'll figure out who's behind it." He gave Lad a significant nod, clearly playing a role for the guards nearby. "In the meantime, come sit down. You look half dead. I'll arrange a room for you here for the night."

"No, I'll be fine. Don't worry about me. Come on, Ryann." Lad held his hand out to me.

At my side, Nox stiffened but didn't interfere.

"Oh, I uh…" I stuttered. I couldn't leave now. "I'm staying here with Nox." *I have to—I have no choice. Davis will kill my mom if I leave. Maybe even Daddy and Grandma Neena, too.*

Lad searched my face. *And that's really why you're staying?* "*Do* you love him?" he demanded.

The two guards came around the corner, standing back, but staring at Nox, clearly asking if he needed their intervention.

I answered Lad's question, conscious of the listening guards. "Yes. I do."

Lad's eyes squeezed shut and his jaw tightened. Oh God, he didn't believe me, did he?

Nox cleared his throat, glancing over his shoulder toward the guards. "Thanks for coming by and telling us what happened, Lad. I'm relieved you made it out okay. And… thanks for looking out for my girl." He slung his arm around my shoulders, pulling me in close to his side.

We all could have done without that last part. I *was* his girl as far as the guards knew, but he shouldn't have rubbed it in Lad's face. Especially right now when there was so much confusion.

The stony look came back into Lad's eyes. He gave Nox a curt nod, then strode through the French doors, across the lanai, and swung himself over the balcony. I didn't worry about his making the two-story drop—I'd seen him do much more astounding things. It was his emotional state that concerned me. And mine for that matter.

Even though we hadn't bonded, the connection between us was so strong I felt like my own heart had gone over that balcony and was sprinting away from me down the beach.

I wanted to run after him.

I also wanted to let him go and make sure I never saw him again.

Because if I did chase him down, if I told him the truth about how I felt... admitted it to myself... I could never go back. I'd be completely vulnerable. If I reopened my scarred heart to him, I'd have no defense against the kind of pain I'd sworn I'd never let myself feel again. There was no loving Lad conservatively, cautiously. It was all or nothing with him.

God, it was this bad *before* bonding. How on earth would I survive if we did take that step and then something separated us? If he sent me away again... if something were to happen to him...

For the first time, I had a real understanding of the mark that occurred when a bonded Elven couple was permanently separated. The white hair was nothing. It was the indelible mark on the heart that could never be covered up, erased, or repaired.

I stared through the open doors at the empty balcony, at the night sky, taking in a shaky breath and releasing it.

I had to let him go. Tonight and forever. It was the smartest thing to do. I simply couldn't *stand* loving someone like that again.

What the hell are you doing?

I spun around to face Nox's aggravated expression. *What do you mean?*

Why are you still standing here? Go after him. Tell him.

Tell him what?

That you love him. That you want to be with him.

I stared at him in shock. Then my gaze dropped to the floor. *I can't. I can't be with him.*

He reached out and tipped my face up with a fingertip under my chin. *Why not? It's not because you love me. I know you don't. And—don't take this the wrong way—I don't feel that way about you anymore, either. After I got home tonight, I started chugging the saol water. You were right—it was the glamour.*

"Oh."

He raised his brows and gave me a confirming nod.

So what's your problem? he said.

I'm scared.

Of course you are. We're all scared—life is uncertain. No one knows what's going to happen. Things can go wrong. But isn't it worth it to try? Haven't you ever heard that everything you've ever wanted is on the other side of fear?

My head snapped up. I stared at him. *Where did you hear that?*

I don't know. I think I saw it on Instagram or something.

Mom said that to me—that exact quote… the last night she was truly herself, the night we went to dinner with Davis. I poked his chest gently. *I could say the same thing to you, you know—about Vancia.*

He shook his head. *We've been friends too long. I don't even know if she—*

She does, I assured him.

Hey—we're talking about you and Lad here. So… what are you waiting for?

I gave the balcony doors a longing glance. *What about the guards? If I leave…*

Nox turned in their direction, and they both appeared within seconds. They looked intently at his face, obviously receiving instructions, then hustled out of the room.

"What did you say to them?"

"I told them I was concerned about the break-in at my cottage only a few doors down from here. I told them to go and secure the mansion and be very thorough about it. You should've heard me. I was very kingly."

"Oh yes, your highness—you are *so* intimidating. So, you gonna give me a lift down or what?"

He smiled. We walked out to the balcony, peering over the edge. Nox picked me up.

You ready?

I nodded, and he jumped down to the sand, holding me securely in his arms. As soon as he set my feet on the ground, I took off running down the beach, calling Lad's name in the Elven way.

CHAPTER TWENTY-EIGHT
MOTIVATION

Slowly, I walked back to Nox's house. As I drew close, his shadowy figure came into sight, standing in the sand beneath his bedroom window. We looked at each other. His sympathetic eyes told me he already knew the answer to what he was about to ask.

Did you catch up to him?

I shook my head. *I couldn't find him. And he didn't answer when I called out to him.*

Don't worry. We'll find him in the morning. For now, we have another problem. The guards are back.

Already?

Yeah. Apparently I was a bit too kingly—they made quick work of it.

Or they're suspicious.

Right—I told them you were in the bathroom. So, get in there and splash around a bit or something, and then, we've got a show to finish.

I did as Nox suggested, going into his enormous bathroom and flushing the toilet, turning on the sink and splashing some water on my face. When I walked back into the room, he was waiting for me.

"Where were we?" he asked with a deliberately naughty tone of voice we both knew was an act. If our sexual impulses toward each other hadn't already been erased by the saol water, they certainly wouldn't have survived Lad's visit.

I put on a faux-flirty tone of my own, leading him back toward the bed. Inside, I was dying. Outside I was a temptress worthy of an Oscar. "I believe we were right. over. here."

The guards were back at their posts inside the doors, and once again Nox and I silently strategized while making intermittent noises of enjoyment.

So what now? he said.

We're going to have to fake your death—for your own safety and my family's. I don't see any other way. If I "fail" or refuse to assassinate you, Davis would only send someone else to do it. So... life as you know it is about to end— temporarily.

Oh wow. You're right. I wish I'd had some warning so I could prepare—make a will or something. Who's gonna get my record collection? he joked.

I know. I'm sorry. If you want to get up now and pack a bag or something, maybe I can sway the guards into forgetting about it. I'll try to make them forget Lad's visit, too. But I need to put most of my focus behind making them believe they saw your dead body. Then I've got to report to Davis and hope he lets me go. Or that he's decided to take me to Boston again now that I've done his bidding.

Well, at least you're not bored, right? Don't worry about the packing thing. I'll just buy some clothes when I get out of here. He grabbed my shoulders, staring into my eyes with a deadly serious expression. *Listen to me—you be careful. And don't worry about Lad. Vancia will get him to Boston. You, too, if you need help getting there.*

What if he won't go? What if he doesn't want to help me anymore?

He'll be there—trust me. I know my brother. There's nothing he wants more in the world than you. I'll meet up with you all there. In the meantime, let's get busy. You have a "murder" to commit.

An hour later, I sat straight up in bed and let out an ear-splitting scream. When the guards came running around the corner into the sleeping area, they found me frantically shaking Nox and calling out his name.

I looked up at the men. "Something's wrong. He's not waking up."

They rushed forward. As they bent to examine him, I put all my effort into my next words, sinking them into their minds.

"I think he's dead. Oh my God, he *is* dead." I screamed again and did my best to fake a realistic cry. "I want my father. I want to see my father."

The taller of the two men, a fair-haired Elf with deep blue eyes, straightened and looked directly at me. "I'll take you to him. He's expecting you."

Kirk, that two-faced S.O.B. Nox's voice snarled in my head.

I tried to discipline my expression, but I knew my eyes must have widened in surprise, and I gasped aloud at my mistake.

It's okay, Rye. It's okay. Somehow Nox, without opening his eyes, knew I was panicking and tried to reassure me. *It's fine to be surprised that one of them is Davis's spy—it supports your story if Kirk thinks you didn't know you were being watched.*

Oh, right. Good. I'm kind of nervous—first assassination, you know. So... I guess this is goodbye for now.

I'm afraid you'll have to let yourself out this time.

That reminds me—should I try to see Vancia before I leave here? Let her know what's happening?

No, that's okay. I can tell her myself from here. We... uh... we can hear each other long-distance.

Oh. Wow. What further proof did I need that they were meant for each other? I'd done the right thing telling him about the glamour and its cure. He was going to be happy with the girl he *truly* was meant for—provided we all lived through the next week.

Following the traitorous guard from the room, I gave Nox's still body one last glance. *See you in Boston. By the way, you look pretty hot for a dead guy.*

I shouldn't have said it—I almost giggled and blew the whole ruse. I sure hoped my glamour held strong on the one remaining guard who was near him—that the mind control would prevent him from noticing the slight twitch of Nox's mouth, the soft rise and fall of his chest as he also struggled not to laugh.

Yeah, well, you'd better drink your saol water, sister. Or when I see you in Boston, I'm going to make you pay for that—one super-sized musical glamour-coma coming right up.

You can try, buddy. You can try. But it won't work anymore.

From now on, I'd only be dealing with my *true* feelings. Like it or not.

The blond guard and I left Nox's mansion and walked in silence down the Pacific Coast Highway. As we neared an upcoming driveway, the nose of Davis's limo peeked out and edged forward.

"Get in," said the guard.

I shot him a side-glance, forcing myself not to spit in his direction. Nox had trusted him. Of course Kirk assumed he and I were allies in the service of Davis, and it would be stupid of me to contradict that assumption. I got in the car.

"There she is," Davis beamed. "My own little deadly weapon. Is it done?"

"Yes," I snarled as the guard opened the other door and climbed into the backseat.

Davis looked at the man for confirmation. "Kirk?"

"Yes. He's dead. I checked the body myself," he said. Davis was undoubtedly swaying him, so the guard must have believed what he was saying. So far, my Sway was holding.

As the car started rolling, Davis brought his attention back to me, questioning me relentlessly about how I'd pulled off the assassination. The entire time, he kept a hand on my mother's knee. She sat in silence, staring out the window.

Knowing that actually carrying out such an assignment would devastate me, I pretended to be devastated. My act seemed to reassure Davis. I guessed he couldn't exactly go inside and check for himself because it would be *unseemly* for him to be at the murder scene when Nox's death cleared the way for him to once again ascend to the Dark Throne.

I stuck to my story—I'd put the poison in Nox's drink and made sure he'd swallowed it by making a romantic champagne toast. Blinded by lust, he hadn't suspected a thing. I'd stayed beside him in bed for a long time afterward, checking his pulse, checking for breathing to make sure it had worked. Then I'd faked horror at finding him dead to throw suspicion off of myself.

"It doesn't matter," Davis informed me in an arrogant tone. "Even if you are suspected, you are my daughter, and I am once again the ruler of the Dark Court. You are above the law now."

I nodded and then tried not to squirm as he tilted his head to one side and then the other, taking inventory of my appearance.

"I assume you didn't have to go *too far* in your efforts to seduce him into trusting you? Your hair color hasn't changed."

At first I was confused. My hair color? And then I realized what he was getting at. Spluttering in very real embarrassment, I said. "Uh… no… I was able to poison him before I had to… uh…"

Davis laughed. "Good. That's good. This is all coming together even better than I'd hoped. I may still be able to arrange an advantageous marriage for you. As it turns out, your former paramour, Lad, survived the tussle with my men. He was seen near Nox's mansion last night, no doubt trying to get inside to see *you*."

Uh oh. So he knew Lad was alive. Clearly another of his spies had been on the job at Nox's house and reported back. I had to fess up to seeing Lad, in case he already knew I had. If he *did* know and I withheld the information, he'd doubt my entire story and Kirk's account as well.

"I saw him. He actually found a way in—he came to Nox's bedroom."

He nodded. "Interesting. Go on."

"We spoke for only a few minutes. He told us how he'd survived the fight. Then he left."

"Hmmm. I'm surprised. Why so quickly?"

"He caught Nox and me making out. He wasn't happy."

"Ah." A wide grin spread across Davis's face. "Excellent. So his attachment to you is still strong. We can use this. It would still be an advantage to have the Light Court on our side when the plan is enacted."

"So… I can be with Lad now?" It seemed like what a pathetically in love, glamourized girl would ask. In truth, I was wondering the same thing.

Davis eyed me and then broke into laughter. "Yes my dear. You will have the young man. As my daughter, you will have the entire *world* at your feet." His eyes shone with a maniacal gleam. "Speaking of your birthright, you must have been… very persuasive to get past Nox's staff and into his private quarters late at night."

Uh oh. Something didn't feel right. I'd thought the interrogation was over. I thought I'd already passed. "Yes… I did my best."

He gave me a dead-eyed chill-inducing smile. "And you did well." Turning to Kirk he said, "Kill the mother."

"No!" I lunged for the huge guard, but he stiff-armed me, holding me back and reaching for Mom's neck.

He got his fingers around it with one hand and opened the back door with the other. Freeway noise filled the car's interior, the pavement whizzing by in a blur as we sped along. I attacked him, pounding on his steely arm, digging my nails into one side of his face, kicking at his legs and trying to distract him as much as possible. Anything to keep him from throwing her from the moving vehicle.

"What are you doing?" I screamed at Davis.

He sat back into his own seat and held his fingernails out, inspecting them as if nothing more interesting were happening in the back seat at the moment.

Finally losing the battle against Kirk's superior strength, I watched him pull Mom from her seat and drag her body toward the open door. Frantic and knowing she had only moments left to live, I did the only thing I could. I swayed him.

"Drop her. And jump out."

Immediately the brawny man released my mother's neck. And then he leapt from the speeding car, his body hitting the freeway with a smack before it whizzed from sight.

I dropped to my knees on the floor, pulling Mom into my arms and holding her head against my chest, rocking and crying.

Davis leaned over and pulled the door closed, and then laughed as if he was in the audience of an A-list stand-up comedy show. The vile laugh went on and on.

"Oh yes. You *are* my daughter. You only needed proper motivation to tap into your natural gifts. I *knew* you had it in you. With your Sway and mine combined, very soon our people will regain our rightful position in this world. You'll see—you will be glad you... and your dear mother..." He reached over and picked up one of her limp hands, which was bruised from his brutal grip last night. "... are with *me*."

CHAPTER TWENTY-NINE
IT'S YOUR TURN

I had a vague idea of what the Opening Ceremonies would be like—music, dancing, fireworks—a spectacle. I'd seen the Olympics on TV before. But being there in person was a whole different thing. It was simply overwhelming. TV might have been great for amplifying glamour, but there was no way it could convey the majesty, the sheer *hugeness* of an event like this.

Mom, Davis, and I were seated in a luxury box at the Olympic Stadium, a gleaming, ultra-modern structure that had been erected in Widett Circle specifically for the opening and closing ceremonies and the track and field events. It stood in sharp contrast to the city's colonial era buildings and made me feel sort of like I was in a gigantic oval space ship that had set down next to the Southeast Expressway.

Davis said the temporary stadium would hold 69,000 spectators, and from the looks of it, every seat was filled.

I couldn't believe the mass of people down on the field, each playing a role, wearing costumes and either dancing, or doing acrobatics, or acting out a dramatic vignette. It was like watching the most elaborate stage show you can imagine—Cirque Du Soliel on steroids.

The production must have cost millions of dollars. There were pyrotechnics, gigantic video screens all around, an incredible electronic light show, glowing props, and an ever-changing set, pieces of which moved on and off the field almost magically.

The music also changed constantly, segueing from one iconic American musical artist's song into another and then into an orchestra piece. Some were slow and heartwarming, then the beat would pick up and a high-energy number would take place. People around us were dancing, too. When I looked over the railing at the general seating area, it was even more energetic.

All at once, there was a balloon release from each part of the stadium. There must have been tens of thousands of white orbs floating up through the crowd and into the night sky.

The show transitioned into the parade of nations. Colorfully dressed young athletes walked around the track with their teammates, waving frantically as their country name was announced.

After that the Olympic flame made its way into the stadium, carried by a single runner and then passed to a team of identically dressed runners, who took turns carrying it all the way around the track, making their way toward one side of the stadium where a high tower stood, illuminated by spotlights, with a giant bowl on top.

The torch carriers ascended a ramp to the base of the tower and handed the flame to an aging athlete—clearly not Elven by the looks of his stooped posture and shaking hands. To the accompaniment of dramatic music, he held the torch high over his head, then lit another torch, which began moving upward and seemed to fly through the air on its way to the top of the tower.

"It's on a wire," Davis said, whispering to my mom, who nodded mechanically.

When the fiery vessel reached the tower's top, the huge cauldron burst into bright, dancing flames, and the crowd cheered wildly.

That was our signal—it was almost time. Very soon the celebrity singers would take the stage to perform their number, and we'd set our own plan into motion.

Nox had passed the schedule of events on to Vancia, and she'd texted it to me before she and Lad flew to the East Coast. All of our communication had been through her since I'd left California. Believing I was under his glamour and his total control, Davis had allowed me to keep my phone.

Vancia was in it under the name, "Roberta."

I had tried messaging Lad in the Elven way—to attempt to explain the scene he'd witnessed in Nox's room—but he'd cut me off with a few terse words.

I don't want to talk about it.

But…

No Ryann. Not now. We'll talk at the Games.

Okay, so it wasn't a total *No*. But it wasn't exactly a yes, either. I only hoped when all of this was over, when we *were* face-to-face again, he'd give me at least a few uninterrupted minutes to tell him how I really felt about Nox. And about him.

Vancia hadn't been in contact for a few hours, which increased my anxiety. Had Nox made it here safely? Had someone spotted him and stopped him before he could reach his position?

I looked around, searching the area near the President's box, where a dark stage jutted out, high above the field. Our luxury box wasn't far away. As the stage was still in darkness, I couldn't make out any faces but emerging from a tunnel and spreading across the stage was a collection of figures wearing red white and blue. As they assembled, a sequin occasionally caught a stray light and flashed, like an oddly-colored firefly.

I knew who they were—some of the world's top celebrities—movie and TV stars, singers, musicians, models, famous authors, professional athletes, and even a celebrity chef. With everything else going on inside the stadium, probably very few people even noticed them gathering there. I only did because I was specifically watching for their entrance.

Cameras were already trained on them from every angle, though they weren't filming yet—the Jumbotrons visible throughout the stadium still showed the hordes of dancers and costumed figures who filled the field.

But it wouldn't be long before the stage would light up and Nox would join the celebrities there for their big sing-along-and-brainwash the world moment. That was the plan, anyway.

And as if his miraculous return from death wasn't enough, he was also going to shock the event organizers by conducting the group in a completely different song than expected—one he'd written himself just for the occasion.

Butterflies in my belly danced along to the deafeningly loud music filling the stadium. If I was going to play *my* part, it needed to be soon. I gave Davis a subtle side glance. He sat completely still, serenely taking in the show.

Was Vancia wrong that he planned to take the stage and introduce the performers, using his Sway to influence the planet during the worldwide broadcast? Maybe he'd changed his mind since sharing that information with her. Maybe he thought the song he'd planned for them to perform would be enough to hypnotize the audience and launch the Dark Elven takeover.

I fidgeted, growing increasingly impatient. I *really* needed him to stick to the plan. How else was I going to get to the stage myself? More importantly, how would I get him to walk through that tunnel?

Before the worrisome thought was completed, he rose from his seat and grabbed my upper arm. "Come with me."

"Where are we going?" I stood to join him, playing dumb and trying to hide my immense relief.

Davis didn't answer, but leaned down, placing his lips close to my mother's ear. He whispered something before dragging me toward the luxury box exit and the stairs beyond, no doubt ordering her to stay put.

We hurried through the walkway behind the seats, heading for a tunnel entrance in the distance—I hoped it was the right one. I knew it was when I spotted two burly bodyguards standing at the mouth of it. They stepped aside when they saw Davis.

We entered the dark tunnel together, and the drumming of my pulse in my ears nearly drowned out all other sound. This was it. It was about to happen. I was either going to help release the world from Dark Elven rule tonight, or if Nox, and Lad, and Vancia, and I failed, I would be forced to help bring the human race under the control of the most power-hungry, malevolent Dark Elf of them all—my father.

Davis's fingers dug into the tensed muscles of my upper arm as he swung me around to face him. In the muffled quiet of the tunnel, his voice was menacing and filled with dark glamour. "Now—you're going to take your place by my side and fulfill your role as my daughter *and* my subject."

Pretending shock, I asked him, "What do you mean? What do I have to do?"

"You're going out on stage with me and you're going to use that oversized Sway of yours *exactly* as I tell you."

"Me? Up there? With all those people watching?" I paused for dramatic effect, catching movement from the corner of one eye. And then I smiled and gave a blasé shoulder shrug. "Okay."

His head jerked back at my flippant tone. He knew something was wrong. "You're not going to fight me at all?"

Lad and Vancia stepped out of the shadows.

"I don't have to," I said. "I think these two can handle you just fine."

Davis's eyes widened with shock as Lad and Vancia grabbed him. The sounds of their struggle echoed through the tunnel, but I wasn't worried about the guards. I'd sent them a very clear message when we passed by them earlier. If my Sway was worth a damn, they were far from here, chin deep in some nachos and beer right about now.

I knew exactly how strong Lad was, and after watching Vancia arm wrestle Nox, I was confident she could hold her own. The zip ties she'd whipped from her pocket would probably come in handy, too.

"Go Ryann," Lad shouted. "We've got this. Help Nox."

He didn't have to tell me twice. I ran for the stage end of the tunnel, through which I could see a small circular glimpse of light and color. Bursting into the brightness and noise of the stadium, I sent a message to Nox.

We're good to go. Where are you?

I prayed he was close enough to hear me. We had to be within sight of one another these days for our silent communication to work.

One of the masked characters from the show—American patriot Samuel Adams, actually—stepped away from the sideline area of the field below me and pulled off his costume head. Nox gave me a brilliant smile as he bounded up the stairs toward me, taking them two at a time.

I grinned back. *Welcome back from the dead. You ready for this?*

Yep. Time to make some music.

With one final wink in my direction, Nox leapt from the stairs onto the stage and grabbed his guitar from its stand. It was time. My pulse felt like it would hammer right through my forehead as I waited to hear which song would come from the speakers—the one Davis had prepared, which would influence viewers worldwide to accept Elven rule—or the one Nox had written, which would have the opposite message.

The first strains of the music began. Stage lighting slowly illuminated the gathering of celebrities who stood shoulder-to-shoulder, and their images appeared out of the dark on the giant screens.

The awed gasps of the attending crowd collected, sounding like an enormous gust of wind blowing through the Olympic Stadium. And then wild applause and fanatic screams broke out as people recognized the famous faces.

Vancia told me this part of the ceremonies had been kept top secret. The song itself would be released to radio stations and for digital downloads the minute the performance was finished, but up until this moment, only those directly involved knew it was coming.

The surprise seemed to enhance the thrill for the crowd. I could only imagine the reaction of viewers all over the world who'd tuned in to this event. They were going to get much more than they even bargained for tonight.

As one, the celebrities began singing. My heart soared as I recognized a tune I'd heard Nox working on many times when we were together. It was his song.

And then the crowd and the television viewers got perhaps the biggest surprise of all. The camera turned on Nox, and the face of a beautifully tragic young rock star—whom everyone believed to have died in a high-speed car accident in Hollywood—filled the Jumbotrons. The roar of the audience was so loud it threatened to eclipse the music itself.

Nox raised one hand in an appreciative gesture, then let it drop to his guitar and strummed his fingers across the strings, striking a perfect chord in accompaniment to his celebrity choir. And the words of his song—brought to life by his inhumanly beautiful voice and those around him—came through the Olympic Stadium speakers and the TV's and streaming devices of millions of viewers around the world.

We're always on, always connected.

And still we grow more disaffected.

What if we all just turned it off?

All the noise

All the talk

And what if we could turn them on?

Our voices, our smiles, our hearts

And become one. Yeah, we are one.

We don't need plans. We don't need screens.

We don't need tabloid kings and queens.

I need you. You need me.

We need each other—let's make it real.

We are one. We are one. All the world.

We are One.

The melody was absolutely stunning. I'd never heard anything that moved me more—and I was already a lost cause when it came to Nox's music.

But as the song continued, I realized his singing hadn't sent me into a glamour-trance this time the way it had the times before. The saol water really did work.

The final notes of his song played, and Nox's voice spoke clearly in my mind.

Join me center stage. It's your turn.

Fighting to control my breathing and basically not have a heart attack on the spot, I crossed the stage and went to Nox's side. His large hand squeezed mine.

You can do this. You have *to do this.*

I nodded, accepting the microphone he held out to me. And then I looked up. And around. I actually turned in a circle. There were faces and the tiny lights of cell phone screens and cameras surrounding me 360 degrees. The walls of the stadium were even higher than the interior walls of Altum's cavernous underground world.

My knees wobbled so hard I thought I might fall down right there and ruin the entire plan. I darted my eyes at Nox.

Does Sway still work when your mind is absolutely completely blank?

His reassuring smile gave me courage, and I put the mic to my lips.

"Let's hear it one more time for Nox Knight and the amazing We Are One band."

The crowd erupted in a deafening roar before quieting enough for me to continue. I took a breath to focus my Sway. There would never be a more important moment to employ it. I had to put all my cards on the table—right now.

"On this special night when we all gather as one world, one people, let us take the message of that beautiful song to heart. There is no better way to connect with each other than face-to-face, voice-to-voice, and heart-to-heart. Let's carry the spirit of these Olympics and this song with us this week. For seven days, I'm asking you—these people…" I held out my arms, gesturing toward the gathering of instantly recognizable faces and names. "…are asking you to put away your electronic devices—your phones, TV's, tablets, computers—turn them off. And turn to your friends, family, neighbors, and co-workers. They are the only fans any of us have ever truly needed.

They are the only ones who deserve our devotion. But first…"

I let the words hang for a moment, and the stadium went eerily quiet. I had to add one more thing, or the extreme change I was encouraging would never stick. I felt so cheesy about it, but there was no other way.

"We must thank our sponsors for the evening… especially Magnolia Sugar Tea… the official drink of the We Are One singers and the best way to quench your thirst this week. And now ladies and gentlemen here in Boston and watching from every corner of the world…" I pulled my own phone from my pocket and held it up. "Let's turn off our devices!"

There was a long moment of excruciating silence… during which nothing happened. What had gone wrong? Had they not heard me? Was my glamour not strong enough to influence them to abandon their electronic lifelines? My belly dropped through the stage to the stadium floor.

Lad… it's not working. In my moment of desperation and fear, my mind called out to him.

Stepping up beside me, he took the microphone gently from my hand. It was the first time I'd seen him up close since the confrontation in Nox's room. I looked into his eyes, not sure what I'd find there.

He gave me a quick smile before putting the mic to his lips.

Together, his voice spoke inside my head.

To everyone else, he said, "Are you with us? We are one. Now… let's Turn. It. Off."

As if a black wave was sweeping across the stadium seating, phone screens blinked out, one by one.

CHAPTER THIRTY
HOPE

The darkness had never been more beautiful. It signaled hope. It meant victory—over Davis and over the evil Dark Elven takeover plan.

The stage lights went out, and the fireworks began over the Olympic Stadium. I had no doubt every pair of eyes there was focused on the colorful light show instead of on a cell phone or tablet.

But what about the people at home? Had the message affected them as strongly? The fact that electronic signals enhanced glamour gave me reason to hope that it had been even stronger.

That would mean they'd turned off their TV's already and were missing the spectacle playing out around me. It was too bad—these were some pretty freaking amazing fireworks—but compared to slavery and subjugation, missing a light show was not so great a loss.

Only time would tell if we had truly succeeded. By the end of the week, there should be reports of a monumental and inexplicable TV ratings flop for this incarnation of the Summer Games. *Sorry Boston.* If I'd been able to figure out another way, I would have.

Warmth enveloped my hand, and I looked up to see Nox's eyes shining with the same hope blooming in my heart. He embraced me in a tight hug.

You did it.

We did it, I corrected. *Your song was brilliant.*

The moment of intimacy was hidden from everyone except those closest to us. Which included Lad. Nox released me and slapped him on the shoulder. Lad grinned and dropped his head—in modesty or relief, I wasn't sure. I couldn't hear what Nox said to him.

But I heard what Lad said to me. He lifted his face again, locking eyes with me. *I'm proud of you... and of Nox. He's a worthy leader.*

He is. I nodded. *So are you. The leadership glamour came through there big time—your dad was right. It took our combined Sway to get the job done.* Here I had to stop and take a steadying breath. *So... you said maybe we could talk...*

He stepped closer. *I'm sorry if I was rude before. I wasn't ready to deal with losing you. I needed to wait until this was over, until I had myself under better control. And until I could look into your eyes again and ask you mind-to-mind... Ryann... I have to ask it again... just one more time. Do you love him?*

Well, it depends on which "him" you're referring to. I took his hand, intertwining my fingers with his. *If you mean the guy standing in front of me now, the answer is… "yes." I love him. Always have… always will.*

A grin slowly developed on Lad's face, lighting up those remarkable eyes that had always seemed to see right into my soul.

Off to one side, there was movement. Vancia and Davis emerged from the tunnel. He was bound and tightly under her control.

I was touched to see pure love shining on Vancia's face when her eyes met Nox's. He stood, looking back at her with unmistakable longing, but not making a move in her direction.

Hey—Rock God—what's your problem? Go to her, idiot.

He glanced over at me. His fear was palpable. He shook his head. *We're just friends.*

No. You and I are friends.

One of his eyebrows lifted.

Okay, we were friends with glamour-induced benefits, I amended. *But the real deal is standing right over there—just on the other side of fear.*

He grinned at me and then took a step toward her. Her flushed face and the obvious connection between them had my emotional glamour pinging off the charts.

And then my gaze went to Davis's face, and what I saw there erased the happily-ever-after-glow from my heart in an instant.

He didn't look defeated. He looked… satisfied. A grin formed and slithered across his mouth. What was there for *him* to be happy about? He'd lost.

His adoptive daughter was reunited with her true love—whom he'd attempted to kill. It looked pretty good for me and Lad as well. And we had freed the earth's human population from the grip of Dark Elven glamour.

There was no way he could get that horse back in the barn even if he were able to somehow free himself. The message was already out there. Nox's song was already playing on radio stations worldwide, influencing those who hadn't been tuned in to the Olympic broadcast tonight. By tomorrow or the next day they'd turn off their radios and other devices and be on their way to glamour-freedom as well.

The effect would multiply and spread when those who *hadn't* seen or heard it went on social media and saw the majority of their friends weren't on and interacting this week. The big influencers—the fan pod members—had no doubt abandoned all online interactions already because if *anyone* had been watching tonight, they were.

Davis's plan had failed.

Still—that smile gave me the creeps. It stole away the joy I'd felt moments earlier.

Congratulations, Ryann. You possess all the glamour gifts of your father… and then some.

I heard his distinctive voice crystal clear in my mind. There was no use pretending I didn't anymore. I had just displayed my Sway for all to see—anyone who could recognize it—and Davis certainly had. And of course he now knew I could communicate mind-to-mind as well.

That's the ONLY way I'm like you. You're a monster.

He laughed. *You must feel very pleased with yourself, daughter. But I wonder... if your mother is as proud right now?*

I whipped my head back and forth, looking for her. Craning to inspect our box seats, I saw she was no longer there. Was she sick? Had she finally collapsed from the cumulative effect of weeks under his non-stop glamour? My insides froze over with arctic fear.

Where is she? What have you done with her?

Davis laughed again, this time tilting his head back and letting the sound flow richly. Then he lifted a hand and pointed to the tower that held the Olympic Cauldron.

Look up. Look to the eternal flame and see how you have murdered your own mother. Now who's the monster?

Heart zooming to the top of my throat, I turned my face to the sky. My gaze landed on the giant bowl that would hold the flame steady above the Olympic stadium for the duration of the games, a symbol of friendship among the nations of the world.

To me, it had morphed into a symbol of impending death. Because just above it, at the highest point of the tower scaffolding, stood a tiny figure.

Mom.

Her face was a miniature pale oval as she stared into the roaring flame, transfixed by the changing colors of the firelight.

Apparently reading my panicked expression, the others also looked up.

"What is it?" Lad said.

"What's up there?" Nox asked.

"It's my mom. She's on the tower near the cauldron."

"Oh God," Nox breathed, his body going rigid as he spotted her. "We have to get to her."

"What have you done?" Lad fired at Davis. "She could fall. She could slip and die."

He looked wholly unconcerned. "That is precisely my purpose in glamouring her to wait there for me and Ryann. Let us go, my dear. Every moment we waste is one in which she could lose her balance or be buffeted by the wind... and reduce our happy family by one member."

He raised his bound hands as if expecting to be set free.

"What do you think is going to happen? It's done, Davis. Your scheme to enslave the human race is over. And you can't possibly believe I'd be interested in being a family at this point. I could never love you."

"I don't need your *love*." He spat out the word like it was spoiled meat. "Only your Sway. You know by now how strong mine is. Only a suggestion from me—even at this distance—and your mother will step off that platform, and well... you can imagine how that will end. But I don't think you'll let that happen. I think you're going to accompany me to the top of that tower where she is waiting for you... afraid and alone."

"And then what? You'll throw us both from the top?"

"Oh no. I need you alive. And if you do exactly as I say, I'll allow your beautiful mother to live as well." Pointing to a cameraman and audio tech standing nearby, he barked an order. "You. Both of you come with me." Then, skewering me with his glare again, he said, "You are going to *undo* the damage you've done, and they will broadcast it to the world."

I shook my head vigorously. "It's too late. You heard me tell everyone to turn off their TV's and phones—not to use electronics for a week."

"Yes, and to drink your nasty tea-and-saol water concoction to break the influence of glamour. But there are still enough people who may have just tuned in to the broadcast—as well as the nearly seventy thousand people present in this stadium who can still be influenced to reverse that suggestion. With your glamour and mine together, working in tandem, we will send a message so powerful no one will be able to resist it. Those people will become absolute evangelists for Elven rule. They'll be *begging* us to rule them, and they won't stop until they convince their friends and neighbors to turn all those devices back on and avoid your poisonous Magnolia Sugar Tea at all costs."

"No. I won't help you make the humans your subjects. I've seen what you and your kind do with that type of power. And I've seen what *it* can do to people."

Davis's calm expression contorted into barely controlled rage. His patience was at an end. "You *will* help me. Or perhaps I was mistaken about the level of devotion you have for your mother."

He gave a pointed glance overhead, and my eyes followed in time to see Mom take another step closer to the edge of the precipice and teeter there. My heart seized with panic as I pictured her frail body toppling over the edge into the furnace below.

"Stop," I yelled at Davis. "Tell her to step back. I'll go with you."

As I started toward my father, Lad stepped up beside me, obviously intending to come along.

"Alone," Davis said, stopping me and Lad in our tracks.

Of course he wouldn't allow anyone to come along and possibly overtake him physically again. It remained to be seen whether I could challenge him mentally.

Turning to Lad, I looked up into his worried eyes. "I'll be fine. I'll be right back."

He shook his head, his brow furrowing heavily as he whispered. "No way. I'm not letting you go with that madman."

I grabbed his hands. *There's no choice. I have to do this alone. I'll be all right. Let me go.*

One finger at a time, he loosened his grip on me but rested his forehead against mine and stared directly into my eyes. *I will never let you go, Ryann. I can't. I love you too much.* And he released me with one last desperate whisper. "Come back to me."

I nodded and turned to go then abruptly swirled back around to face him. "I will. I love you." *I love you.*

The brilliant light that flashed in his eyes bolstered my courage. I *would* return to him. Somehow. I had to. There was so much more I had to say to him—so much lost time to make up for.

But first thing's first.

"Release him," I said to Vancia.

CHAPTER THIRTY-ONE
TOWER OF TERROR

An elevator took us up through the center of the tower to the top. The doors opened on the eerie sound of the night wind whipping the brightly hued flags of the world. It was the only sound way up here, far above the crowd.

I imagined Mom making that elevator ride alone, walking out onto the tiny walkway that lined the scaffolding, completely at the mercy of Davis's mind control. The image terrified me too much, so I put it out of my head and forced myself to focus on the circumstances at hand.

Which were also pretty terrifying. We were so high above the Olympic Stadium that the people below seemed like a mass of indistinct color.

We stepped out of the elevator onto a fairly wide platform then walked around it until we reached the side where the flame burned at nearly eye level. A blast of heat hit my face as it came into view. Just to the side of a narrow walkway intended for specialized construction workers, hung a sign.

DANGER: NO TRESPASSING.

Beyond that sign, which flapped in the strong breeze, stood Mom. She was far out on the walkway, nearly at its end. Her expression was blank, her eyes empty. She didn't register our presence—didn't seem to see me there at all. I wasn't sure she even knew where she was.

Or maybe she saw everything, felt everything, and was so strapped by Davis's mind domination she was unable to express her terror.

Terror was exactly what I felt as I watched her rail-thin body sway in the wind so close to going over the edge I thought I might vomit. My main focus was getting her away from that deadly drop-off—and the flaming death below.

I shot a quick side-glance at Davis. If I could kill him, his control over her mind would be released. But could I manage to do it before he had an opportunity to make her jump? I had no weapon. He was much larger and stronger than me. And even if I had the physical strength, could I do it at all? *I* wasn't a killer. I didn't want to be a chip off the beastly block.

I tried reaching out to her in the Elven way. *Mom? Can you hear me? Mom, look at me.*

No response. As far as I knew, she had never communicated mind-to-mind. But she *was* susceptible to glamour—I'd seen it first with Nox and then Davis. If only she'd look in my direction, maybe I could catch her eye and speak the words aloud. I might be able to influence her to step back out of the danger zone.

"Mom, it's Ryann. I'm here. I'm going to get you out of here," I said.

"Not quite yet—and *don't* try anything tricky." Davis motioned to the video crew who'd ridden the elevator with us. "You have a job to do before there can be any 'happy reunion.'"

Reaching toward the woman, who held two stick microphones, Davis said, "Give one to her. Then tell Federic in the booth to be ready to switch to us live within the stadium and for broadcast."

He took one of the mics from the woman, and she immediately obeyed his order, stepping forward and handing me the other then speaking into her headset to Federic, who I assumed was in charge of the broadcast. Once again, Olympics viewers were about to get an unscheduled event in their coverage.

Davis was smart. What *we* were about to broadcast would definitely stand out as bizarre. So bizarre in fact, it would probably be rebroadcast for the next few days on newscasts worldwide, in case any un-glamoured human being out there happened to miss it.

The producers of the Olympics coverage would probably claim some lunatic had taken control of the airwaves temporarily—and they'd be right—but none of them could know just *how* devastating the aftereffects of our live and recorded messages might be.

Davis was convinced our combined glamours would be irresistible. What if he was right? I'd come here to *stop* the worldwide takeover. I couldn't let myself be used as an instrument to *cause* it to occur after all.

Looking at the heavy microphone in my hand, I evaluated its usefulness as a weapon. Could I knock Davis out with it? In a moment of hysteria, I imagined a light saber type battle with microphones, and him saying in a deep, iconic movie voice, "I am your father, Ryann."

And then my eyes wandered up the chest and shoulders and neck of my very large and thoroughly Elven father, and any hysterical visions vanished instantly. This wasn't a movie. This was real life. It was life and death.

Two hundred and fifty years old or not… Davis was more than a match for me physically. And he could order Mom to jump before I'd be able to get in one blow. No— I'd have to find another way to stop the broadcast.

"Tell her to come in first," I demanded.

Davis eyed me with something that resembled boredom. "I think not."

"Do it—or I won't say a word when those camera lights come on. Or maybe I'll sing Nox's song again…"

"Fine," he snapped. "Maria, darling, please step away from the edge. Not too far. One more step toward me— good—yes. Right there will be fine."

She was so close now I could almost touch her, but I didn't dare.

Davis *could* touch her. His hand caressed her shoulder, the gentle touch an ugly lie. Because he didn't love her.

Any man who loved a woman would never put her in danger. That's what I'd come to understand about the decision Lad had made to send me away. Though I was what he'd wanted most in the world, he chose to let me go—for my sake. To protect me. That was love.

This was evil.

Davis and I stood on the central platform, but Mom's feet were still on the precarious walkway. She was no longer teetering on the edge, but he could easily shove her right over if he wanted to.

Her vacant expression never changed as she stared at her toes. We were both in the greatest danger of our lives, and though they didn't know it, so was the rest of the human race.

Davis tossed a contemptuous glance at me. "Now—no more stalling. When the on-air light comes on, I will begin, and *you* will repeat my words—and *mean* them. Remember—I've seen your Sway in action now. I'll know if you're not using it."

He nodded toward the camera crew and raised one finger.

"One minute," the woman said into her headset to Federic or whomever was on the other end.

One minute. One final minute of freedom. That was all the human population of our planet had left.

My eyes darted up and down, left to right. What could I do? How could I prevent this catastrophe? The robotic cameraman and audio woman were obviously not going to do anything to help. I'd read their emotions—they were completely under Davis's control.

"Thirty seconds."

My pulse exploded. This was happening. It wasn't just Mom and me—not just Lad, and Nox, and Vancia down below. This was everyone. This was all the people back in Deep River and my friends in the fan pods, and Daddy, and Grandma Neena. All the kids in my high school, all the benevolent Light Elves, and the innocent Dark Elves who didn't even know what their nefarious "leader" was up to.

If I went along with this and did nothing to stop him, I'd be no better than the most vile of the Dark Elves, no better than this man who called himself my father.

But I am better than that. The thought flashed through my mind, and its rightness burned in my gut.

Yes, I had more Dark Elven blood in me than Light, but as Nox had once said, just because you're born a certain way—it doesn't mean that's who you *are.* I had a choice. I could *choose* who I wanted to be, how I wanted to live.

Even if it meant dying for that right.

Was I afraid? Oh yes. But everything I wanted—life, love—was on the other side of that fear.

I gripped my microphone tighter. Just as the red camera light clicked on, I made a grab for Davis's mic. I must have really surprised him because it came right out of his hand. In one jerky motion, I threw it with all my strength, sending it careening over the edge and down to the sidewalk on the outside of the Olympic Stadium.

As Davis lunged forward and grabbed at the empty air in an attempt to recover it, I locked my grip around Mom's wrist and pulled her to me, spinning so she stumbled off the walkway and onto the platform.

Her dazed eyes locked with mine. "Ryann."

I had just enough time to scream, "Run to the elevator," before Davis recovered and turned to face us, his face red with rage.

"No. Stay right where you are Maria." His enraged voice was filled with malevolent and powerful Sway.

He made a move toward Mom, whose nose started gushing blood, but I backed up to the edge of the platform and held the one remaining mic over the drop-off. "Let her go. Leave her alone, or I'll drop it. You'll have a hard time broadcasting your message with no audio."

Davis froze in place, gritting his teeth and clenching and unclenching his hands as Mom made her way to the elevator and pushed the button. Clearly he wanted to choke the life from me. Knowing that would leave him without a microphone, he settled for a ferocious command.

"Give it to me."

I shifted the mic even further from his grasp. "Your glamour doesn't work on me, *Father*. One of the lovely 'gifts' you've given me. I believe I'll hold onto this until Mom is safely on her way."

"And then you'll go on television with me and fix this mess you've created?"

"I'll go on. But I won't say what you want me to. If you put me on camera, I'll tell the viewers the truth—that you're a corrupt senator and not worthy of their trust. Then not only will your plan have failed, you'll be disgraced and probably out of a job."

His face erupted in fury. "You *cannot* do this to me. You are my daughter. If you won't join me, your Elven heritage will be wasted. You really *will* be human." His tone said he did *not* mean that as a compliment.

"Thank you," I said, taking it that way anyway. "I *am* human *and* Elven. And I choose to be the best of both."

Instead of exploding in rage or trying to wrestle the microphone from me as I expected, Davis wilted. His broad shoulders drooped. His head hung down. "Very well."

I froze, unsure of what was happening. "Very well what?"

"That's it, I suppose. There is no point in continuing to fight. It all means nothing if I have no family—no one to leave my throne to."

"It's not *your* throne," I reminded him quietly.

Maybe I should have kept my mouth shut. It was looking like he was going to just give up and go away at this point, which was more than I could ever have expected. And he looked so defeated, there was no point in rubbing it in.

For a moment Davis stared at me, sad eyes cataloguing my face, perhaps because this was likely to be the last time we ever saw each other. For the same reason, I stared back, memorizing his face, the features strangely reminiscent of my own.

Then I extended my emotional E.Q. toward him, so I could not only see and hear him, but feel what he was feeling. This final snapshot would be all I'd ever have of my biological father, and I wanted it to be vivid and complete. It wasn't sentimentality. I wanted to make sure I'd never forget what great power without compassion looked like.

Hatred and vengeance flashed through my brain in a bright burning path—not mine for him—but his for me.

Breathless and jolted from its power, I doubled over and dove to the side just as Davis lunged toward me and made a grab for the remaining microphone. He succeeded in stripping it from my fingers. But he must have underestimated the distance to the edge of the platform.

Or maybe he had meant to push me over.

Instead, he was the one who slid over the side, disappearing from view with a shout and the scrabble of fingertips as he tried desperately to cling to the platform edge. For a few seconds it was quiet, and then the screams began.

I scooted to the edge, unable to stop myself from peering over. The cameraman and audio tech, as if suddenly freed from a spell, broke position and ran to the edge as well.

"Careful," I cautioned them.

After that, there were no more words as we stared at the unfolding horror. Davis had fallen directly into the brazier holding the eternal flame, a spectacular, searing conclusion to his own eternal life, his immortality terminating in agony and fire.

"Oh my God," the cameraman breathed.

"Um, we're live," said the sound tech. The confusion in her voice and the clarity in her eyes told me the glamour over her had completely lifted the moment Davis died.

So sick I could barely speak, I said, "Tell them to turn it off. There's nothing to see up here."

CHAPTER THIRTY-TWO
WE ARE ONE

The halls of Altum had never been so brightly lit. Candles and colored stones glowed in every direction, held aloft by the Elven people who filled the cavernous valley of the underground kingdom, Dark and Light standing side by side.

Missing were the popping flashes of the paparazzi, though one of the world's biggest music stars was here today.

The song Nox had written for the We Are One singers had immediately vaulted to the top of the music charts, although the Boston Olympics had inexplicably turned out to be the most poorly watched Olympic Games since the advent of television coverage. TV in general had a horrible ratings week, which experts could only blame on a bizarre summer slump.

There were some other strange stories on the evening news, such as the mysterious disappearance of venerated Georgia Senator Davis Hart, who according to witnesses, had attended the Opening Ceremonies and hadn't been seen since.

And the extreme downturn in cell phone usage for one week across the globe following the Games' first night.

Since Hart's disappearance, the aggressive cell tower expansion legislation he'd been pushing had suddenly lost support and failed to pass a Senate vote. The box office saw an unprecedented number of flops as A-list stars failed to draw audiences the way they had before. NFL quarterback Reggie Dillon had abruptly retired and left the country, claiming he needed to "find himself," and would be going on a walkabout in Australia for the next few years.

And entertainment news venues were shocked by a surprise announcement from iconic Hollywood agent Alfred Frey regarding the disbanding of fan pods for all his clients.

"It was a good idea that had its day. It's run its course now," he'd been quoted in one Los Angeles newspaper.

A certain small beverage manufacturing company in North Mississippi was enjoying phenomenal success, though, driven to hire hundreds of new employees to meet worldwide demand. Its owner pledged to donate all proceeds to a new charity set up to help families reconnect and reunite with missing children who'd joined fan pods and disappeared over the past few years.

Enchanting Elven music played as the bride moved slowly through Altum with her bridesmaids, the procession crossing a flower-strewn bridge over its central crystalline river toward the wedding shrine, which was raised so that all would have a view of the graceful and ancient ceremony.

Atop the shrine waited the King of Altum, dressed all in white... waiting to officiate the event.

Beside him, the beaming groom waited, watching his bride approach with love shining in his hazel eyes. To his other side stood a tall, beautiful raven-haired woman. Her resemblance to her son was unmistakable. Nox leaned down and kissed his mother's cheek then looked over at his brother, his ally.

For the first time in centuries, the rulers of the Dark and the Light courts stood together. In peace. In total agreement on their approach to the human race. Live and let live.

I watched the ceremony with Lad's mother and my family—Grandma Neena, her sister and her parents. Mom was at home recovering, with Daddy as her devoted nurse. She had very little memory of the events in Los Angeles or Boston, and in my opinion, that was for the best.

He looks the part, doesn't he? I said to Lad's mom Mya.

She nodded, her lovely face glowing with pride. *I only wish his father were here to see this.*

I hugged her, and her happiness flowed around me in a warm glow. She had her son *and* her sister now. When Alfred had disbanded the fan pods, he sent representatives to check the properties of all his clients. Sophie Jerrick had been discovered in a tiny soundproof cell in Reggie's basement. It was possible Nox and I had been right next door to her when we'd been held prisoner there ourselves.

The ceremony was breathtaking. And yes—I cried. Not just from the beauty of it and certainly not from envy. It was the overwhelming sense of joy surrounding me. My emotional glamour receptors were filled to capacity and beyond from the gathering of all these thankful and contented hearts.

There might still have been a few bad apples like Audun in the Dark Elven court, but for the most part, the Elven people wanted peace. They wanted to love their families and live their lives.

After the vows were said and the happy couple had shared a very passionate kiss, the crowd began to stir and eventually, to make their way to the royal residence for what promised to be one heck of a reception.

I waited beside the river to give my congratulations to Nox and Vancia. When she saw me, she actually picked up the hem of her dress and ran to hug me.

"Oh, wow. Hi. Congratulations. It was beautiful. *You* look beautiful," I told her, and I meant it.

"Thank you, Ryann. Thank you so much for everything you did." The words bubbled from her mouth. "I'm so happy."

"You two belong together," I said, watching Nox approach as he caught up to his vibrant bride.

I stretched out a hand to shake his, but he ignored it and swept me off my feet in one of his patented bear hugs. "There she is. If we were doing this at *my* place, you would've been standing up there as my best man, you know." He laughed and set me down, leaning down for a loud stage-whisper. "These Light Elves are kind of uptight about all the *rules*. We're gonna have to loosen them up."

We laughed, and Lad joined us, slapping his brother on the back. "Well, now that we're ruling jointly, we'll certainly consider some policy changes."

Happy as I was, my heart sank a little at that statement. I knew what one of those policy changes would be—now that Lad had an ally and friend to share responsibility, he would want to travel, to leave Altum—and Mississippi—and see the vast world his father had forbidden him to explore.

No doubt he was jealous of Nox and Vancia's upcoming honeymoon, which would double as The Hidden's world tour. In addition to the homes and the bank accounts, she'd inherited her father's two airplanes, so they'd be traveling in style.

"You must be excited about your trip," I said to her.

"Oh yes." She beamed. "I've already got my art supplies packed. I'm ready to capture the world on canvas."

Nox gave Lad a conspiratorial grin. "She thinks she's actually going to *leave* the hotel room."

Lad laughed softly, then blushed as his eyes drifted over to meet mine.

The subject of bonding was one we hadn't really discussed since returning to Mississippi. Like Nox and

Vancia, Lad was eighteen. I knew it was getting more difficult every day for him to wait. Heck, it was hard for *me*, and I was only a partial Elf. Kissing Lad and being close to him made it seem like a better idea all the time.

But I had a year of high school left. I couldn't just leave and wander the world. Besides, my family and friends, my life, were here.

"Have a good trip, brother." Lad shook Nox's hand. "I have no doubt you will. You, too." He leaned over to kiss Vancia's cheek.

"And I have no doubt you'll do a fine job running things while we're away," Nox said. "Don't change the place too much. I kind of like it here."

The newlyweds moved off together, drawn away from us by other well-wishers toward the entrance of the royal mansion.

I folded my arm through Lad's as we slowly strolled together, taking our time, enjoying the music and the beautiful river reflecting the wedding flowers. "So—*are* you going to make any changes? Or try to do what your father would have wanted you to do?"

"You know what?" He looked down at me with a nostalgic smile. "I think he would have wanted me to have my own leadership style… as long as my priority is our people's well-being. I will change a few things, ease up on the rule prohibiting Light Elves from venturing out of Altum, for instance."

"Your people have no experience with the human world. Won't they be afraid?"

"Probably, but I think a good leader encourages his subjects to move beyond their fear. You can meet some pretty amazing people that way." He winked at me and stopped walking, pulling me to face him. "And I'll make sure they're prepared before sending them out into the world."

I looked down at his chest, the V of smooth tanned skin visible where his shirt parted, then brought my eyes up to meet his again. "What about you? You must be eager to get out there yourself—finally see all those things you've missed."

He smiled. "There's only one thing I'd *ever* miss if I didn't get to have it. And she's right here. This is where I'm going to be—as long as you are." He kissed me again, this time a little longer. A little deeper. Then he pulled back, wearing a mischievous grin. "Not that it isn't good to get away from time to time. For special occasions, you know. Like a honeymoon?"

I looked around and realized we were on the bridge leading to the wedding shrine. "Honeymoon," I repeated. And then I got it. "You mean…"

Yes, I do. Will you? When you're ready of course.

I stretched up on my toes and brought my lips to his, returning all that love I felt flowing from his heart. *Oh yes. Yes I will.*

"After all," I said, pulling back to look into those unearthly beautiful green eyes. "We are one."

THE END

AFTERWORD

Thank you for reading HIDDEN HOPE, Book Three of the Hidden Trilogy. If you enjoyed it, please consider leaving a review on Goodreads and wherever you purchased your copy. Reviews help other readers find great books.

If you haven't checked out THE SWAY yet, I think you'll love getting Vancia's story and more insight into the world of the Dark Elves and her childhood connection to Nox. There's also a fun crossover scene with HIDDEN DEEP in the novella, so it's a must for Hidden Trilogy fans.

Read on for an excerpt of THE SWAY...

Sometimes the more a person talks, the less you want to listen. Even when he speaks without making a sound.

"This legislation will lead to more jobs for the middle class—this country needs to move forward, not backward." Pappa's voice drones on and on, flowing from the surround sound system in our living room like the underground river in Altum. Slow. Deep. Never-ending.

I reach over and click the remote, and the image of his unnaturally young, unusually handsome face disappears from the big screen, the manufactured smile and slick speech replaced by soothing blackness and quiet.

"Why'd you do that?" Carter whips his head around to face me across the low table where we're working together, surrounded by piles of books and trays of snacks prepared for us by Edda, my family's chef.

I shrug, not taking my eyes from my laptop, continuing to peck away at the art history senior paper Carter *should* be working on as well. Instead, his eyes have been glued to the TV for the past ten minutes.

"It's distracting," I say. "And boring."

"It's not boring. It's awesome your dad's on TV all the time."

Finally I look up. "It was *awesome* when I was thirteen. Now—it's boring."

Carter throws his hands up in an exaggerated pose of surrender. "Well *excuse me* for being impressed, Miss I-Have-Mansions-In-Two-States-And-Had-Dinner-At-The-

White-House. Some of us *country bumpkins* could listen to him talk all day."

I gesture toward the row of floor-to-ceiling windows that look out from the living room over our manicured suburban neighborhood. "Atlanta is hardly the country. And you're not a bumpkin. And you wouldn't be saying that if you actually *lived* with him in those two houses and had to *listen* to him talking all day."

Carter shakes his head, the light blue of his eyes matching the color of his frayed button down. "No. He's not like other dads." Rolling his pen between his fingertips, he looks up at the soaring cathedral ceiling, obviously searching for words to explain the unexplainable. "Your dad's so… so…"

I know it's the glamour at work, and like all the other humans in our sphere, Carter can't help himself, but still, his reaction to Pappa's televised interview is bugging me. It makes me feel sorry for my new friend. It makes me feel guilty.

I lighten my tone a few degrees, adding a note of humor. "You're *kind* of creeping me out here with the hero worship."

Now his gaze comes back to me along with a sheepish grin. "Sorry. Not being weird. You know I want to go into politics, so to me, he *is* kind of a rock star. I guess to you he's just 'Dad.'"

"Exactly."

Only he isn't.

Pappa adopted me five years ago after my parents were killed in a small plane crash. He doesn't feel quite like a father—I remember what a real father feels like—but I'm lucky to have him as a guardian. There aren't many people (especially among *our* people) who'd take in a stray teen girl and raise her as their own.

"Anyway, you're not getting any work done with the TV on. And we've only got a few days left to finish this. So get on it." I lift my hand and flip it, making a cracking noise with my mouth to approximate a whip.

Carter flinches and laughs, places both palms on the table between us, and drops his face to his knuckles in a reverent bow. "Yes, master."

I laugh along, but only weakly, as a sick twinge hits my stomach. I don't like the sight of him bowing to me. It's too close to what Pappa actually believes all the humans should be doing.

Of course, Carter has no way of knowing about that, and he can never know. I'm not even supposed to have friendships with humans, much less confide in them.

Pappa would probably flip if he knew Carter was even in our house right now. But he insists on my going to school with them—public school of course—*man of the people* and all that politician garbage—so he'll just have to put up with it when I have a partner on a project. The school library where Carter and I have been working together closes at three-thirty, and I have no doubt Pappa would like me going over to a human boy's house even *less*.

"They're only interested in one thing, Vancia," he's constantly warned me. "And that's the one thing you absolutely must not give them. You know the consequences."

Oh, I know. Believe me, I know. How could I not, when it's been preached to me so often? *Our kind have one partner for life. Separation from that partner results in the mark—and a solitary life for eternity.*

Though eighteen is the age of bonding for us, we all get The Talk in early childhood because even before our eighteenth birthdays, if we choose to bond ourselves with someone, that's it. No take-backs. No oopses.

I glance up to check that he's working and can't help but smile at Carter's concentration face as he scribbles in his notebook. The tip of his tongue is in the corner of his mouth, and his light brown hair is flopped to one side, revealing cute little frown lines across his tanned forehead.

A sweet warmth spreads through my chest, and I pull my gaze away, forcing it back to the screen in front of me where it belongs. No point in looking. A human—like Carter for instance, with his short human lifespan—would be a tragically bad oops.

I hear Pappa come in long before Carter does. Of course, he's calling to me in the Elven way, so Carter can't hear him at all.

Vancia? Are you home? Where are you?

In the living room, I answer without making a sound. *And I have company.*

Now he repeats his question, using his voice this time. "You home Vancia?"

I scoot further away from Carter as I hear Pappa's quick footsteps echo through the marble foyer, hurrying toward the living room.

He steps into sight, surveying the wide open, sunlit space, his eyes dropping to me and Carter sitting on the carpeted floor at opposite ends of the low wooden coffee table, our shoes kicked off, our school papers intermingling. From the expression on his face, you'd think he caught us half-undressed in a lip lock.

Both Carter and I scramble to our feet, and my heart stops at the look Pappa directs toward him. It makes me feel like throwing myself in front of Carter—like I'm taking a bullet or something, but I hold my ground.

"Hi Pappa. I didn't think you'd be home for a while. We saw you on the news."

"That was recorded," he growls, never taking his eyes from my project partner.

"Pappa this is—"

"Carter Fields." Carter steps forward with his hand extended. He's got stars in his eyes as big as our TV screen, but I'll give him credit. Most humans who find themselves face-to-face with Davis Hart, Senior Georgia Senator and Science and Technology Committee Chairman, are speechless for a few minutes. Maybe

Carter's debate team experience is coming in handy. "It's an honor to meet you sir," he adds.

Pappa must be surprised as well because the frown drops momentarily, and he grips his hand and shakes it. At the appearance of Carter's charming dimples, my father's scowl returns.

A few monosyllabic answers later, my project partner apparently gets the *No Trespassing* message. "Well, I guess I'd better get going. My mom will have dinner ready soon. It was nice to meet you sir."

Pappa nods, and I come quickly to Carter's side, helping him gather his papers and books so he can stuff them into his backpack.

"I'll walk you to the door." Pulling Carter along with me, I speed-walk toward the foyer and open the front door to the view of a wide double staircase flanked by stately planters overflowing with blooms. At the bottom, in our circular drive, Carter's old Jeep looks sorely out of place parked next to my convertible Mercedes and Pappa's new Bentley.

"Sorry about the cold front back there," I say as we step outside together.

He blows out a whistling breath and nods. "An ice storm is more like it. He's different than he is on TV, huh? Does he always act like that when you have someone over?"

"I don't know. I've never had anyone over before." *Great.* That was stupid. Not only am I the weird art geek girl, now he knows I'm friendless as well.

Carter's puzzled expression warms into a pleased grin. "So, I'm the first guy who's been to your house then."

Not the reaction I was expecting. His flirty tone makes me suddenly aware of the humid warmth of the evening air. What does it mean? Does he talk like that to all girls or is it actually something to be worried about?

We've been working together after school on our senior project for about two weeks now, and what started out as awkwardness has turned into a fun daily exchange of ideas and jokes… and sometimes long, loaded glances. Or maybe they're only significant on my end.

I study his face, trying to calm my racing pulse and wishing I could read his thoughts. Unfortunately, that's one thing we can't do. Some of my kind can read emotions, which is pretty close, but I don't have that glamour. Mine is artistic giftedness, which is almost laughably useless. Reclusive artists aren't exactly the poster children for winning fans and influencing people.

I know Pappa would rather I had some really badass glamour like hypnotic musical ability, or acting or athletic prowess, so I could be groomed for celebrity and have a fan pod of my own, do my part to advance The Plan. I can almost feel his disappointment when he walks into my painting studio and looks around, as if he's thinking *What am I supposed to do with this?*

Like all of my people, I have the Sway, but mine seems rather weak compared to the others I know. Or maybe I just haven't tried very hard to convince people to think or do things they otherwise wouldn't. Another disappointment to Pappa, who is the *king* of Sway. He could convince a cattle rancher convention to go vegan.

It might be worth it to use whatever Sway I *do* have on Carter now—nip this in the bud—if there even *is* a *this*. But when I open my mouth to do it, I find myself unwilling to influence him after all, so I try subtle redirection instead.

"Usually when I *study* with someone, I do it after school in the library, like we've been doing. We can work there tomorrow again—I think we got enough done today that we'll wrap it up on time."

"I don't mind coming back here. Your old man doesn't scare me." Carter's face breaks into a sunny smile, showing me that he knows how ridiculous his tough talk sounded.

What he doesn't know is that he *should* be scared of Pappa. And he'd be terrified if he knew *how* old my "old man" really is.

To learn about other books and upcoming releases from Amy Patrick, sign up for her newsletter. You will only receive notifications when new titles are available and about special price promotions. You may also occasionally receive teasers, excerpts, and extras from upcoming books. Amy will never share your contact information with others.

And check out http://www.hiddentrilogy.com/ for more goodies on the Hidden series.

You're invited to follow Amy on Twitter at @amypatrickbooks https://twitter.com/AmyPatrickBooks, and visit her website at www.amypatrickbooks.com. You can also connect with her on Facebook https://www.facebook.com/AmyPatrickAuthor

ACKNOWLEDGMENTS

This is an important part of the book for me because without the people named here, HIDDEN HOPE wouldn't exist.

First to you, my beautiful reader... thank you for giving my books a chance to entertain you and touch your heart.

Huge thanks go to my lovely editor Judy Roth for her wonderful work and to Cover Your Dreams for another fantastic cover.

I am forever grateful for my amazing critique partner, McCall, for her words of wisdom and huge heart. I'd be nowhere without my brilliant and hilarious Savvy Seven sisters (I'll make sock puppets with y'all anytime) and the special Dauntless girls. Love and thanks to the rest of the fabulous Dreamweavers and my Lucky 13 sisters for their support, good advice, virtual Prosecco, cupcakes, and cabana boys. #teamworddomination.

I'm blessed to be "doing life" with some amazing friends. Love to Bethany, Chelle, Margie, and the real housewives of Westmoreland Farm. Special thanks to Mary and CM and Bria for all the great book (and life) talks.

To my first family for your unconditional love and the gift of roots and wings. And finally to the guys who make it all worthwhile—my husband and sons. And thank you to the rest of my friends and family for your support and for just making life good.

ABOUT THE AUTHOR

Amy Patrick grew up in Mississippi (with a few years in Texas thrown in for spicy flavor) and has lived in six states, including Rhode Island, where she now lives with her husband and two sons.

Amy has been a professional singer, a DJ, a voiceover artist, and always a storyteller, whether it was directing her younger siblings during hours of "pretend" or inventing characters and dialogue while hot-rollering her hair before middle school every day. For many years she was a writer of true crime, medical anomalies, and mayhem, working as a news anchor and health reporter for six different television stations. Then she retired to make up her own stories. Hers have a lot more kissing.

I love to hear from my readers. Feel free to contact me on Twitter and my Facebook page.

https://twitter.com/AmyPatrickBooks
https://www.facebook.com/AmyPatrickAuthor

And be sure to sign up for my newsletter and be the first to hear the latest news on Ryann, Lad, Nox, and the Hidden Trilogy.

The Hidden Trilogy

Hidden Deep

Hidden Heart

Hidden Hope

The Sway- A Hidden Novella

Other Books by Amy Patrick

Channel 20 Something

Still Yours (20 Something, Book 2)

Still Me (20 Something, Book 3)

Still Beautiful (20 Something, Book 4)

Still Waiting- coming soon